The Unfortunate Victim

Greg Pyers grew up in the small Australian town of Daylesford. He is the author of more than 160 non-fiction books and three novels for children. This is his second novel for adults.

For Di and George

OTTO BERLINER INVESTIGATES...

The Unfortunate Victim

GREG PYERS

SCRIBE
Melbourne • London

Scribe Publications
18–20 Edward St, Brunswick, Victoria 3056, Australia
2 John St, Clerkenwell, London, WC1N 2ES, United Kingdom

First published by Scribe 2017

Typeset in 11.5/16.5 pt Janson by the publishers
Printed and bound in Australia by Griffin Press

The paper this book is printed on is certified against the Forest Stewardship Council® Standards. Griffin Press holds FSC chain of custody certification SGS-COC-005088. FSC promotes environmentally responsible, socially beneficial and economically viable management of the world's forests.

Scribe Publications is committed to the sustainable use of natural resources and the use of paper products made responsibly from those resources.

9781925321975 (paperback)
9781925548136 (e-book)

A CiP data entry for this title is available from the National Library of Australia.

scribepublications.com.au
scribepublications.co.uk

Author's Note

This story is based on a murder committed in the gold-mining town of Daylesford, Australia, in 1864. The names of some characters have been changed, but all characters herein are based on real people.

PART 1

1

9.00 A.M., THURSDAY 29th DECEMBER 1864
ALBERT STREET, DAYLESFORD

THE COCKATOO ON THE roof let up its screeching, and the gurgles and squelches from Maggie Stuart's body claimed the room. They were sounds to unsettle Constable Irwin, as if the commotion outside had cast a veil over the examination in plain view before him. Doctor Doolittle went on with his specimen collecting as the policeman looked to the dead woman's slashed throat. He leant over the deep rents either side of the windpipe, and noted the blood — congealed on the sheets and sprayed on the wall, and darkening as it aged.

Doolittle smeared a second glass slide and fitted a cover, and, along with hair samples already taken, made a parcel and addressed it. He wiped his fingers with a damp cloth.

Irwin stood back from the bed now to regard a corpse that could not have been more immodestly positioned: chemise lifted high, legs wide and hanging to the floor from the knees. It looked to him a deliberate arrangement, a taunt to the husband who would, and did, make the grim discovery on his return from his shift a little after midnight.

Doolittle tapped a bruised thigh with a spatula.

'My belief is that forcible connection took place.'

'Bastard,' Irwin breathed, and shook his head, despairing that such depravity should be found in his prosperous little gold-mining town.

Doolittle was detached, unmoved. Not two years had lapsed since he was a young Union surgeon in the thick of it at Chancellorsville; here was just one more mutilated body. He held out the parcel.

'Be careful with this, Constable, and prompt. Undue delay to Melbourne will compromise the microscopic analysis.'

'Rely on me, Doctor. God help us all, the monster who did this will hang!'

With resonant steps across rough-hewn boards, Irwin exited to the only other room of the Stuart cottage, one sparely furnished with a meat safe, table, chair, small bed, and two-seater bench. A chimney of mullock and coarse mortar stood within a wall, framed by a mantelpiece. Detective Walker was there, examining in lamplight the surface of the fireplace, all whitewashed for the summer, when cooking was for outside.

Early blowflies droned by in search of the corpse.

2

WEDNESDAY EVENING 21st DECEMBER
SEVEN DAYS BEFORE THE MURDER

THE DOG HAD BEEN amusing company, for a time, with its playful yaps and lunges. David Rose tossed his visitor morsels of gristle and fat from his plate, and let it lick the grease from his lips and beard, such was his appreciation. He scrunched the dog's ears and upturned it to slap its taut belly. The animal grinned and squirmed beneath broad, callused hands. Its tail thumped the dust.

'You're a hungry un, you are,' he said. 'Aren't you, eh? A hungry un!' He set it on its feet and stood. 'Now be off, go on, go home!' A stamp of a boot sent the dog slinking into the shadows of the gathering dusk.

He turned and poked at his fire. It was the same most nights; eat, then time to sleep the hours till dawn. And tomorrow, the same most days, look to pick up a stretch of work. Maybe moving cattle, digging a water race, swinging a pick.

He stretched, looked into the orange west, and farted. The sound and smell amused him —

The dog was back, circling his feet.

'Get away!' A boot breezed the dog's ear. The animal cringed and withdrew. A fling of gravel elicited a yelp and a hastening.

He pulled back his tent flap and settled himself full-length within. His dark eyes closed, and in minutes his thick whiskers were shivering to a deep snore.

The night stilled. A chill descended.

A clattering of metal brought the sleeper to his feet and out to a starry sky.

The dog was there, standing among scattered contents of a swag, tail beating and jaws working a block of cold meat.

He regarded the animal for a few moments and returned to the tent. He beckoned from within, 'Come here, boy! Come on.'

The dog bolted its find and trotted over.

'Good boy.'

The dog entered the tent, and its skull was shattered by a single hatchet blow. Even before the quivering had died away, David Rose was back in his bed.

PEARSON THOMPSON POURED HIMSELF tea from a porcelain teapot he'd brought with him to Daylesford, all the way from Cheltenham, fifteen years back. He still smiled at the trouble he'd taken with it, though he had long since stopped caring that Dorothy probably missed it more than she missed him.

He sipped and sat back to rest his slicked old head against leather upholstery. He closed his eyes and heard the familiar *crock* of cup on saucer, the tick-tocking of the Ansonia on the mantelpiece, and the clopping of a horse out on Duke Street —

A thumping on the front door cancelled his evening reverie.

'Pearson!'

'Oh, for the love of Jesus, Eliza, not now,' he sighed.

The door rattled in its frame.

'Pearson! I know you're in there.'

He breathed, set down his cup and saucer, and got to his feet. In the passageway he tied his dressing gown and opened the door to a woman thirty-five years his junior, with two small children; one riding her hip, the other clutching her skirts with a filthy hand.

They looked at the man in the doorway with indifferent stares.

'Oo, look! Here's your daddy,' the woman said. 'He's going to give me money what he owes so's I can feed you proper at Christmas. Isn't that right, Pearson?'

'You can't stay here, Eliza, if that's what you're —'

'Stay here! You flatter yourself, Pearson. Now give me the money what you owe.'

Pearson's hesitation over compliance was short. Any delay, and he'd have a banshee at his door, and the whole street would know about it. He returned inside and promptly re-emerged with notes.

'Here, ten pounds. Take it and leave.'

She scowled at the offering.

'It's all I can spare, and more than you deserve,' Pearson said.

She snapped the thin wad from his hand and stowed it in her skirts.

'To think I have to come knocking, to feed your own flesh and blood. And at Christmas, too!'

'We all have our crosses to bear, Eliza. Why not be thankful you're still young and pretty enough to make a living.'

Yes, he thought, it was her face that had drawn him into this regrettable entanglement; that, and an absence of the education and refinement that can make a pretty woman out of reach to an aged gent of limited means.

'You're a cold fish, you are, Pearson. You ever think of your wife and children back in England? Of course you don't. I'll tell you this for nothing: you're not leaving us in the lurch. Oh no. I won't let you. You hear me, Pearson?'

'AN ARSE LIKE AN onion,' John Pitman said, slapping that very same backside as Maria Molesworth swanked it by. 'Makes a man's eyes water!' Glasses clinked amid the laughter as Maria stopped to hip the bar and flaunt her cleavage. The proprietor regarded her. He'd never have made so bawdy with that Maggie Stuart from just up the road. She was altogether in a higher stratum than the likes of Maria, and Squeaking Betsy and Cockeyed Pat — and Waxy Venus, Polly Price, and all the rest he'd pulled from that stream of destitutes come to town to relieve stupid men of their hard-dug gold. He smirked at Maria, with the knowing that she needed him; that she was too cheap for anything better, and too commonplace to be irreplaceable. Maria was watching him back with the kind of don't-touch look the punters couldn't resist. For how much longer, though, Pitman wondered; the woman wasn't getting any younger. He'd always fancied her; imagined her bent over his bed ... He looked away, into the bush-timbered, bark-roofed lean-to that was his business premises. And there was Joyce, his wife, the great frump, wiping a table and all conversational with a half-pissed regular who'd soon be off home to a missus of his own. She looked up and caught the disgust in her husband's face.

Pitman had been thinking much about Maggie Stuart these past weeks. A neighbour of not more than fifty yards distant, he first saw her when Joe Latham and his wife moved in with their litter a year back. She was Maggie Latham back then. He'd see her by the house, or walking by, a sweet young thing — cheeks and lips unpainted, but rosy with a virginal glow that Maria Molesworth and her ilk had long since bade farewell, if ever they had such a thing. Maggie smiled so sweet and shy, and walked straight and easy; her clothes were clean, her bearing dignified, a real lady. He would think a man'd feel very satisfied squiring Maggie Latham about town on his arm. But not once she was Mrs George bloody Stuart! How did such a plain man land such a beauty? She was still living in the old house, and she was still walking by. At times, he could get to thinking she was taunting him, reminding him of the life he could have led —

A bleat intruded on Pitman's musing. He looked through the back door to see his wife, out in the yard with the Christmas lamb. He watched her secure the animal between her knees, pull back its chin, and draw the knife across its taut throat.

3

THURSDAY 22nd DECEMBER
SIX DAYS BEFORE THE MURDER

THE CHILDREN WERE OUT early, calling across the moguls of mine spoil that lay at the head of Connell's Gully. From high on his hill, David Rose heard the strain in their cries. He looked at the corpse stiffening at his feet, with dawn flies mopping blood from its breached scalp and drool from its grin. In one move, he stooped and pulled it by the tail across the red coals. Amid the reek and fizz of burning hair, he laid on wood. By the time the youngsters came up, the flames had concealed the carcase, and the crackling disguised the sizzling.

'Morning to you,' he said, herding them away from the pyre. 'And a fine mornin' it is to be out for a walk.'

The tallest, a girl in plaits and bonnet, spoke up.

'I'm Anna Spinks. We're looking for our dog. His name is Wombat. Have you seen him? He's black, and he's got a white nose.'

David Rose grimaced and pulled at his neck.

'No, I can't say I have, Miss Anna, but I'll be sure to keep an eye out. Wombat, you say?'

Anna Spinks nodded. He shrugged his regret that he was unable to shed any light.

He raised a finger. 'Would you like some sweets?' he said, and darted into the tent. He returned, sweets like coloured jewels in a cupped hand. 'For Christmas.'

The siblings looked to their sister. She nodded, and they moved forward to accept the offering.

GEORGE STUART LOVED TO feel Maggie's fingers claw at his soft white arse.

'Squeeze,' he breathed, and with voice, 'Squeeze, my love!' He loved to watch his wife of five weeks staring up at him like a child. God, was she pretty. Seventeen, and so lovely. And his! Thighs slapped, and the bed creaked and juddered on the boards. Maggie whimpered, George grunted. And then he was done, and sagged over her, blowing like a mill horse while she held his thick, sweaty neck and gazed vacantly at the blowfly bouncing across the ceiling. Days had often begun like this since they'd wed; and then he'd be gone to start the eight-hour shift at the New Wombat mine.

George pulled up his trousers, and sat on the bed to lace his boots.

'You'll mend those socks, won't you, love? And there's that shirt.'

She nodded and stood to dress.

'And love, I'm nearly out of tobacco, so when you're in town, you could stop by Kreckler's. He'll be closed over Christmas.'

Maggie had no plans for town, but she did have to shop, today or tomorrow. Flour was low, and the stores'd be closed Sunday through to Tuesday for the Christmas holiday. Yes, she would shop today.

George had moved through to the other room. Maggie heard him open the tin that sat in a recess above the mantelpiece. Coins shuffled and slid within. She heard him scrabble among them and place a few on the table, and the tin being returned.

'On the table,' he called.

She came out.

George was at the door. 'Don't forget my tobacco, now.'

'I won't.'

He smiled at her and was gone. And then he was back, darting for the top of the meat safe.

'Left me bloody pipe, would you believe!' he said, retrieving it from between dishes and cups stacked there, and leaving with it between his teeth.

DAVID ROSE POKED A stick at the charred dog, at the unlipped teeth gleaming from a skull sheathed tight in burnt flesh. A scrape of a boot, and the grin was banished under ash. He took out a clay pipe, loaded it from a pouch, and lit up from a stick of burning bark. It was a good spot he'd found for himself, all right; there on the edge of town, a pair of gum trees close together to sling the rope for his tent, a stump for a seat and table, and a fine westerly view. He looked at that view now, out over the diggings and on to the dull forest fading into summer haze. He could watch people come and go along Albert Street; women with shopping, men with tools, children with each other. There was a small house — bark roof, weatherboards, two windows — not a hundred yards away, that enjoyed the same view to the west. He'd gone by that house several times these past weeks on his way to town, for food and for the fortnight of work he'd had at Hathaway's blacksmith and livery stables. He'd seen a young woman come out of that house. Her hair was a dark reddish-brown, and framed a face that had not a single line. He'd once had a woman of his own, but she was a withered leaf to this pretty petal. What was her name? he'd wondered. Did she live in that house? Was she in need of a husband? Such a one ought not be without a husband.

VINCENT STREET WAS WIDE and busy, as the commercial centre of a town of three thousand would be. Albert Street brought Maggie Stuart to its bustling midpoint at the Prince of Wales Hotel corner around two. There the summer air was abruptly pungent with dung and dust, and noisy with voice and vehicle.

She began up the street, for Mills' family grocery, negotiating a way among wide skirts, hat brims, and wicker baskets, all constricting the available space, at a premium two days shy of Christmas. From the stream came a hand. It grasped Maggie's forearm and pulled her round to a halt.

'Maggie my dear, heavens, aren't you keeping well!' said an abundant woman of disciplined hair and unruly dentition.

'Thank you, yes, Mrs Homberg, I am keeping very well.'

'Marriage must agree with you then. But it is only six weeks, mind!'

Maggie blushed.

'Oh, take no notice of me. But look, my dear, if ever you'd fancy to come back to the Argus, you know you'll always be welcomed with our open arms. Mr Homberg still says you're the best waitress outside Melbourne.' She squeezed Maggie's arm and leaned in to add, 'And the prettiest!'

DAVID ROSE HAD ARRIVED at the Prince of Wales Hotel at one-thirty, just before the free counter lunches closed. He'd paid his threepence for a pint, in case his entitlement was questioned by the painted lady behind the bar. Rouge and powder may have masked the pocks, but did nothing to hide her wrinkle-nosed disdain for the man before her, with his thick black curls, his beard with the strange shaved gap below his large nose, and the teeth that jutted over his lower lip. Yet she took his order for vegetable soup and bread, and left him to settle in at a table by the window. And while he waited, he gazed out through grimy glass upon a scene of great animation; of drays, of women with baskets and children, of old men smoking and gesticulating, a Chinaman with his vegetable barrow, youths loafing, the well-dressed and ragged, young and old all drawn for whatever was their business to the throbbing and dusty heart of this booming town. And the thought came to him of just how far from Gloucestershire he was, yet how remote he felt from the world just outside this window —

There she was! The pretty woman from the house! He saw her, her hair worn up under her hat, the broad brim shading her lovely face from the glare and heat. She walked upright, with assured step, but he could see that there alone amid all the noise and dust and movement she was vulnerable, like a flower in a storm —

The Castlemaine coach burst into Vincent Street in a great snorting, pounding, and rattling. Dawdling pedestrians quickened their step as this juggernaut of horse, metal, wood, and leather touched down and slowed towards its point of disembarkation.

He swept his eyes along the footpath, but she was gone.

ALICE LATHAM WAS AT the counter when her daughter Maggie entered Mills' store. The women each caught the other's eye and smiled, as in the manner of acquaintances, though there was longing in the older one's gaze. Her lower lip was swollen and split.

'Hello, Maggie,' she said. Her tone was tentative, as if in expectation of a snub. 'I were thinkin', if it's all right, that maybe you an' George might like to come over Saturday afternoon for tea? Seein' as it'll be Christmas Eve. The girls would love to see you; they've hardly seen you at all these past weeks.'

She waited, hopeful.

'Thank you, ma, but George will be out.'

'Oh —'

'Will that be all for now, Mrs Latham?' the shop assistant said.

Alice nodded a thank-you and paid. She continued as she loaded her basket from the counter.

'You could always come on your own. And you do know I wouldn't ask unless Joe were going to be out.'

The assistant had turned his attention to Maggie. She took the opportunity this afforded and avoided the question.

'Four pound of flour, a half-pound of sugar, a half-pound of butter, a pound of dried apples, and four candles, thank you,' she said. 'And soap. I need soap. Though not quite as much as my husband does!'

She chuckled along with the man serving, as much to distract herself from all the awkwardness.

Alice was regarding her daughter. 'It does warm my heart to see you happy, Maggie,' she said. She waited, and walked with Maggie back out to the street, where they stood, the two still figures on a busy boardwalk. Alice placed a hand on Maggie's arm, and had to wait till the clanging bell of the town crier and his bawling of some notice passed them by.

'Please, love,' she said. 'For Christmas.'

Maggie looked at her mother. The fat lip was no surprise, and Maggie felt no longer obliged to enquire as to how she came by it, or of any other bruisings she might bear on any particular day.

'My husband comes first, ma. You taught me that.'

Alice stiffened. 'And rightly so, if you want a roof over your head, and food for your children.'

And to be safe, Maggie thought to say, but she knew the words would be lost on her mother.

'I gave you my consent,' Alice said, in the exasperated tone of it having been said a hundred times. 'So's you would be happy. You know that.' She squeezed Maggie's arm and offered a kindly face. Maggie's was impassive. She felt sorry for her mother, blinded by fear and wifely obligation to Joe Latham. *So help me, Maggie Latham, I swear I will cut your very throat if you defy me.* That's what he'd said, her own stepfather, not two months past. And this was no idle threat uttered in a moment of lapse. He'd bided his time, till they were alone in the house, and the menace was all the greater with a blade in his hand. Ma saw the evidence of his violence; in the bruises and welts, in the tears and frightened face of her daughter, but it was for the violence that left its stain on Maggie's sheets — but could never be spoken of — that Alice gave her consent for her daughter to wed.

4

FRIDAY 23rd DECEMBER
FIVE DAYS BEFORE THE MURDER

A ZEPHYR WAS ENOUGH to quiver the front door in its housing, and a knuckle-rap to shake it, but late at night the quick agitation of the handle would make the distinctive rat-a-tat by which Maggie would recognise her husband's hand. She would slip out of bed, and, with the candlelight from the front room, skip through to let him in. When Louisa Goulding came over, she never knocked; the timber was too hard and coarse for eight-year-old hands. Rather, she would call, 'Maggie!' like the trill of a tiny bird.

She visited early that afternoon, just as George Stuart was leaving. To Louisa, George was no more than the man Maggie lived with, just as she lived with her uncle William Rothery and aunt Emma. Maggie was young and soft and pretty; George was like uncle Rothery; old and whiskery and lined, with chipped fingernails and hands callused and thick. George even seemed old enough to be Maggie's father, though Louisa did know that, like her own father, he'd passed away long ago, before Maggie even knew how to walk.

George nodded a greeting to the girl, and pulled the door shut behind him.

'Maggie won't be long. Just tidying up,' he said with a quick smile and a touch of her cheek as he walked away. At the brow of the hill, he looked back, catching Louisa watching him. Quickly, she turned. When she looked back, he'd gone.

PEARSON THOMPSON ENTERED THE small reception area of the London Portrait Gallery to a tinkling of a bell and a cheery call from a room beyond.

'Be with you in a moment.'

He removed his top hat and patted down the slicks of grey either side of his bare pate to the genial pitch of a happily married husband and wife in conversation. The wall before him was squared with framed photographs; portraits in the main, with a few street and rural scenes. He nodded to himself that he was in the hands of a skilled practitioner.

Footsteps sounded.

'Mr Thompson?'

The customer swivelled on his polished shoes to see a man wearing the smile of one who was content in his work and life.

'Ah, Chuck. Good afternoon.' They shook hands. Thomas Chuck stepped back, and looked his client up and down.

'If you will allow me, Sir, that is a beautiful silk jacket. London?'

'Every stitch.'

'And the cravat the perfect complement.'

Thompson shifted on his feet. Chuck took the hint.

'Well, Sir, I think we should begin.'

'Splendid.'

Chuck ushered his client through into the adjoining small room bright with light from an overhead window. Against the far wall was a padded leather chair by a small round table, upon which a woman was placing a vase of blooms.

'May I introduce my wife, Adeline. Adeline, this is Mr Pearson Thompson, the barrister.'

Thompson bowed his head. Mrs Chuck nodded a how-do-you-do and excused herself while her husband moved to the large brown camera that sat atop a tripod some ten feet from the parlour-room set.

'Please,' he said, pointing to a long mirror on a stand in the corner. 'Should you wish to make sure all is as it should be.'

Thompson took the opportunity provided, mainly to check with angled glances that his hair was shown to best advantage. Also, that his sideburns were well primped, and with a quick comb ensured that the luxuriant moustache which linked them was straight and symmetrical. So satisfied, he settled himself on the chair, though uncertain as to what to do with his top hat.

Chuck relieved him of his indecision.

'I think it best to leave your hat off; it will cast a shadow. But please, why not place it on the table; it is such a handsome hat, after all, and ought to be in the picture.'

Thompson took the advice, and watched as Chuck stooped and disappeared beneath his blackout hood. From a fold, a hand reached around to adjust the brass lens that fixed Thompson in its black stare. Chuck reappeared and placed a cap over the unsettling aperture.

'All in focus. I just have to prepare the plate, so if you'll please bear with me a few moments …'

He smiled and retreated through a door he shut behind him. 'Dark Room. Please Do Not Enter' was painted across it in cursive letters, the florid style strikingly at variance with the authority intended.

Pearson Thompson sat still. The room was rather too warm — his unseasonal portrait attire notwithstanding — and sweat beaded on his scalp. He mopped it away, and considered that at this very moment mild summers were what he missed most about England. Then again in winter, when Vincent Street was a quagmire and its buildings were rendered all the flimsier for the fog, it would be the grand, sweeping façade of his beloved

Lansdown Crescent in the family seat at Cheltenham that had him pining. This portrait was something he'd been looking forward to; court victories are forgotten soon enough, buildings crumble, but a photograph is for the ages.

The dark room door opened, and he watched Chuck return, clutching a wooden box the dimensions of a folded backgammon board. In his wake came a strong and not altogether disagreeable waft of ether. Thompson watched him lift the blackout hood, open the back of the camera, and insert this box. From another part of the camera's back he pulled out a black screen.

'And now for the exposure,' the photographer said, his hand ready to remove the lens cap. 'Still as you can, Sir. Ten seconds ought to do it. Ready? On the count of three ...'

THE GROUND IMMEDIATELY WEST of the Stuarts' was not long cleared, and the detritus of the original forest was still plentiful enough to provide fuel for stoves and open fires. And so it was for sticks and broken roots that Maggie and Louisa ventured into this untidy terrain.

The sun was high and benign in this early day of summer. A breeze was gentle and cooling, flowers nodded, and insects clicked and buzzed into the air. Seemingly involuntarily, Louisa skipped with the joy of being there with her friend on such a day, but promptly tripped on a root and fell with a squeal. Maggie rushed over to find Louisa turned on her back and laughing.

'Oh Louisa, you are silly!' Maggie said, then pretended a trip of her own to lie with her, laughing and beaming with the pleasure of being silly together on a beautiful day.

'What will your aunt say if you break a leg?' Maggie said.

'Or much worse, tear my dress!'

They giggled some more, neither wanting to get up just yet.

Maggie thrust a finger skyward.

'Eagle,' she said.

They watched the bird bank and soar, letting it be the reason to be silent and in their contemplation to enjoy togetherness all the more.

Louisa was suddenly to her feet, squealing and stomping, and slapping at her dress.

'Ants! Ow! Maggie!'

Maggie was up, searching across Louisa's clothing and then to the ground, where an angry swarm was flowing.

'Have you been stung?' she said.

'Yes! Oh Maggie, look how many there are!'

'Well, come away from there!'

Maggie took Louisa by the hand and hurried her away.

'We can gather wood another day.'

'No. I'll be all right.'

They hugged, and when Louisa was quite sure she was ant-free, began their collecting.

Soon, their meanderings took them near the tent that had been there for some days. Maggie had seen the man who resided in it on a few occasions. He was there now, twenty yards distant, seated on a stump by his fire.

He stood.

'Good day,' he said.

Maggie smiled. She looked for Louisa and saw her sitting astride a log, arranging a posy of wildflowers. Maggie's bundle was large enough now. She took the first step towards home.

'You're a nice-looking girl,' the man said.

Maggie turned just far enough to make a small smile, to acknowledge a compliment.

'You live over there?' he said.

Maggie nodded. 'Yes.'

'It's a pity you've not a sweetheart,' he said.

She faced him fully now.

'I'm a married woman.' She glanced at Louisa, and was all the gladder for her being there. But the man seemed unaffected by the bluntness. He even smiled, and added as he sat down, 'Oh, 'cause I'd like to marry you myself.'

Maggie nodded and turned away to leave for home.

'Who's that girl?'

'Louisa, she lives next door to me. I have to go now.'

'You have a good husband?'

'Yes.'

'Where does he work?'

'At the Wombat mine. I expect he'll be home soon.'

'Best I not be asking more questions then, else I get my nose broke!'

5

SATURDAY, CHRISTMAS EVE
FOUR DAYS BEFORE THE MURDER

ONE STOMP OF A boot crushed the skull to splinters, and so was eliminated the last identifiable remains of dog. David Rose scraped the skeleton's disjointed, naked bones into an anonymous jumble among the ash, and sat on his stump to load a pipe. He felt easy, though he'd found no work yesterday, and had no particular drive to look for any today. What he did have was a belly full from another free counter lunch. Dinner had been secured, too. He hadn't quite managed to talk a forequarter of mutton out of the butcher in Albert Street, but a story of hardship and an appeal to old Gelliner's Christian charity had netted him three sausages. No, he'd decided, with tomorrow being Christmas Day, the Wombat Park Boxing Day picnic everyone talked about would be the place and time to find work. He'd be sure to get a good feed there, too, most like. Till then, he'd rest up, keep his own company. Maybe even wash some shirts, if the mood took him.

He sucked on the mouthpiece and drew the smoke deep. He closed his eyes and raised his face to the afternoon sun, its kick mitigated by thin eucalypt foliage nodding in a benevolent breeze. A magpie warbled there, and distant voices drifted in and out on the shifting air. He opened his eyes and beheld the world at his feet: men toiling at the Trafalgar Mine way below, a woman hanging a sheet, a horse turning a Chilean mill. And here he was, David Rose, the burglar from Blakeney, thirty-four years of age, fed, feet up on his stump and smoking a pipe, would you believe! He had such sweet moments from time to time, and was very glad of them, for they reminded him of his good fortune, scant though it was. But he was a free man, with a full belly, and tobacco in his pipe. What else could he want? He looked across the hill to the cottage. She was there, in the yard, singing while she washed clothes in a bucket. He emptied his pipe, stood, and walked towards her.

IN THE CHANGING SHADOWS one hundred and fifty feet below, a man had to mind his head walking along the tunnel to reach the head of the lead.

'No place for the tall man, George,' Aitken observed from ahead as he ducked beneath an irregularity of basalt in the ceiling. 'None for the short either,' he added with a chuckle once the constriction had been negotiated.

'Or the fat,' George added, for want of something else. He preferred to say little — he found reverberations of voice and sloshing water through flickering light and dark disorientating.

'No, they're all at Bleackley's, getting drunk on the profits of our hard graft.'

George let the remark pass. He'd heard it all before from Aitken: the resentment, the jealousy. It was childish; there was no law that said he had to be down here, no gun at his head.

They'd reached the lead, the compressed remains of an ancient river where gold lay for the taking. They fixed their lamps to the shoring.

'You must feel like a pig in shit, married,' Aitken said.

George Stuart grasped a boring rod, ready to hold up for his mate to drive it into the seam with a hammer blow.

'To her, I mean, a bloke like you. I mean, she's a very good-looking woman, your wife, and young. She could be the wife of a gentleman. Instead, she's with you. I don't mean no offence by that, understand, George. I'm just saying, that's all. I mean, good luck to you.'

MAGGIE WIPED DOWN THE table with a damp rag. With the afternoon light reaching across it from the window, she could see she'd done a good job. She smiled at her work, because she loved keeping house, and it very much pleased her to please her husband. And tomorrow was Christmas Day, and they would be hosting two of George's workmates for tea and scones. Later, Mr and Mrs Homberg from the Argus would be their dinner guests. Nothing fancy — sausages and salad, and pleasant conversation with her favourite former employer. This was how she had hoped married life would be, and the anticipation of a lovely day was a joy to savour. But for now there was washing to be done.

Bless George, she thought, filling the butt for her earlier in the day — this was no easy job, loading two buckets at a time and walking a hundred yards to and back from the shaft. Now, as a dutiful wife, she would carry out her side of the enterprise. She filled her wash bucket and, with soap in hand, sat on the threshold and worked up a lather. First in was George's shirt. She squeezed and rubbed, and in the shade of the doorway began to sing softly to herself.

Maggie wasn't aware that she was being watched, and when she saw that she was, knew that the man from the tent hadn't just arrived there on the road frontage. His stance was too square, his carriage too settled, to have been just walking by. No, he'd been there a minute or more, she was sure of it. She stood in the open doorway, with a wet petticoat dripping from her hand.

'You live here?' he said.

Maggie nodded.

He seemed unsure of himself, holding his large hat over his waist and rotating it by the brim. Maggie stooped to collect her bucket.

He stepped forward a few paces, ostensibly to let a dray go by. He pointed. 'I'll be camping across there … till the Christmas holidays are over.'

Maggie's fingers flexed around the bucket handle. She stepped back, and felt for the door.

'Well, good evening to you, Missus,' the man said.

'Good evening,' Maggie said.

She nodded, closed the door, and locked it.

CANDLE-HOLDERS, ASH PANS, AND household containers from tea caddies to flour bins were typical of the assortment of items manufactured, and repaired, by Cockney tinsmith Joe Latham in the shed at the rear of his residence in Bridport Street. In all practical regards this address was an undeniable improvement on his last, the tiny cottage he'd built in Albert Street for his family and business. In fact, with one child from his wife's first marriage and eight since, the move was a necessity. Though he had been the builder, in Latham's head there was no fond nostalgia for the old place, no dreamy musing or cherished memories of humbler beginnings. There was only a deep loathing, such as he might have for a lover who'd wronged him. The simple two-roomed wooden abode, with its makeshift chimney, rough-hewn weatherboards and shingles, one door, two windows, all put together by his own hand, had become for Joe Latham a monument to betrayal, for now it was the place where Maggie and George Stuart lived.

Late that afternoon, Alice returned from town to find Joe at home making repairs to a chair. With her were four of their girls: Maggie's half-sisters. In expectation that Maggie might accept her invitation after all, Alice was made anxious seeing him still there.

'Aren't you going out drinking at the Union?' she said.

Joe looked up from his work. He was a short man, broad and muscular, with sandy hair and eyes that were blue from the scantest pigmentation. They lent him a menacing mien, which he was not loath to exploit.

'In good time,' he said, in a practised tone that let it be known that he considered himself the master of his own life.

Alice was just as practised at ignoring the implication.

'Of course, Joe. Only let me know when you might be home for dinner.' She smiled and went inside. Joe followed, hammer in hand.

'I won't have her in this house, you hear me?' He didn't shout the words, which for Alice didn't make them any the less tiresome.

The girls were by their mother, watching their father as sheep watch a dog. Alice motioned for them to go outside.

She turned to her husband. As usual, she would hear him out, so as not to provoke.

'Margaret defied me,' he said. 'If she don't respect the rules of the house, she's got no place in it. Simple.'

'Why are you still tellin' me this, Joe? I know this is how you think —'

'Because, woman, I don't think you give me the support a wife should give her husband. I turn my back, and she'll be here, laughin' at me. Both of you, most like. Well, I won't have it, you hear me?'

'I think you need to calm yourself, Joe. All them angry words do you no good —'

'You went behind my back, you did, Alice, givin' permission for a marriage that should never be.'

'I did what I thought was right, for my daughter, for all of us. And now she's happy. Don't you want her to be happy, Joe? And please, Joe, would you put that hammer down?'

Joe glared at her a moment, and began to leave the room. At the door, he turned and said, 'George Stuart is no man for

Maggie. He's twenty years older, whatever he says; soon enough she'll be alone, with no means of support. How fuckin' happy will she be then?'

He turned and kicked open the door; he was going back to work.

'More happy than stayin' here,' Alice muttered as she turned her back and began to unload her basket. *For heaven's sake*, she thought, *the wedding is five weeks past*. And to support her husband, she hadn't even attended it. To think of it, having to miss her own daughter's wedd —

Her wrist was suddenly up by her ear, and she was being swung in close. Joe's eyes and nostrils flared. She flinched from his breath, and braced herself for whatever she had coming.

CAN YOU BELIEVE IT, Sarah Spinks fornicating with Angus Miller all Christmas Eve! Yes, and her with six children and a husband, such a good man he is.

Sarah could hear the gossip. When blissful thoughts should be stirring her mind on this walk home, imagined conversation drove them out. *Well, they can all be damned*, she thought. *What business is it of theirs? They know nothing!* She and Edward had not been matrimonial in a year or more, not since the mine accident. Who would know that two days alone in the dark under collapsed rock could so change a husband? Well, it changed hers. Edward had turned anxious, he jumped at shadows, was feverish in thought, quick to temper. He wasn't the husband, let alone the man, she'd wed. Who knows the mind of a woman in her place? Who knows that her love could evaporate as fast as a summer puddle? She hadn't deserted him, and never her children. It's just that there was Angus now, for the manly company, and where was the harm in that, she kept asking herself.

She passed by the Stuarts' house and began down the Perrins Street hill. It was six o'clock, and she ought to have been home an hour ago. Edward would be there from the mine — they all said what a good worker he must be for Roman Eagle to keep him on up top, since he would no longer go below — and the children would be circling for dinner. And thus, with every step closer to home, she felt the weight of the everyday increase.

The sun was still strong in the west, and she paused a moment to lift her face to it. She closed her eyes and reminded herself that it had been a grand afternoon, and ought not be spoilt by guilty thought …

She heard their happy squeals before she saw her children. Across the hill they were, all six of them: Anna holding the baby, the others spearing sticks into a fire and shrieking at the spitting sparks. There was a man sitting there, too. He could have been the man she'd seen these past few days on her way into town. She began walking across the rough ground of debris and stumps of the bygone forest. She drew close and saw that it was him, with his imitation sealskin coat and high-domed hat; the man who had given the children sweets. Had she not told Anna that strangers offering treats were not to be trusted! And didn't Anna know that a fire was not for playing with, and in the summer dry, too!

She reached the children, and their mood became at once respectfully subdued. She took the baby from Anna and admonished her eldest with a look.

David Rose twisted at the waist and looked up.

'Good evening,' he said.

'Good evening.' She hesitated a moment. This man was polite enough, but so brutish. His face was thick-boned, thick-whiskered, and with eyes dark and deep-set. What was she to make of such a man keeping company with young children? Her young children?

He tapped his hat rim, nodded, and turned away. Quickly, Sarah marshalled her brood and left him alone.

6

SUNDAY, CHRISTMAS DAY
THREE DAYS BEFORE THE MURDER

REVEREND WILLIAM 'CALIFORNIA' TAYLOR stood tall in the pulpit and held out his arms in a grand gesture of greeting to the early-morning congregation. The murmur died away and, save for sporadic coughs, the crowded church was silent. From a pew at the rear, Maggie Stuart looked up at the preacher, standing there in his black vestment, his bearded head held high, waiting, as if for a sign from his maker that it was time to begin. She felt the gentle squeeze of her husband's hand around hers. There was such expectation in George's face, in all the faces around her. And so many people were there, and not just the Wesleyans. George had said on the way in that it was for all people that the Yankee evangelist had come, to save them from the profanity, immorality, and drunkenness that had taken such pernicious hold in the goldfields these past years.

Still the minister waited. He waited while, outside, cockatoos screeched, even more as a horse cantered by, and yet more as men greeted each other raucously across the road. Only when the faces before him began to turn to one another did he speak, in the rich and resonant baritone one might have expected.

'Twelve murders in twelve years,' he said. He shook his head and let his chin drop to his chest, as if he had known each and every one of the poor victims as a dear friend. He looked up, and in the gravest cadences, completed the pairing of the awful fact with its starkest interpretation. 'Friends, you don't need me to come across the vastness of the great Pacific Ocean to tell you that something is terribly wrong in this beautiful little town.'

And so began a sermon like no other Maggie had heard. Sermons had always been so dour, incomprehensible, removed from experience. It was for the singing that Maggie came to church. How she loved the singing! Sermons were boiled cabbage; hymns were pudding. But this Christmas Day, this visitor, with his voice, his great gestures, his striding up and down, his vehemence — his charisma — simply insisted that she listen. And believe.

'WE WILL GO TO hell, I think.'

'Then hurry up and climb in here with me, my beautiful Latin lover. You know Lawrence will be home soon, bellowing for his Christmas lunch.'

'And I don't want to be on the menu!'

'No, but you're on mine. Now let me at you!'

Serafino Bonetti had been fornicating with the ample, libidinous, and neglected Mrs Lawrence Telford every other day since the day he first met her. That put their affair at a fortnight — the most exhilarating two weeks she'd had since arriving in the town as the dissatisfied wife of a dour country police sergeant. Serafino was young, attentive, and priapic, and conveniently and fortuitously building the extension to the police cottage, where the sergeant lived. They'd had to be careful, with the cottage immediately adjacent to the police camp, though not so careful as to kill the frisson that the risk of discovery brought to their lovemaking. Still, by now there were times that Penelope wouldn't have minded her husband finding out, if only so she might show herself as a woman of spirit and independence, and not the dutiful, unquestioning accessory he assumed she was.

'Can you sing?' she asked her man. The timing puzzled him.

'What, now?'

Mrs Telford chuckled. 'If you like, though I'd rather you keep your mouth free! No, I mean, do you like to sing? Because if you do, you could join the Philharmonic Society — we're rehearsing *The Messiah* for our opening night in March. At the Theatre Royal. It would be fun!'

Serafino smiled. 'I will think about it.'

MARIA MOLESWORTH HAD WORKED at Pitman's Refreshment Room for more than a year now, on her way, she hoped, to greater things; specifically, a husband and a house. And children, too, of course. But she was nearing thirty, and lately a creeping dread that her dream would never be realised was sinking her into bouts of melancholy. In these troughs, she would dwell on her unchanged circumstances: she was no respectable wife keeping house, but a tart at a goldfields grog shanty. Then sober self-examination would pull her back from the lip of despair, and she would find comfort in acknowledging that at least Pitman's presented her with a steady stream of prospects, and fixed though her lot seemed, her world could change with the very next customer. And until it did, she had room and board, and was safe. She earned good money, too; no one knew better than she how to pout and preen a way into a punter's purse.

Christmas Day was a busy day for Pitman's, and to cater for the holiday patronage, the house standards of beer and whiskey had been augmented with grog of a more eclectic taste, such as absinthe, champagne, claret, and sherry. Yet, with limited kitchen facilities, the menu kept to its standard offerings of meats, bread, and cheese — the kind of tucker most amenable to the palate of the drunkard. And indeed the west end of Albert Street was the haunt of the drunkard, with Pitman's on the West Street corner, the Union Hotel a few doors along, and the West of England Hotel across the road. These establishments didn't so much compete as collude for trade in their luring of clientele from other drinking precincts of the town. Cut-price liquor and pretty young women with a willing disposition were the chief enticements of this informal cartel.

Nonetheless, as a self-interested businessman, Pitman strove always to give his modest premises an edge on his larger neighbours, and so he invested in women he fancied were a little more willing, if not prettier, than those next door or across the road. For this Christmas season, he'd secured the services of Ellen and Susannah. The girls arrived mid-morning from Castlemaine, saucy-dressed and painted. Pitman did the introductions.

'This is Maria,' he said. 'Our grande dame. Ain't that so, Maria?'

Maria stretched her mouth to approximate a smile. For her boss, it was adequate. He turned back to the recruits.

'Any questions?'

They shook their heads, but Pitman was already gesturing to Maria that the girls were in her hands.

WITH HIS CHRISTMAS LUNCH eaten, his wife out, and his afternoon entirely at his disposal, Sergeant Lawrence Telford sat himself on a chair at the front of his residence, the police cottage, and searched through *The Argus* of the 22nd. There was something of the poking at an aching tooth about this, he knew, but he wasn't going to take on faith the report of 'brilliant detective work in Melbourne' that Tandy was going on about. Tandy was barely a constable and barely knew Otto Berliner, much less how pompous and difficult an officer he'd been in the few years he'd endured at Daylesford. It was the cold that Berliner said his health couldn't abide. Ha! Some detective. And there was never a hair out of place; that said enough. Telford scanned the newsprint, muttering, 'Forgery … forgery …' He found it.

'Apprehension of a Forger of Bank Notes,' the headline read. 'Patrick Lennan was charged with committing forgeries on the Bank of New South Wales to the amount of £10,000 …' Telford swallowed, resentful in anticipation of what was sure to follow:

> Detective Otto Berliner … stated that for two months he had been keeping watch over Lennan, who had been accustomed to change his residence every seven or eight days, and his style of dress — sometimes in blue shirt and trousers, or in a suit of black.

There was nothing brilliant about basic surveillance. Telford felt the tension within him ease a little, and read on:

> Lennan had approached engraver Troedl of Collins Street, to make engraved plates for the forging of £5 notes. When Troedl informed the police, Berliner conceived to work in a disguise of wig, whiskers, and spectacles as assistant to Mr Troedl. Under Berliner's direction, Troedl completed the plates and handed them, with two thousand forged notes, to Lennan, with Berliner witness to the whole transaction. It is supposed that Lennan intended to take the spurious notes up the country and buy gold with them. It will thus be seen that Detective Berliner has saved a great number of people from being victims of a most impudent fraud, and it is satisfactory to know that the accused was not able to get rid of any of the notes, for the detectives have not lost an hour in watching him since they were put upon the scent. Detective Berliner has actually been in his company several times, and this circumstance induced him to adopt the clever disguise …

Telford folded the paper, placed it on the adjacent seat, and decided that an aching tooth really ought to be left be.

7

MONDAY, BOXING DAY
TWO DAYS BEFORE THE MURDER

PEARSON THOMPSON STRODE ALONG the sweeping and newly tree-lined gravel drive of Wombat Park, feeling conflicted, for it brought crisply to mind the day he'd first walked Montpellier, his father's estate, as its ambitious new owner. He'd been just twenty-six, home free from chambers at Gray's Inn, with a head full of vision and drive — and a fat inheritance — to see his vision realised. And how! To think, he was hailed as 'The Maker of Cheltenham', no less. False modesty it would be to dispute the accolade, for the lovely gardens, the grand buildings, the wonderful entertainments had made Cheltenham a town of wide renown. It may have been the father who discovered the spa, but it was the son who turned it to gold! So, yes, he was conflicted, for here he was now, an aged man of very modest means, back practising law in an outpost of empire — a spa town, too, just to render the comparison all the more odious — confronted, nay, taunted, by this reminder of what he once was and once had.

At the end of his tormented walk, he found the sun-bathed lawn by William Stanbridge's splendid house comfortably populated with townsfolk gathered there at the owner's pleasure to picnic. A most convivial scene it was, with women seated on chairs and blankets, men standing and drinking by a beer tent, children chasing one another, and dogs wandering for scraps. Beyond, people strolled along meandering paths through tidy young gardens, and in an adjacent paddock, a football match was on. All this diverse activity took place amid jaunty tunes being played by a bright little band set up beneath an ancient eucalypt, a relic of a time long gone when another people gathered here. Pearson Thompson stood at the edge of the action, awkward in his aloneness and searching across the scene for someone he might talk to.

THE BALL BOUNCED FREE, Constable Robert Tandy swooped and gathered it, shoved an opponent aside, and ran on to kick it high and long between two trees serving as goal posts. The small crowd of spectators cheered — none more enthusiastically than pretty young Susannah, there to be seen with Ellen, her friend and colleague from Pitman's. Tandy strutted for his admirer, and reached out a hand to pull to his feet the player he had flattened.

'Nothing broken?' he said.

David Rose reassured the policeman with a shrug that all was in working order. Tandy righted Rose nonetheless — a gesture he knew would be sure to impress those at the fence.

ON A BLANKET BY a line of shrubs at the back of the busy lawn, Maggie Stuart sat with Louisa Goulding. A neighbour in West Street, Elizabeth Shier, came by with bottles of mineral water, taken from a dray put there by their host for the refreshment of all. She saw Maggie and offered one. Maggie took it.

'You must look after that lovely complexion of yours, Maggie. The sun's fierce today, so drink plenty.'

'Thank you, Mrs Shier. That's very thoughtful of you.'

Mrs Shier smiled. 'Your mother's here,' she said. 'Over by the beer tent.'

Maggie nodded, and felt the familiar gnaw in her stomach that Joe might be with her. She looked about. The lawn was crowded, and as Joe was likely to be in the company of drinking companions all afternoon, she decided she would just stay put and enjoy the day. Besides, Louisa was with her for company, and now, two more arrived to share their patch of lawn.

'Hello, Maggie Stuart! How lovely to see you.' Mrs Buckley and her husband were precisely the kind of company Maggie might have wished for. They were elderly and respectable, people with whom she could feel safe.

'We have missed your service at Tognini's, haven't we, dear?' Mr Buckley said.

Maggie blushed. Tognini's Hotel in Burke Square was Maggie's last place of employment before she became Mrs Stuart.

'All I can say is that George Stuart is one very lucky man,' he added, which did nothing to ease Maggie's discomfort.

'Would you like a scone?' she said, and opened a tea towel in her basket. 'Louisa baked them.'

The Buckleys smiled at the girl, who blushed even redder over cheeks already rosy from a touch of sunburn.

'Is your husband here?' Mrs Buckley said.

'He's at a wrestling match, at Browne's Hotel in Coomoora,' Maggie said.

'As a spectator, I hope!' Mr Buckley quipped.

Some women walked by and greeted Maggie with friendly hellos and promises to see her later in the day. She beamed back at them, happy to be there, and for the moment unconcerned by the chance that she might bump into Joe Latham sometime that afternoon.

DAVID ROSE SLIPPED BEHIND the stump of a once-mighty gum, unbuttoned his flies, and aimed his piss at a yellow daisy. The flower bent before the stream and bobbed back, only to be slapped away again. He smiled at his puppetry and how well satisfied he was with himself coming up here today. He'd cadged lunch and beer, and, what was more, a steak for his dinner. And Mr Stanbridge's foreman had told him there'd be a chance of some work if he'd like to come back tomorrow — though no promises, mind. He'd enjoyed the football game as well, the knocks and bumps nicely cushioned now by alcohol. He closed his eyes and let his head loll back for the mid-afternoon sun to fill his face as his bladder emptied. It had been a grand day all right …

A moan came from somewhere nearby. And a whimpering — like that of a woman, it sounded. He drew back foliage. There was a hayshed, cleared out ready for this year's harvest. And in the shadows within, a naked arse was hard at work, with a woman's bare legs crossed over it. He crept forward for a better view.

BY FOUR, THE CROWD had thinned to the point where any sensible people still remaining felt it was time to be going home lest they be left in the company of those who never knew when enough was enough. Maggie had chatted at length with Mr and Mrs Buckley, and in their company two pleasant hours had slipped by. Now, as they had left, she was homeward bound herself. She stood, and it took a moment for a sudden surge of dizziness to abate. An arm grasped her elbow.

'Maggie, are you all right?'

It was Johanna Hatson, a woman Maggie once worked with in the bar at Blanket Flat Hotel.

'A touch of heat, I think. Thank you, Johanna.'

'I'll walk with you.' The pair was joined by Louisa, and together they began back down the drive. Many other returning picnickers were strung out the length of the young avenue, chatting, laughing, or in quiet contemplation of the lovely day they'd just had.

'Did you see that man?' Johanna said suddenly, with open-mouthed alarm. 'I think he was Italian. And filthy!' She shook. 'Ooo, he sent a shiver down my spine, I can tell you.'

Maggie didn't much care for stories of such men, and now resented Johanna's being there.

'What did he say?' Louisa said. Johanna seemed taken aback by the girl's boldness, but more gratified that some interest was being shown in her report.

'Oh, he didn't say anything — not to me, anyways. He was just so strange, looking at me and Mrs Telford and the other ladies on our rug. I'd wager he was staring at you, too, Maggie … Oh, there's my boy. I must go. It was lovely to see you, and you,' she added with a smile for Louisa, and bustled away.

'Let's not talk about strange men, Louisa,' Maggie suggested with a smile.

'She probably made it up.'

'Yes, she probably did.'

They'd reached the end of the drive, on Glenlyon Road, and enterprising young men were offering a taxi service for anyone preferring to trade the discomfort of walking the hot mile back into Vincent Street for that of a hard ride on the back of a dray. There was still room, and for tuppence the deal still seemed more than reasonable.

'Come on,' Maggie said. They clambered aboard, the boy flicked the reins, and they were away.

MARY FOLEY WALKED WITH her new lover along the Wombat Park drive.

'You won't forget now, will you?' she said with a grin.

'How could I?' Pearson Thompson said, head up and looking to the front.

'A fair exchange, I think — flesh for brains. Don't you think so, a fair exchange?'

'I thought we'd established as much already.'

Mary chuckled. 'Ooh, you have a way with words! Mind you speak like that in court, now.'

Pearson looked down at his diminutive companion, smiling up at his stony face. She was indeed a pretty young thing, he thought.

'What are you thinking, you old devil?' she said, poking a finger into his side. Actually, Pearson was considering how he'd arrived at this place in such a funk, yet here he was, a few hours on and the object of desire to this erotic creature of full mouth, ample breasts, and gyrating hip. It mattered not a jot to him that the attraction from her point of view might well be entirely commercial.

'I was thinking, Mary, that it would be prudent to begin the preparation of your case as soon as possible. Drunk and disorderly is a very serious charge, you know, and as it's not the first time for you, I think a thorough briefing is called for.'

'What are you getting at, Pearson?'

'I just thought you might, um ...'

'Pay twice? Is that what you thought?'

A change in mood had come over Pearson's picnic mistress, and he feared she might not have the self-restraint to keep it discreet in this public setting.

'We have a contract, you and I have, Pearson, and I've kept my side. Now you keep yours!'

MAGGIE LIT A CANDLE and placed it in its brass holder on the table. Though intense orange light from the setting sun beamed through the cottage's two windows, Maggie liked to even out the transition from light to dark.

'Your uncle will call for you soon?'

Louisa nodded and Maggie smiled. She would be glad of her young companion's company a little longer.

'What shall we sing?' Louisa said, a moment before a pebble struck the stone base of the fireplace and bounced out onto the floorboards.

Maggie stood, and backed away, as if it might explode or leap at her.

'It's all right, Maggie,' Louisa said, retrieving it from under the bench 'It's just a stone come loose, that's all.' But another rattled down the chimney and skittered out to come to rest at Maggie's feet. And then came two more together.

Louisa was standing now.

Maggie turned for the door, grasped the knob and the key for turning … and stepped back as the door was pushed from the other side and George swayed in, red-nosed and grinning.

'I didn't scare you, did I, love?'

Someone else appeared there, behind George. He swung around and extended a hand to William Rothery.

'Will, me old neighbour. Come to collect the lass?'

Rothery seemed unimpressed at the tipsiness, and motioned for Louisa to come along.

As she had done on many occasions, she hugged Maggie and left with her uncle.

George had seated himself on the bench.

'A fine day, Maggie,' he said. 'See your ma?'

Maggie nodded.

'That's good,' George said, nodding that he was pleased to hear it. 'Joe there — ? Hey, I see that tent's still up across the way.'

Maggie didn't reply. George was rambling anyway. She took scones from the safe and placed them on a plate.

George swung a leg over the bench and craned his head around to catch her eye.

'Are you not feeling well, love? I'm sorry about them stones down the chimney — I meant no harm.'

'Please, George, I don't want to talk about it.'

George stood, and put a hand on Maggie's shoulder.

'About them stones?'

Maggie swung around.

‘Please, George. About Joe, or about the man in the tent.’

‘Well, I’m sorry, love, but when a man comes round asking his wife questions —’

‘George, please.’

‘You think I’m jealous?’

Maggie didn’t reply. She felt George’s arm enclose her, and the squeeze of his right hand on her upper arm.

‘Well, Maggie, I’m not jealous. You are my wife, and will be till the end of time.’

8

TUESDAY 27th DECEMBER
THE DAY BEFORE THE MURDER

DAVID ROSE'S CALICO WAS folded and stowed in his swag by nine, before the heat could intimidate him into delaying for a day. For the comfort of having a few quid in his pocket should illness or injury lay him up, the imperative was to work. And strong though he felt in his bones and sinews, age would soon enough see infirmity intervene. What then for David Rose, he wondered.

The good-looking woman wasn't there when he went by up Albert Street. He watched in case she came out, and even when he was well past, he turned about-face for a final look. But no. Such a modest cottage she lived in, but how happy a circumstance it would be to live in it with such a beauty to keep him! He adjusted his load across his back and set a course for Wombat Park.

A woman was approaching. She'd emerged from the next house along — Pitman's refreshment room, a ramshackle affair of lean-to additions and an undulating bark roof. David Rose had never entered the place; no free counter meals were ever on offer, and fights seemed all too frequent for his liking.

He nodded and tipped his hat to the woman, but a blank look was all she would offer. He turned to watch her bustle over the ground in her skirts. Like a giant lampshade she was. He saw her stop at the cottage and knock. He paused a moment. He saw the door open, and there she was. He stayed long enough to see that her visitor gave her no reason to smile.

THE FOREMAN DRIVING SHEEP at Wombat Park remembered him.

'Rose?'

'Aye, David Rose. You were sayin' I might come today for work?'

The foreman grimaced and gave a regretful shake of the head.

'I can't say right at present there's work, but I tell you what, if you pitch your tent by the yard, tomorrow morning I'll see.'

'No promises then?'

'It's the best that can be done. The men aren't yet back from holiday, and if my reckoning's right, one or both of them could well be in no fit state. But there'll you be, all good and ready. You don't drink, yourself?'

'Not so's I get drunk, I don't.'

The foreman nodded.

'You'll camp then?'

Rose shrugged.

'I might keep looking, if it's all the same. I was wondrin' if there might be picnic left-overs?'

'I reckon enough to fill that huge bloody hat o' yours!' The foreman pointed to the house, an elegant weatherboard building at the end of the drive, its sunny eastern side luxuriously cool and dark under a long and low veranda.

'Elsie will show you the kitchen.'

'WHAT DO YOU MEAN, you daren't go?' Mrs Pitman said, with irritation. 'I run a business, and I pay your mother good money to wash. And now, I'm telling you to go fetch her.'

Louisa Goulding sat in the corner, caught between wanting to tell the big horrible woman to go away and leave Maggie alone, or to slip through a gap in the boards and pray she left soon. Maggie, agitated to the point of a reddened face, was pleading. 'I can't go to my mother's, not today.'

'Why ever not!' Mrs Pitman said. 'What else do you have to do!' She swept an exaggerated gaze across the spartan interior. 'You seem to do nothing but walk back and forth into town all day.'

Maggie drew in her breath, and put her face in her hands. Louisa went to her and put her arms across her back. Mrs Pitman scowled and hurrumphed.

'Well?' she said.

Maggie straightened, and with steady eye on her interrogator, said, 'I can't go — I won't go — not when my stepfather's there.'

Joyce Pitman shook her head and blew out a loud breath as the door swung open and George entered. He nodded to Mrs Pitman and sensed the air.

'Trouble?' he said.

Mrs Pitman deflected him.

'Goodness no, Mr Stuart. I just came by to see if my husband might borrow a gimlet from you. A few screw holes need drilling. He'd need it only a day.'

'He can have it two if need be, Mrs Pitman. I'm back at the mine tomorrow.' He faced Maggie. 'Night shift, Maggie. I start at four tomorrow afternoon, so I won't be home till after midnight. Sorry, my love, but there it is.'

SWEAT HAD MADE A feeding ground of David Rose's back for a seething multitude of flies. All across it they settled and resettled, mopping the dirty fabric of his dark coat as he trudged along the Glenlyon road under a severe sun. His swag, the sum total of his possessions, pulled at his shoulder; his hat grew hot, and his boots swung heavy. But he was well used to the enterprise of tramping, and, by turning his mind from the discomfort, found the miles took care of themselves.

As the afternoon wore on, with the heat and miles mounting, asking for work had become begging for work. The best anyone would do was give him a mug of tea, tell him he was too early for the hay, and that maybe he could try at Porcupine Ridge to the north where the grass was advanced by a week. Or, as one farmer, John Sherman, advised, there was George Cheesbrough in Glenlyon; maybe he was in need of help. Rose ate the remains of the picnic leftovers, a date scone, and set off in that direction.

At five o'clock, when at last the day was on the turn, and in a mood of quiet resignation, he rapped on the front door of the Cheesbrough cottage. It promptly opened, and a kindly face appeared from the dim interior. The woman didn't have to smile — there were good reasons for not doing so — but she did, and it disposed him to believe that prospects here were good, or else to accept rejection without protest.

'Good evening, Missus,' he said, raising his hat from its sweat-flattened seat. I'm told hereabouts that your husband might be hiring? I can tell him I'm an honest worker, strong, experienced with horses —'

A dog loped from the side of the house, barking. The woman called it to her.

'A good watchdog, is he?' Rose said.

The woman darted out and took the dog by the collar. She smiled, seemingly relieved to have averted an incident.

'If you'll wait here a moment, Mr … ?'

'Rose, Ma'am, David Rose.'

'Well, Mr Rose, I'll fetch Mr Cheesbrough. I'm his wife.' She smiled again and retreated with the dog into the house, leaving the door open. A good sign, he thought; a sign of trust.

He let his swag slip to the ground, and felt his muscles and bones spring back with the relief. A nice place, this; a garden with shade and sun and pretty little blue birds scampering and twittering through it all. A faint breeze brought sweet and earthy smells of grass and manure. A cow lowed. He could live in such a place. Yes, with a good wife.

SERGEANT TELFORD PICKED UP a pillow from the marital bed and pressed his face into it. What he expected to detect, he wasn't sure; the smell of adultery maybe, for future reference. He scanned its floral surface for an errant black hair, to no avail. No matter, he'd have the evidence soon enough. Penelope had always underestimated him. He replaced the pillow and smoothed out the indentation. He stepped back and gazed dead-eyed at the bed. What greater humiliation was there than to be cuckolded, he wondered. He felt anger should be rising within him, but he found it was well in check; hidden, in fact. He decided he would keep it that way, until an appropriate, satisfying course of action could be decided upon.

DAVID ROSE NODDED ACROSS the kitchen table at his new boss. The evening was warm, and its light fast-fading. It felt good to have made a start already, feeding the cattle. Jane Cheesbrough had made them a scone and tea supper. She arrived now from the house to clear, the dog following.

'He sleeps in here?' Rose said.

Cheesbrough chuckled. 'You don't like dogs?' he said.

'Some dogs.'

'Well, your bed's in here, the dog's is under the tank. I'll call you out at five-thirty tomorrow morning. There'll be oats for breakfast, and a brew —'

A man appeared at the door. His clothes were in need of changing, and his face of a wash. He removed his tattered hat, and held it flat against his chest.

'Beggin' your pardon, Sir, you're the master of the house?' this tramp said to Cheesbrough.

'That I am, master and lord of the manor is me.'

'Spare a traveller lodging for the night?'

'I'm sorry, but I have no convenience,' Cheesbrough said, with a gesture to Rose that all vacancies had been filled.

The man wasn't so easily put off.

'Just the night, and I'll be gone,' he said.

Cheesbrough grimaced, and shrugged that he was sorry but he'd already given his answer, unfavourable though it was.

'But you ought to let a man stop. For just a night! It's dark out now and —'

David Rose took this as his cue. 'We have got no convenience here, man!' he said, with glowering look. The tramp looked at Rose a few moments, the set of his face making it plain that he would not be intimidated.

'I'll be square with you,' he said to Rose, 'you have no business to put in your word.'

At this, Rose was on his feet. 'Don't I, now!' he bellowed as his chair overturned and clattered to the stone floor. This, at last, was too much for the man at the door, and he vanished from that dark opening and into the night.

9

WEDNESDAY 28th DECEMBER
THE DAY OF THE MURDER

AT AROUND THREE, WHEN his wife had settled in to her cooking, John Pitman thought it a good time to return George Stuart's gimlet. Why she didn't ask him first, he had no idea; he had one of his own. He slipped out beyond his woodshed and along the goat track to his neighbours, fifty-odd yards to the west. A sturdy breeze was up, and undergarments, both male and female — and a dress he recognised — were flapping loudly on the Stuarts' line, strung across his way. He ducked beneath the washing, and the cottage stood before him across five yards of patchy ground. The emptiness of the yard was stark, unexpected, and a sudden feeling of apprehension and disappointment halted him. The breeze lulled, and sounds came from within the building. He stole closer, and heard the rhythmic creaking so familiar to him. He pressed an ear to the wall, straining to hear Maggie's whimpers over the scraping and grunting …

It stopped.

Pitman hurried away, watched by his wife from inside the woodshed.

DAVID ROSE TOOK A swig from his water bottle and wiped his mouth. He took out a pipe and lit it. Strange, he thought, the same hot sun — foe yesterday, yet friend today. What a difference work made to a man's view of things. He looked about, across yellow fields to green forest and to blue sky. He could believe he owned it all and that no one could deny him. Yes, it was grand to be out under the sun today. He picked up the scythe and swept it through the sward, hearing the swish of blade, the fall of grass, and the click and whirr of insects disturbed. A week of this good life he'd been promised, with meals, a soft bed, and four shillings a day. *A good man, Cheesbrough; a good woman, his missus.*

ALICE LATHAM HAD WORN many blackened eyes in her years with Joe, and this one wasn't the worst, at least not to look at. But as the latest in the series, it attested most to a helplessness that was beyond remediation. At least, that's what others might think. She prayed only that Maggie wasn't one of them. She looked at herself in the mirror that swivelled on the dresser in the bedroom, and noted that the colour had faded since Monday night. *Doesn't Maggie know the risk I took for her, defyin' Joe like that*? George Stuart, she was certain, would never raise a hand in anger to her beautiful daughter. With George, Maggie was out of harm's way —

The outside door squealed. Boots rang on the boards. Alice turned away from the mirror and busied herself with the bedding.

'Still in here?' Joe said.

'Just tidying. I know how you like the bedclothes straight.'

'You know there's no bread for supper, or butter?'

'Don't worry yourself, Joe. I'm going to shop this afternoon.'

'And plannin' to see Maggie, no doubt.'

Alice stood up from the bed. She looked at her husband square-on, if not a little to the side, to present his recent handiwork to greatest effect. The man was capable of some shame.

'I had no plans to, Joe, but now that you remind me, I might well make some,' she said, with a defiance that exhilarated her.

'Whatever you like,' Joe said. 'Just don't be out so late our girls go hungry.'

'When have I ever let our girls go hungry, Joe?'

She was following him now, demanding answers, but he was smiling at her, compounding her exasperation.

'When, Joe?'

He sat at the table, smirking as she railed as never before.

'How dare you say such things. I know why you do, because I dared to allow my own daughter to be happy, to be safe from you, you ...'

He sprang out a hand and caught her wrist, and twisted it so that she had to arch her back awkwardly.

'What?' he said. 'What am I?'

'Please, Joe, you're hurtin' me. Please.'

He let go. She left the room.

'Go and see Maggie all you want. I don't give a tinker's. Just don't bring that whore here.'

MAGGIE FINISHED HER SHOPPING at Mills' family grocer late afternoon and began for home. First day back after the holidays was as busy as the last day before, and she regretted not making an earlier start. Still, she was done now, and thought to get home to cook and eat before the sun set on this evening that she would be alone, now that George was on night shift. Louisa had said she'd come over, so there was that to look forward to.

Briskly, Maggie made her way down Vincent Street, and was on the point of turning into Albert Street, for the half-mile home, when she collided with a woman whose face she recognised, but for which she had no name.

'Oh, I beg your pardon,' Maggie said.

A can of fish had been jolted from her basket, and she knelt to retrieve it from the gravel.

'You're Margaret Stuart,' Maria Molesworth said.

Maggie stood. 'Yes.'

This woman seemed tense, as if a wrong had been done her and that Maggie was responsible for. But she wasn't elaborating, so Maggie smiled feebly and made to continue her journey.

'Do you know me?' Maria said.

Maggie looked back, and shook her head. This was already very discomforting.

'I'm sorry, no I don't. I have seen you before, I'm sure —'

'My name's Maria. I work at Pitman's. You would have seen me when you go by.'

'Yes, yes,' Maggie said, smiling and nodding as if this might ease the apparent tension. 'I have seen you, Maria.'

'Your husband knows me 'n'all — George Stuart.'

At this, Maggie abandoned any belief that this was simply a civil exchange between passers-by. Why was she saying this? To upset her? Because it did upset her. And if it continued, it would anger her.

'I have to go home now, please, Maria.'

'Don't you go walking off with your nose in the air.' She pressed a hand to Maggie's chest.

'Please, Maria. I have no quarrel with you. I want to go home.'

Maria suddenly seemed to have decided enough was enough. She removed her hand and walked away into Vincent Street.

ON THAT LONELY EVENING, Louisa Goulding appeared to Maggie like an angel from heaven. She welcomed her young companion with a hug and a wide smile.

'Some broth? It's vegetable.'

Outside, a pot was resting on the bricks by the cooking fire. Maggie ladled them each a mug, and tore pieces from a loaf. Stumps served as seats for their dining. At a little after five, the sky was still blue, but the heat had been seen off by a cool and intrusive breeze from the south-west.

'The man's gone,' Louisa noted, nodding to where David Rose's tent had been.

'Where, I wonder,' Maggie said, idly. With an exchange of smiles, both agreed this was something to be glad of, and that there would be no more mention of him.

'I brought my hymn book, Maggie.'

'Then we shall sing. Inside, though — we don't want to trouble the neighbours!'

They put their mugs down and walked to the door, Louisa leading. Behind her, a shape among the stones and untidy grasses caught Maggie's eye. She bent down and picked up a clay pipe. It had a curved stem and a large bowl, chipped on the inside. It didn't look much like any pipe George smoked, but, just in case, she took it inside and placed it on the meat safe.

SERGEANT TELFORD STOOD AT his back door, a mug of tea in hand, watching his hired Italian builder nail a final ceiling joist into place. Sweat plastered the young man's shirt to his back, and dripped from the thick, black hair he kept swept back from his face with occasional rakes of his slender hands. Telford found it impossible to behold the view before him without thinking of his wife's legs splayed beneath that lean, muscled body.

Bonetti looked up and smiled. Telford was more than a little irritated to note that he did so without the slightest sign of apprehension.

'I hope you'll be pleased with this new room, Sir,' he said.

'Yes. I'm sure I will. You've done a good job,' Telford said, and in that moment hating himself for not just throwing the greasy little bastard into the street. But he knew there was a better way.

'*Grazie*, Sir. Well, if you don't mind, that should do me for today. I leave you now, for you and your wife to have dinner.' He began to gather his tools.

'Please, Mr Bonetti, join us, why don't you? I've got to eat early — I'm on duty tonight.'

Serafino hesitated. He began to make noises that unfortunately he was unable to stay, but Telford wasn't waiting for an answer. If he couldn't bring himself to do violence, he could at least make the man squirm. And Penelope, too.

'Penny, dear,' he called to the kitchen, 'I've asked Mr Bonetti to dine with us, to thank him for all he's done. We've plenty to spare?'

Mrs Telford was promptly at the door. If her husband was hoping to make her uncomfortable, he was to be greatly disappointed, for she showed no sign of it. She even embraced the suggestion.

'How thoughtful of you, Lawrence,' she said, and pecked him on the cheek. 'He has done such a wonderful job; I'm completely satisfied with his work. You'll stay then, Mr Bonetti?'

'*Grazie*, Mrs Telford, but I do have an appointment.'

'Oh, that's a pity,' Penelope said with a frown. 'We shall have to arrange another time.'

'You're very kind, Mrs Telford,' Serafino said.

'My pleasure, Mr Bonetti.'

Telford looked at these two. Utterly shameless, they were — not even a blush or an awkward glance. They didn't care what he thought, let alone whether he knew. But in the end, they would pay; he would see to that.

AT AROUND 9.00 P.M., a firm knock rattled the door.

'Louisa, are you there?'

The voice, a man's, startled Maggie. She'd been resting with her head on her hands on the table. She sat up. 'Who's that?'

'Are you ready to go home? It's time to go to bed.'

'It's my uncle,' Louisa said. She collected her hymn book and hugged her friend. 'I'll see you tomorrow,' she said.

'Yes, tomorrow. That would be good. Goodnight then, Louisa. Sleep well.'

Louisa opened the door. Through the gap, Maggie and William Rothery smiled and exchanged goodnights, and with a brief look and a wave back, Louisa disappeared with her uncle into the dark.

Maggie locked the door and stood there, stricken by the sudden emptiness in the room. She heard the wind across the roof and in the trees, and saw it in the flicker of the candle, and decided: she would go to bed. She lit a candle from the one on the table, and, with a hand to shield the flame, crept through into the bedroom and closed the door. With her light placed on the bedside table, she undressed, folding her skirt and blouse and placing them neatly on the trunk. She put her brooch on the dresser. She'd already taken off her boots, but left her stockings on for the chill. George had suggested that.

Maggie retrieved her chemise from under a pillow, pulled it on over her head, climbed onto the bed, and edged herself between the cool sheets, taking care not to untuck them. She settled, lying on her side, with the bedclothes tight and drawn up close. At last, by lying still, the creaking of the bed timbers was stayed; she could hear nothing now, bar the occasional rattle of the outside door before the gusts. At that moment, she felt safe. She licked a fingertip, ventured an arm from the covers, and snuffed out the flame. Light from the gap beneath the door waxed and waned in the draughts. Through the window, a star appeared. She gazed at it, quietened by its constancy amid all the turbulence. She could believe that it was her star, watching over her. *George'll be home soon*, she told herself, and closed her eyes …

It must have been on the cusp of sleep that Maggie was disturbed by the rattling door. She listened … It shook, hard, as if taken by the handle. She breathed into the still space beneath the blankets. *There's no one there, there's no one there*, she whispered to herself. *It's the wind …*

The shaking stopped. She held her breath, straining to hear. She turned on her back. She sat up. The bed creaked. The wind soughed and the door rattled. Something blew over outside; there was a hollow clatter, like wood striking rock. It was the barrel on the chimney. A fragment of rock bounced off the hearth and skittered across the floor in the other room. A shower of smaller stones and sand now ... Maggie's breathing was rapid and shallow; her heart thumped in her neck. The wind whistled, and branches swished and tossed. The door rattled again.

She had known other moments of terror, when she could let her brain go numb to the senses, when she could shut out the smell of Joe Latham's tobacco breath, the rough glide of his callused hand ... She got out of bed and stood in the darkness. The sounds from the other room had stopped. *There are tricks the wind can play*, she thought, *in the dark* —

The front door rattled.

'George? Is that you?' she said.

10

9.00 A.M. THURSDAY 29th DECEMBER

CONSTABLE IRWIN LEFT THE Stuart cottage with his package of evidence, and plunged into the milling, murmuring crowd. It was already of nuisance proportions, and was becoming all the more so by the minute as it continued to swell. Speculation was rife, and in some quarters not principally over who had perpetrated this monstrous act, but rather why the victim should have found herself in such mortal danger. That she was violated had already been decided among the crowd; she was a pretty young woman, after all, and robbery could hardly have been a motive, as word was that nothing had been stolen.

Sergeant Telford detailed three constables to keep the spectators well back, with orders to arrest transgressors. Another policeman, Constable Mansell, was on guard at the cottage front door, where through the throng a man lugging unwieldy equipment had just arrived. He introduced himself with a hand extended from between the legs of a tripod.

'Good morning, Constable. Thomas Chuck — London Portrait Gallery. I'm here on the order of Detective Walker. On account of the coroner —'

'Being away. Yes, yes, Mr Chuck, you are expected. The

deceased is through there.'

The sentry made room. Chuck gathered his apparatus and hefted it across the threshold.

REVEREND TAYLOR HAD RISEN early and slipped away from a back room at Pitman's with a nod of thanks to the proprietor for his discretion. He passed unseen by George Stuart, seated at the bar and throwing down a double whisky. Stuart had just come from Detective Walker, who'd checked with the mine and so cleared him of suspicion — a development that brought him some guilty comfort.

'That's on the house,' John Pitman said. 'Another?'

Stuart didn't reply. Pitman replenished the glass.

'What's on your mind?' he said, as Mrs Pitman arrived with a basket of wet clothes. She put it down and pulled her husband away.

'He shouldn't be here, drinking. It'll do him no good,' she said in coarse whisper.

But Pitman wasn't quite done. He put a hand on Stuart's shoulder. 'She was a beautiful young woman, your Maggie —'

The front door creaked. Pitman looked up, to see a man there.

'She should never have married you, Stuart.'

Stuart spun around; Joe Latham had announced himself in his coarse cockney. He stood there in the doorway as if to gauge the odds before committing further to the room. But Stuart was already on his feet and striding towards the short man, jaw set and fists tight. Latham didn't flinch. Stuart pulled up. Pitman appealed to reason and self-restraint.

'Now listen, fighting won't do no good.'

'Go on, Stuart,' Latham taunted, 'but I know you're not man enough.'

Stuart was blowing hard, unsure of whether to attack or leave. Latham scoffed at the indecision.

'I always said you were wrong for my girl. I never meant for you to have her.'

At this, Stuart found voice, and his fists. He leapt at Latham, 'You cut her throat, you bastard!'

They pushed and twisted in each other's grip. Latham broke free and landed a blow on Stuart's cheek. Pitman was onto them to spare furniture and glassware. He tried to pull Latham away, but it was Mrs Pitman who proved effective. She bustled over and inserted herself into the fracas.

'For the love of God!' she cried, glaring at one and then the other. 'Never have I seen the like of it. Your own wife, your own step-daughter, lying up there like that, all exposed, violated, drenched in her own blood —'

Pitman pulled her away. The combatants straightened themselves. George Stuart collected his hat and departed.

11

FRIDAY 30th DECEMBER

WILLIAM STANBRIDGE LIVED BY a maxim of taking the initiative. Whether it was to emigrate at the age of twenty-four from England, to invest in property and mining, or even to live among the Boorong Aboriginal people to record their astronomical knowledge, he was never one to wait for instructions, permission, or approval. And so it was that now, as a Daylesford magistrate with a young woman viciously murdered within his jurisdiction, he wasn't about to change a life's habit just because the coroner happened to be out of town. No, Stanbridge decided that it fell to him to take charge, and at ten in the morning of Friday December 30th, at Daylesford Court House, before a packed public gallery, he began his magisterial inquiry into the death of Margaret Stuart. Joining Stanbridge on the bench were Mayor George Patterson and local solicitor Joseph Dunne. Representing the police was Superintendent Francis Reid from Castlemaine. Before proceedings could begin, Reid rose to seek leave to express an opinion.

'Your Worship, while I am prepared to leave this case in the hands of the bench, I feel that as this is a case of such importance, and seeing as the coroner has already taken the initiative and ordered a post-mortem examination, and that I do have some doubts as to your power, Sir, with respect, to empanel a jury —'

'Come to the point, Superintendent,' Stanbridge urged.

'Well, Sir, I think that as the coroner may well return from Woodend within an hour or two, we might best be advised to wait. Nothing we do, after all, will bring the woman to life, or this inquiry to a conclusion today. And the police will have additional information to bring to bear, and so might not wish to hurry the case. However, as I said, I am happy to leave the matter in the hands of the bench.' He sat down.

'Thank you, Superintendent Reid,' Stanbridge said, with a hint of a smile, 'then we shall proceed.'

Stanbridge took a moment, sufficient to distance Reid's misgivings from the serious business at hand. When the gallery was silent and all attention directed his way, he began, and on the front foot.

'The delay that has occurred in this case is a disgrace to this district. Here we have the body of a murdered woman corrupting for thirty-six hours with nothing done. Nothing. I don't blame the police — they have their orders — but they have not shown due respect to the local magistracy, which, instead of communicating with, they have telegraphed all over the country. The police well know magisterial inquiries are conducted every day, but why not in this case? And now, the coroner has ordered a post-mortem —' He paused to consult Reid. 'Completed last evening?'

Reid nodded. 'Yes, Your Worship, as the body lay in the Stuart bedroom. It was around seven, I believe.'

Stanbridge continued, 'A procedure which will have resulted in such mutilation of the body that no jury would be able to tell the cause of death, whether by suffocation or otherwise. In effect, the coroner has done away with a jury.'

Stanbridge's exasperation was apparent in his tone, and was now openly expressed in every word. He took the opportunity to indulge.

'It seems that local magistrates are deemed efficient only in the signing of summonses or dealing with drunken men. It is my feeling that out of respect for ourselves, and in defence of the locality that has so grossly been neglected, we shall go on without further delay!'

Cheers and applause erupting from the gallery were promptly suppressed by a disapproving glare from the speaker.

Reid got to his feet, looking a little chastened.

'Sir, in reference to the "mutilation of the body", referred to by the bench, means have been taken to obviate this; a photograph has been taken of the deceased woman as she was found. This has been received as evidence.'

Stanbridge twitched with irritation at this circumvention of procedure. Reid sat down, as Stanbridge resumed. 'Even so, a coroner's jury would now be a farce. No twelve men could go now and look at the body and form any idea of the cause of death. In my experience, I have never heard of a body being moved before a jury had seen it. I do not blame the police, mind.' He addressed this remark to Reid, who nodded his acceptance of it. 'I mention this only so that we have a more defined course of action. If the Minister of Justice himself would line up here and defend us, well and good; but if our men are to be murdered, and our women violated, it is our duty to protect ourselves, and so this inquiry will go on.'

Mr Dunne took the floor in support. 'It is my belief that this magisterial inquiry will be thoroughly effectual, and given that the body has been moved, any subsequent inquiry by the coroner and a jury would likely, in my opinion, be unnecessary. I, for one, will render any assistance to the bench without fee, reward, or emolument.'

Stanbridge nodded his appreciation, and after a brief pause in proceedings to mark the end of the preliminaries, called the first witness, Doctor Frank Wadsworth Doolittle.

Murmurs in the gallery faded, and the men and women who comprised it fixed their gaze on the young man rising to give his testimony. At last, what many had been waiting for would be presented: the grisly details.

Doolittle was a native of New York, and for those in attendance his experience on the bloodiest of civil-war battlefields leant him credibility and gravitas beyond his years. This, they understood, was a man who knew the horrors that men do.

Having been duly sworn, Doolittle took out a notebook, to which he referred as needed to recall details. Stanbridge led the questioning.

'Describe, doctor, how you came to be at the house of the deceased.'

'It was half an hour after midnight, on the morning of the 29th, that I was called by Mr Pitman, who told me a woman at Albert Street had had her throat cut. I went with Pitman to the house at the extreme end of Albert Street, arriving there at ten minutes to one, to find George Stuart and Joseph Mounsey in the house.'

'Could you describe the house, briefly. And then what you saw.'

'Yes. The house is about 20 feet by 12 feet, containing two rooms — one a sitting room, and the other a bedroom, where I found the deceased. She was lying across the bed, on her back, her head somewhat inclining to the head of the bed, her legs hanging over the side. The bed was about six feet by four feet. She had on a chemise and stockings. The chemise extended down to her knees. Her legs were in that recumbent position which might have been expected from that prostrate posture. The left arm was lying nearly by her side, the hand firmly clenched — violently clenched, I should say. The right arm was extended at nearly right angles with the body, the right hand open. The head was upon a bolster and slightly turned towards the left shoulder. The eyes were about half-open and looking straight ahead; there was a glaze over the eye. The mouth was open, conveying to my mind the act of screaming —'

Gasps and stifled shrieks emanated from the public gallery. Stanbridge admonished the observers with a stern look, and returned to the witness. With a nod from the bench, and a brief look at his notes, the doctor continued.

'I noticed that the tongue seemed natural in the mouth. The deceased was about eighteen years of age, well formed and healthy. Her hair was dishevelled. In her throat was a combination of wounds, forming one jagged wound about three-and-a-half inches in length and an inch-and-a-half in depth. There was a second wound on the left side of the neck merely under the skin, making, as it were, a sheath for the blade; the weapon had then been drawn back till it cut into the other wound. I believe that this second-mentioned wound was made after the larger injury. From the position of the wounds, I would consider it barely possible that she could have inflicted these injuries herself. The wounds were made with considerable violence.'

A cry of 'monster!' came from the gallery.

Stanbridge swept a schoolmaster's gaze across the faces of this cross-section of Daylesford citizenry.

'Ladies and gentlemen, notwithstanding the graphic and appalling content of the testimony, I will ask the constable to eject those who are unable to restrain themselves. These proceedings are not to be disrupted further.' He turned his eyes to the witness. 'Did you form an opinion as to the kind of knife used to inflict such grave wounds?'

'I did, Sir. From a close inspection and probing of the wound, I believe it may have been caused by a sailor's sheath knife, or a butcher's knife. It must have been a sharp knife; a common house knife would not likely make such a wound. It would seem as if the party using the knife had made several cuts, as though to make assurance doubly sure, by cutting down deeper with a fresh cut.'

'Thank you, doctor. And there was much blood?'

'There was, Your Worship. Much had been partially absorbed by the bedclothes, but the deceased had probably lost three quarts of blood.'

'And did you form an opinion as to a time of death, or at least the time these injuries were inflicted?'

'The extremities were cold, but the heat had not entirely left the body. So, from the appearances presented, I am of the opinion that the injuries were inflicted between half-past ten and half-past eleven p.m. Death would have been almost instantaneous; the carotid artery on the left side and both jugulars were severed.'

Here, even Stanbridge had to suppress an urge to cry out in horror at such brutality. He paused a moment, then raised his hand to invite Doolittle to proceed. The doctor obliged, with reference to his notes.

'The face of the deceased was greatly disfigured, as if scratched by a hand being held over the mouth; a piece of skin had been torn off the upper lip. There was also a cut upon the second finger of the left hand, and one on the first finger; the hand was so clenched as to cover these cuts. They had been made apparently by the knife being grasped, and then drawn through.' He demonstrated the action. 'Upon the inside of the left hand were two bloody finger marks, which I can confidently swear could only have been made by a second person. These marks presented evidence of sufficient pressure to prevent the action of her arm. Both wrists had been grasped by bloody hands. Her thighs were marked with blood.'

'And there was a struggle?'

Doolittle nodded. 'Yes. The bed presented the aspect of a fierce struggle having taken place. The bedclothes were gathered in a heap at the foot of the bed.'

Stanbridge took a moment to complete his note-taking, then the three men of the bench conferred a moment. After some head-nodding, Dunne cleared his throat to address the gallery.

'I must now warn the court that I have to put certain questions to the witness, questions of such a nature that any woman who has regard for her character should now leave.'

The gentlemen of the bench sat stonily, as if to convey that for the twenty or more females present, they had no choice in the matter. And so they stood, bankers' wives and barmaids alike, with the men rising to allow them passage out along the rows. And when the last had left the building, and the courtroom was the exclusive domain of men, Dunne put his questions.

'Doctor Doolittle, were you able, through your examinations, to form an opinion as to whether sexual intercourse had taken place with the deceased?'

Some in the gallery exchanged looks. Stanbridge reproached them with a glare.

'Not at that time, Sir. I did take samples when I returned later, at 9.00 a.m., which have been sent for analysis. Until the results are known, I can't be certain that coition took place. But it is a possibility, and the signs exhibited incline me to the opinion that some violence had been used.'

'Violent connection, you mean?'

'Yes.'

'So to be clear, doctor, what samples did you take?'

'Mucus from the vagina, Your Worship, and from the rectum.' Doolittle's bluntness took the bench aback a little. And then he added, perhaps unnecessarily, 'For this I used my finger, not a spatula, lest blood be drawn and contaminate the sample, you see.'

Stanbridge consulted here with Mayor Patterson, and the questioning struck out on a different course.

'You mentioned the dimensions of the cottage — the rooms and so on. Did you form an opinion as to how the murderer gained access to the building?'

'Yes, Your Worship, I did. The end of the house, where the bed was, faced Albert Street. The chimney is on the upper side of the house. The barrel which forms the chimneypot had been removed and lain against the roof of the cottage. Inside, in the fireplace, there was a pole across the chimney for hanging pots on. A man coming down the chimney could have this to hold while he slid himself into the room.'

'A man could fit down the chimney?' Patterson said.

'There was sufficient room for a man's body to pass, yes, Your Worship. The back of the fireplace had been whitened to such an extent as to form a sort of crust. About two-thirds up the fireplace, there was a scale of the whiting knocked off, as if by the heel of a boot coming down, and in addition, for about a foot and a half in width, a cloth had apparently been rubbed over the surface. It was an irregular or corded substance that had so rubbed — evidently, indeed, made by the trousers of some person as he slid down.'

'And having entered the building by way of the chimney, did you form an opinion as to how the murderer exited after the crime?'

'I did, Sir. I observed finger marks of blood on both sides of the door leading from the bedroom to the sitting room. I observed the outside door. The knob had finger marks of blood on inside and outside. I saw no blood on the key in the lock, and nothing else in particular, except as regards the appearance of the husband. His face was very white, and I remarked to him that he seemed to be in a kind of trance; he was the first to discover the body, it must be said. And I learned later that his wife's chemise had been pulled up, exposing her person. It was Mr Stuart who'd pulled it down before I arrived.'

Stanbridge shook his head, for want of a better expression of sympathy for the poor husband.

'And then had you completed your initial investigation?' he said.

'Yes, Your Worship. It was nearly 2.00 a.m. when I left the place. I left the covering of the body precisely as I found it.'

Stanbridge held up a hand for Doolittle to pause. He motioned to Reid to hand a photograph to the witness.

'As indicated in the photograph?' he said.

Doolittle looked at the grisly image with professional detachment.

'Yes, this accurately represents the position of the body as I saw it when I left the house. And again after 9.00 a.m. when I had taken the samples.'

'Very well, thank you, Doctor. I commend you on your

thoroughness. Your note-taking is an example to us all.' Stanbridge glanced at Reid, as if to suggest that the police might sharpen their own practice in this regard. Reid averted his eyes from the magistrate's accusatory gaze.

Stanbridge consulted his watch and then the mayor, and, given that it was midday, adjourned proceedings for an hour.

AS SERGEANT TELFORD LISTENED to Johanna Hatson's story, an irresistible conclusion began to take shape in his head. In the wake of the horrific murder of her former colleague, she'd come to the police to report the very strange man she'd seen at the Boxing Day picnic, a man who had been ogling, among other ladies that day, poor Maggie Stuart.

'Ogling?' Telford said.

Hatson was irritated that the meaning seemed lost on the policeman.

'Yes, ogling. Staring in a most unsettling manner. I'd look up, and there he was, his eyes all over our party. And again later.'

'How near was he?'

'Near enough!'

'Well, as near as you are to —'

'Oh, across the lawn, twenty yards, I don't know.'

'Margaret Stuart was in your party?'

'No, but I'm sure he would have been watching her, too; she is — was, a very attractive young —'

'I assume you do not know this man's name?' Telford said.

'Well, I'd never seen him before, much less know his name. But he sent a shiver down my spine, I can tell you!'

'There were other ladies who noticed him?'

'Yes, of course! Mrs Shier, for one, and Mrs Pitman, I'm sure—'

'Describe his appearance.'

'Well, I didn't care to get any closer to him, but he had a very disagreeable look about him. His hair was black, or very nearly. Down to his neck. And curly, it was. I'd say he was an Italian.'

Telford took a moment to transcribe into his notebook.

'Clothes?'

'Filthy. Moleskin trousers, a crimson shirt, lace-up boots. He had on a hat the second time I saw him, a dark-plush one, high dome and wide brim —'

'A billy-cock, or a wideawake perhaps?'

Hatson shrugged. 'I don't know, but he wore it low over his eyes. And I might add that Mrs Louchet was there, too, with her two poodles; this man was watching them, too, so I said to Mrs Louchet, I said, you'd better watch your dogs, because that man surely wants to steal them.'

'You'd recognise this man if you saw him?'

'Make no mistake of that, Constable!'

'Sergeant.'

THE MAGISTERIAL INQUIRY RESUMED at one o'clock. Stanbridge had lunched on shepherd's pie with Mayor Patterson at the Manchester Hotel in Vincent Street; but, given the intrusion upon their dining by inquisitive patrons, the men conceded that their choice of venue had probably been ill-advised.

'This case, George,' Stanbridge had said on their return to the Court House, 'must be resolved if the public is to have any confidence in those charged with dispensing justice in this town, from the police to the borough council. Five unsolved murders, George, in five years. We can't have a sixth.'

The mayor pulled a newspaper from his coat pocket. 'Perhaps we should heed the ready wisdom of the press?' He jabbed his finger at the print. 'Yesterday's *Mount Alexander Mail.*'

Stanbridge craned to read the words:

We have very little doubt that the miscreant who sacrificed to his depraved appetite the existence of a virtuous young woman will prove to be an offshoot of Vandiemonian stock …

Stanbridge tut-tutted. 'Put it away, George. Wild speculation has no place here.'

The wooden benches of the public gallery were again fully occupied as Stanbridge recalled the first witness to the box.

'Doctor Doolittle, you have completed a post-mortem examination?'

'Yes, Your Worship, at the request of the police, and assisted by my colleague there, Doctor McNicoll. We commenced at five o'clock yesterday afternoon.'

'Had the body lain unmoved since last you saw it?'

'Yes, Sir, it had.'

'Please now describe your examination to the court.'

'We examined the wounds first, then the viscera. The organs were in a perfect state of health —'

Stanbridge stopped the witness with a lift of his hand. He looked to the gallery, where a young woman was finding her way along the rows to leave.

'Now would be an opportune time for others so disturbed by such testimony to depart.' He paused. 'No one? Then I urge the gallery to remain silent, or I will have it cleared. Thank you. Now, please proceed, Doctor.'

Doolittle consulted his notebook a moment. 'We opened the uterus and found it unimpregnated. We then examined the brain, and found it normal, without any effusion or disease of any kind. There was no indication of spiritous or fermented liquor in the stomach. I would judge that the deceased had been in a perfect state of health. I would go so far as to say you might examine a thousand and not find one in a more perfect condition.'

Stanbridge nodded and made a note. 'And the cause of death?'

'Severance of the carotid artery.'

'Yes, you did say as much earlier. Please, continue.'

'Next, I examined the nails of the deceased. There were indications of hairs attaching. I found in the grasp of the left hand two hairs, evidently not her own. They have the appearance of a man's hair.'

'You have the hairs?'

'Not here, Sir. They are preserved, sealed up in an envelope.'

'You examined the body of the deceased?'

'In minuteness, Your Worship. I found no marks on the ribs nor the hips. There was blood on the left hand, from the cut there as the knife was pulled through.' Doolittle paused here to clear a dry throat. 'Pardon me, Sir, but might I have some water?'

'Of course, Doctor.' Stanbridge indicated with a finger and a raised eyebrow to the constable if he wouldn't mind.

As the doctor sipped from the glass handed to him, Solicitor Dunne put a question to him.

'Did you find the knife?'

'A search was made by myself and a constable, but no knife could we find.'

Stanbridge nodded, and seeing that there were no further questions forthcoming, asked the witness whether he had concluded his evidence.

'I have, Your Worship.'

'Then, may I say, on behalf of the bench, how high an opinion we have of the zeal and interest, combined with the most observant care, exhibited by you, Sir, in these proceedings.'

'Thank you, Your Worship,' Doolittle said.

'And might I add,' Dunne said, 'that in an experience of eleven years, I have never met with more professional ability and observation than that brought to bear by Dr Doolittle on the present occasion.'

'Hear hear,' chimed in Mayor Patterson and Stanbridge. Doolittle's deposition was then read out to him, and, at a little before three o'clock, he was excused.

By now, Stanbridge had almost had enough for one day;

indeed, he was feeling the burden of office more than he had at any other time in his two years as magistrate. 'That poor, bloody woman,' he muttered.

'William?' Patterson said.

'I'm all right. Thank you, George. Has Mr Pitman arrived?'

'He has.'

'Good. It's half-past three. We'll adjourn for the day after his testimony.'

John Pitman had gone to some trouble to present as a respectable business proprietor, however unrespectable that business was. His dark-blond hair was clean and sharply parted down the middle, and his usually untidy beard had been neatly trimmed. Despite the heat of the day, he'd buttoned himself up in a smart vest and coat that the mayor himself might well have envied. When asked to state his name and occupation, he spoke as a man proud of his station.

'John Pitman, Your Worship, owner and manager of Pitman's Refreshment Rooms in Albert Street.'

'And where were you, Mr Pitman, on the night of Wednesday last?' Dunne asked.

'I was in bed, Your Worship, about nine or ten.'

'Can anyone vouch for that?'

Pitman was quick to answer, not pausing even a moment to recall whether there might have been someone.

'No, Your Worship. My wife, and my employee Maria Molesworth, were out that night, at Jamieson's Theatre to see the Christy Minstrels. They went out at eight o'clock, and came home at about five minutes past eleven.'

'"About five past"?' Stanbridge said. 'That's very precise, Mr Pitman. Tell the court what happened after five past eleven that night.'

'Well, an hour later, at five past twelve, Mounsey came by. He wanted some ale. I let him in and went back to bed. I had a cold, you see, Your Worship. Then, about ten minutes later, there was a pounding on the door. I told the wife I'd see to it.'

Pitman paused here, looking across at George Stuart, sitting alone and expressionless.

'And what happened then, Mr Pitman?' Dunne said.

Pitman faced his questioner. 'I heard George Stuart yelling, "Johnny, for God's sake get up — my wife has had her throat cut." He was agitated all right. He looked like he'd just come back from the mine, being in his work clothes. Anyway, I got up, put on my trousers, and went with him and Mounsey to his house.' He paused, as if to give time for the bench to digest the story.

'Go on, Mr Pitman,' Stanbridge said, 'and please face the bench when you're speaking.'

'Yes, Your Honour. Well, there was a candle burning on the table in the front room. George Stuart picked it up, and we followed him into the bedroom ...'

'Yes, Mr Pitman?'

'Well, I saw the deceased on the bed. Her legs were over the bed, and her shirt was up to her breasts. Stuart pulled it down to hide her person. It wasn't right that a lady should be so exposed. Whoever would do such a —'

'What happened next, Mr Pitman?'

'I went to the camp, for the police, and left the others behind. I saw Sergeant Telford and Doctor Doolittle, and we went back to Stuart's house. Oh, and Constable Irwin came with us, too.'

'Mr Pitman, did you hear any screams that night, around or before midnight?'

'No, Your Worship. I should think I would have heard screams if there were any, because the wind was blowing towards my place, and I wasn't asleep.'

At this point, with the clock showing four, Dunne leaned across to consult with his colleagues.

'My main object today was the identification of the body, so the poor mother can get on and bury her daughter. So may I suggest that we now adjourn proceedings?'

The other two were of like mind. Stanbridge addressed the court, advising that the inquiry was adjourned till ten o'clock on Thursday next, January 5th.

IF CORONER WILLIAM DRUMMOND was irritated by Stanbridge and his so-called magisterial inquiry treading all over his territory, he didn't spend time voicing it; he simply started his own inquest as soon as he reached town. Within an hour of the five o'clock coach from Castlemaine pulling in, he had empanelled a twelve-man jury and had taken them off to the Stuart house to view the body, by then in its forty-third hour *post mortem*. William Stanbridge, well satisfied with his day's work, and more than happy to hand back responsibility to the usual authority, gave the coroner the witness depositions on their return from the murder scene.

'Not much to see?' Stanbridge said. 'A damaged body in a coffin, and a clean cottage.'

'Yes,' Drummond said with some resignation, 'it seems the post-mortem might have been delayed until my return.'

'Well, there ought to have been a jury, and had I been informed, steps might have been taken earlier. Instead, the poor woman lay there corrupting all day in the summer heat —'

Drummond raised a hand in surrender. 'Thank you, William. I do concede the point. Despite the delay, what we — I — need to do now is ensure that a proper inquest is undertaken as expeditiously and as thoroughly as can be done. I've called the jury for nine o'clock tomorrow morning. I am indebted to you, William, for making a start.'

SATURDAY 31st DECEMBER

A HOT NORTH WIND threw grit and dust across the flat and treeless grid of Daylesford cemetery. Maggie Stuart wouldn't have known most of the mourners who defied the gusts to see her buried that last afternoon of 1864. They came, two hundred perhaps, because they knew her. Not just as a sister or daughter, or as a friend, or as a shy young waitress, but as the precious embodiment of all that was soft and sweet in a coarse town. They came in protest, to renounce violence and murder. A covered wagon had conveyed the coffin the mile and a half from house to grave, followed on foot by husband, mother, stepfather, and four half-siblings. The cortege swelled as it progressed down the very street along which, not five days before, a dray had taken Maggie and Louisa home from the Boxing Day picnic.

When the rites were done, Louisa was the first to empty a handful of dry, dark soil into the grave. Behind her stood the minister, exchanging nods, contorted smiles, and solemn looks with mourners. Joe Latham was silent and motionless, perhaps still subdued by George Stuart's charge, or simply trussed up by a suit in want of letting out. Stuart stood off aways, receiving condolences and avoiding the Lathams. Some — Maria Molesworth, Mr and Mrs Rothery among them — had to leave promptly to give testimony at the inquest.

Louisa stood and took her uncle's hand. The wind eased as the congregation began to unravel and disperse. There was calm in the blessed release that ritual brings, but it rendered the unearthly screaming that followed all the more disturbing. All turned to the grave, to a bereaved mother bent double at the lip of her daughter's tomb. Latham went to his wife to restrain her, but she would not be restrained. She reached into the void and toppled, the hollow thud of her landing resonating with the depth of the grave, and the comedy of the action heightening the distress in all who saw it. Latham at last found his mettle and grasped his wife's arms, as he had so many times before, but this time to lift her from the ground, and then to hold her as she sobbed and wailed. People turned away to leave her to her grief, but she pulled free to stand back at the graveside, and in a moment of unlikely composure, declared, 'I pray to God the assassin of my poor Maggie is brought to justice.'

AT DAYLESFORD COURT HOUSE, the jury had heard testimony from various witnesses, but, with no further evidence to present, and with the police investigation proceeding, Coroner Drummond decided it was appropriate to adjourn his inquest for four days, to reconvene the following Wednesday January 4th at 9.00 a.m.

GEORGE STUART RETURNED TO his cottage late in the afternoon. For two nights he'd bunked at a workmate's house while his dead wife had lain in her coffin above the bed on which they had held each other. The police had assured him the place had been kept secure until their investigations were done and the body removed. Well, he thought, now that he was back there, they might have secured the place for a few hours more, because from the state of the place now it had been royally turned over. The furniture, modest at best, was all gone — taken while poor Maggie was still on the wagon to the cemetery. So, too, the crockery and cutlery; all of it. He went through into the bedroom. The bed remained, stripped of its blood-soaked mattress and sheets. Maggie's crinoline wasn't there, nor her trunk. He spun around, as if it were possible that in a tiny, bare room it had escaped his notice. All her clothes she kept in that trunk! He sat on the slats of the bed. The wood creaked; a sound so familiar, a sound to remember her by. They took her clothes. Who would so deny a grieving man? What was there left of Maggie? Not a petticoat or a blouse in which to bury his face and breathe her in. He collapsed to the floor and let his agony contort him how it would.

12

SUNDAY, NEW YEAR'S DAY 1865

DAYLESFORD WAS ON EDGE. Police activity had increased; additional detectives and constables had been assigned to assist the local force. Victoria's Superintendent of Detectives, Charles Nicolson, and even Chief Commissioner Frederick Standish, were up from Melbourne.

Sarah Spinks would always have considered her own life and the workings of the police to be on parallel paths, so the realisation that she might have a part to play in the apprehension of a murderer was a few days in coming. It was first thing Sunday morning that she presented herself at the police station in Camp Street.

Four mounted constables and Sergeant Telford were leaving the yard as she arrived, but still saddling his horse was trooper Tom Mansell. He was a tall man, twenty-six years of age, with dark eyes and the carriage of a soldier. He regarded her for a moment, long enough to know he didn't fancy her. He continued attending to his horse while she spoke.

'Excuse me, Constable. I have some information that may be important to the murder.'

Mansell tightened the last strap and faced her. 'The Stuart murder?' he said.

'Yes,' Sarah said, before wondering whether there had been another.

'And you are?'

'Sarah Spinks, of Connell's Gully. I was walking home —'

'Can I help you?' The question came from a man appearing from the timber building behind the horse yard. He ambled towards Sarah, loading a pipe. 'I'm Detective Walker,' he said, and stopped to light up. Smoke drifted up and around his bearded head as his lips worked the mouthpiece. 'You'd better come inside and tell me what you know, Miss Spinks. Take notes, would you, Mansell.'

'It's Missus Spinks,' she said, and followed the detective through the mounting yard, picking up her skirts to clear the dung. The air was warm, already thick with flies, and pungent with new manure. For now, in the still of morning, dust lay undisturbed. Inside the bare-floored station house, furnished with stove, chairs, and a central wooden table, Walker bade Sarah be seated. He preferred to stand, propped against the wall and sucking his pipe, the smoke going some way to masking the earthy aromas from outside. In appearance, he was an unremarkable man, Sarah considered, of normal height and build, and lank, light-brown hair. His ordinariness put her in mind of Angus Miller, her lover, but only by way of contrast, for Angus was a man who could never be described as ordinary.

Mansell came in, sat at the table, and dipped a pen in ink. His witness and scribe ready, the detective began.

'Tell me everything you know, Mrs Spinks.'

'I —'

'One thing, before you begin. Why didn't you come to the police before today? The woman's been dead more than three days.'

'And buried for two,' Mansell said.

Walker rebuked his colleague, indicating with a look and by pointing his finger to keep to his writing, as Sarah began an explanation for the delay.

'I wasn't sure that what I'd seen was important, Detective. And I heard a rumour that a man had been arrested. For all I knew, the police already had a suspect —'

Walker was waving her to stop.

'Never mind, Mrs Spinks. Please continue.'

And so she did, though with the sense that her interviewer was more sceptical than appreciative.

'On Christmas Eve, I saw a man sitting with my children, not far from Stuart's. He had a tent up there.'

'Describe the man. Slowly, for the constable.'

'He wore a drab felt hat, much slouched over the eye; he had long, dark hair, extending to the neck; his eyes were very large and dark; and he had dark whiskers, but I didn't notice any moustache; he wore an imitation seal-skin coat —'

'Trousers?'

'I think his trousers were moleskin or corded. A pale colour, they were.'

'Height?'

'Not tall, Detective. About the same as you.'

Walker caught Mansell's eye, and quickly looked away.

'So, there was a man living in a tent near Mrs Stuart's, and you saw him there with your children?'

'Yes. And they had spoken with him once before, a few days earlier. They'd lost their dog, you see, and, well, anyway, my daughter told me —'

Walker put his pipe on the table, pulled up a chair, and sat forward in it, resting his elbows on his knees.

'What makes you think this man has anything to do with the murder of Mrs Stuart?'

The tone was suspicious, and put Sarah in a mind to doubt her decision to come forward, or even to question her own thinking. She looked away, to Mansell, who, with the slightest tilt of the head, encouraged her to take no notice. She faced Walker again.

'On the Wednesday evening, the night of the murder, I was at

Jamieson's Theatre, to hear Christy's Minstrels.'

'You went alone?'

'I was with a neighbour.'

'Name?'

'Angus Miller.'

Walker raised his eyebrows.

'My husband was home, Detective Walker. He's not been well. Angus kindly —'

'What time did you leave Jamieson's? Are you getting this, Constable?'

'Every word.'

'Mrs Spinks?'

'I left soon after ten-thirty. We waited a while to see if anyone else was walking our way and would like to join us.'

'Yes, well, tongues would wag, you being out alone with a man not your husband.'

'They do wag, Detective. And they can wag until they fall off, for all I care. Now, do you want me to continue?'

For the moment, Walker was speechless. He could feel Mansell's eyes on him, feasting on his discomfort.

'Please go on, Mrs Spinks,' he said.

'Well, our way home took us close by Mrs Stuart's, and near there I saw a man. I thought it was a stump at first, but then he started walking towards the town.'

'This is the same man with the tent, the man you saw with your children?'

'I couldn't swear to it, but I am confident from the hat and coat it was the same man. It was the hat and coat, you see.'

'You can't be more certain than that?'

'It was dark that night; clear and starry, but there was no moon.'

'How near was he?'

'He passed me by about ten feet. I looked round, being suspicious of him, and saw he was walking slowly back in the direction of Mrs Stuart's. I could see Mrs Stuart's then. I was on a track that goes into the gully towards my house.'

'You saw him go to Stuart's house?'

'No, I saw him go in that direction.'

'Did you speak to him?'

'No.'

Two riders entered the yard and dismounted. Someone spoke to them.

Walker looked up.

'Telford's here,' he said to Mansell. He went to the door to tap out his pipe. 'Well, thank you, Mrs Spinks. If you think of anything else ...'

'I can go?'

Walker nodded. 'Oh, and a happy New Year to you.'

Sarah reached the doorway as Sergeant Telford arrived there. He made room for Sarah as she departed, touching his hat as she passed.

Walker brought the sergeant up to date. 'She saw a man loitering by Stuart's on the night.'

'Italian?'

'Pardon?'

'Was he Italian?'

'She didn't say.'

'He might be Italian, Sir,' said Mansell, 'from her description. Black hair and all.'

Telford continued. 'I have a witness who said she saw an Italian leering at women, Mrs Stuart included, up at Wombat Park, Boxing Day. And, what's more, I know an Italian whose whereabouts on the night of the 28th might be well worth our while investigating.' Telford turned for the door and bawled out to the two constables in the yard. To Walker he said, 'I'm sending Tandy and Dawson to bring him in.'

Walker nodded. 'I'll call Mrs Spinks back, too; he might be the same —'

Telford's hand was up.

'Let's just hear what Mr Bonetti has to say for himself first, eh?'

IT WAS THE PREVIOUS afternoon, the Saturday, that Serafino Bonetti had come around to finish laying shingles and attend to the last of the weatherboards on the Telford extension. He finished early enough to attend to Mrs Telford, too, against the newly lined wall. By the time the sergeant returned home for his lunch, Bonetti was packing away his tools.

'A fine job, Mr Bonetti,' he said. 'Don't you think so, dear?'

Penelope Telford appeared from the open doorway, her face flushed and her manner uncertain.

Telford felt the hideous clench of jealousy in his gut, but reminded himself of what Johanna Hatson had told him not an hour earlier, and soothed himself with the knowledge that satisfaction would soon be his. But not just yet. He took himself on an inspection tour of the work, testing the floorboards with comical little jumps, lining up levels with an eye closed, feeling the finish with his fingers, and all the while nodding that he was pleased. He also took care to note the exchange of looks between wife and worker. *Oh yes*, he thought, *I see all.*

'All is just as it should be, Mr Bonetti. If you will bring me an invoice next week, we can conclude our business.'

And so it was that he'd delayed acting on Johanna Hatson's information until Bonetti had finished the job — a fool of a policeman he'd be to put his builder in gaol with the roof not finished. Telford was more than a little satisfied with himself; there was the sweet revenge he would exact on the man who would cuckold him, the embarrassment his wife would have to endure, and, who knows, perhaps a free extension to the police house. Whether Bonetti actually had anything to do with Margaret Stuart's murder wasn't important. Unknown to Telford was that even as his two constables were en route to question Bonetti, word was being put out on the telegraph all around Victoria to be on the lookout for a man fitting the description given by Sarah Spinks.

Talk of the man with the tent up by Stuart's was getting around among the public, too. The absence of the tent now only confirmed in the minds of many that its occupant was surely the killer. There was no gossip entertaining the possibility that the two were merely coincidental. Besides, until the police determined otherwise, people were free to speculate as wildly as they liked.

MONDAY 2nd JANUARY

ON A BRIGHT MORNING of magpie song and busy streets, the first business day of the new year, Detective Walker and Constables Irwin and Tandy paid a visit to Rothery's, specifically to speak to young Louisa.

'We'll have her home in an hour, Mrs Rothery,' Walker said.

'Please, Detective, no longer than that. It's been only a few days, and —'

Walker showed his palms. 'I quite understand, of course. You have my word Louisa will be home in good time for lunch.'

Suspicious activity was going on at the Stuart house as the police and their young assistant walked by.

'Can't you tell them to keep away?' Louisa said. 'People keep coming to nosey about.'

'I'm afraid that's up to Mr Stuart, Louisa,' Walker said, which didn't impress the girl.

Irwin saw as much, and took matters into his own hands. 'Oi,' he called out to the man and woman who had their hands at the window to peer in. They looked up.

'Yes, you. Have you business there?'

They looked at each other. The man shrugged; the woman fidgeted.

‘Then piss off!’ Irwin said. And they did, to Louisa’s delight.

Louisa led the men to the gum trees where David Rose had tied the rope to support his tent. The remnant of the cooking fire drew Walker, who used a stick to scatter the ashes. Nothing like a weapon was uncovered — only empty tins, bones, and sundry pointy teeth in a remnant of a jaw.

The police now took Louisa a few streets away to where a tent had been erected in a manner similar to Rose’s.

‘Might this be the tent of the man you saw, Louisa?’

‘It is like his tent. But it’s not his tent.’

‘You’re sure?’

‘Yes. I want to go home now, please.’

‘All right,’ Walker said, incautiously enough that his disappointment was revealed to the girl. ‘One of the constables will take you. But, Louisa, it will be very important that you remember all that you know about this man, so that when we find him, we can be certain he is the right man. We all want to catch the man who killed Maggie, don’t we?’

DETECTIVE WALKER RETURNED TO the police station to the news that a suspect had just been arrested at Geelong Railway Station and had been remanded at Geelong watch-house.

‘Any other details, Tandy? Name? Appearance?’

‘James Mason’s the man’s name. As to his appearance, no word. He’s been remanded for 24 hours. Another thing, there’s a Serafino Bonetti in the lock-up. He was brought in this morning. He’s Italian —’

‘Is he really?’

Tandy ignored the sarcasm. ‘As Sergeant Telford said, the man can’t vouch for his whereabouts on the night of the 28th.’

‘I’ll have a word with him. What else?’

‘We have a report that some cove with a swag and miner’s clothing was on the Melbourne train to Malmsbury last Friday.’

'And?'

'Witnesses said the suspect was in an excited state, whatever that is, Sir. And the description is scant. The husband says he reckons the father-in-law Latham done it.'

'He can reckon all he likes, because the mother's given Latham an alibi.'

'From what I've heard, she'd be too afraid not to.'

Walker narrowed his eyes. 'My advice to you, Constable Tandy, is to leave pointless speculation well alone, and confine your attention to investigations that might actually lead to a conviction.'

THE LOCK-UP BEHIND THE police station was a solid block of a building, thick-walled of brick, with a gabled slate roof. Its three cells opened off a small vestibule, entered through an iron gate. Each cell, three yards by two, was fitted with an iron-panelled door, a bucket, and a bunk, and a vent beyond reach high in the wall allowed light and air. If there was any consolation for the only inmate that hot summer day, it was that no cooler refuge could be had in the district. Detective Walker observed as much to the prisoner once he'd been escorted across to the station for interview.

'Now, Mr Bonetti, to business. I have a description of a man seen ogling women at the Boxing Day picnic. Good word that, "ogling". You know what it means?'

'I was not at the Boxing Day —'

Walker stopped his prisoner there with a raised finger. 'I should have said, I have several witnesses, Mr Bonetti.'

'Does that make a difference, seeing that I was not there?'

Walker continued. 'I also have an eye-witness account of a man fitting your description lurking by the late Mrs Stuart's house at around eleven on the night of December 28th. I'm wondering now, where were you that night, Mr Bonetti?'

Walker sat patiently, to give his suspect a little time to decide the most sensible course. Bonetti did seem to be mulling over what that might be. At last he spoke.

'I can't tell you that.'

'Can't, or won't?'

Bonetti shrugged, as if he didn't understand the distinction, or else he saw no point in making one.

'Your lodgings will be searched, Mr Bonetti, for evidence.'

Bonetti shrugged again.

'Do I need to remind you that, right at this moment, you are the main suspect in a murder investigation?'

'No.'

'No?'

Bonetti sighed. 'No, Detective Walker, you don't need to remind me. I know this.'

Walker shook his head, confounded. 'Then why not take this opportunity to clear your name? Isn't one night in here enough? Just tell me, for pity's sake, where you were the night Margaret Stuart was murdered.'

The men stared at each other across the table, but it was the interrogator who grew tense. Bonetti read it in the unsteadiness of Walker's eyes, the fidgeting of his fingers, the thickening of a vein in his neck.

'Detective Walker, I do not have to prove I wasn't at that woman's house that night; you have to prove that I was. And you never will, because I was never there.'

Walker slapped the table hard, and stood up. 'Then where were you, for Christ's sake?'

Bonetti folded his arms and looked away.

'Irwin!' Walker called.

'Sir.'

'Take this stupid dago back to the cell.'

TUESDAY 3rd JANUARY

TROOPER HENRY BRADY WAS young, tall, blue-eyed, and Irish-born, and fancied himself as a man no fugitive could long evade. This was a fine attitude for a trap to have on a manhunt, and today he had every expectation that he would be bringing in the suspect before the day was out. With him was his antithesis, Constable Harry Wilkinson, a short Yorkshire newcomer with no ambition as a police officer other than to reach the end of each working day, with or without a suspect. Together this odd pairing had struck out along the Glenlyon Road at eight in the morning, in search of 'the man in the tent', the as-yet unnamed dark-featured individual who alarmed ladies and frightened little girls.

Encouraging information had come from William Stanbridge's foreman that a man fitting the description had passed by Wombat Park the Tuesday before. As this man had mentioned Glenlyon as a place he might find work, the small hamlet was made prime hunting territory within the ten-mile search radius determined by Superintendent Nicolson and Chief Commissioner Standish. Accordingly, several teams of constables and detectives, local and from further afield, were conducting property-to-property searches of this area to the north-east of Daylesford.

Brady had some familiarity with the Glenlyon district, and decided their best bet was to the north of the village, where abundant cleared land offered the best opportunity for hay-harvesting work. The decision was promptly vindicated when they encountered John Sherman, out mending a perimeter stone wall on his property. Not only had Sherman actually spoken to a man so described, but he had directed him on to George Cheesbrough's place.

'I think we have him, Harry!' Brady said, and with a wink spurred his mount to a canter. Wilkinson wanted to share in the excitement of the moment, but it had puzzled him from the moment they'd left Daylesford why a murderer would still be in the district, however good the work might be, or how desperately he might need it. It was a thought he just couldn't air with Brady, fearing that his logic was somehow flawed — that fleeing only brings on suspicion, that the best bet for a murderer is to hang about. Anyway, he really didn't care all that much; it was a hot day, but more than pleasant enough to be out riding. And so he gee'd up his bay and rode along in the dust of his partner.

JANE CHEESBROUGH POURED WILKINSON tea from her best china teapot.

'Thank you, Mrs Cheesbrough,' he said, with a smile. He took a sip. 'Ooh, there's nowt like a good cup o'char to quench —'

'Just to be certain about this, Mrs Cheesbrough,' Brady said, jotting down notes. 'He called himself David Rose, and your husband gave him employment on the afternoon of Tuesday the 27th, but dismissed him on Thursday the 29th?'

'That's right, Constable. If you wait a minute, George will soon be here; he'll be able to tell you —'

'Rose was here on Wednesday the 28th?'

'Yes.'

'What time did you last see him on that day?'

'Nine o'clock.'

'In the evening?'

'Yes, in the evening. Why —?'

'And you saw him when the next day?'

'In the morning, after breakfast. Maybe eight o'clock?'

Brady walked to the door and looked out over the stubble, which was standing stiff and golden in the very paddock where David Rose had been cutting hay a week ago.

'Where did he say he was going, Mrs Cheesbrough?'

'He didn't.'

Brady turned to see a big man with sun-parched cheeks and a pallid, bald pate in the room. His wife poured him a cup and handed it to him. He took it with a fond smile, and turned to Brady. 'He was late to turn out Thursday morning, so after he brought up the horses I sent him away.'

Brady's eyes sparkled at hearing this information. He straightened to be front-on to Cheesbrough.

'How late Thursday morning?'

'He should have been up at half-five, six. I didn't see him out till near eight. He was in the neighbour's paddock. I sent him away around ten. Why, what's he done?'

Brady was looking away, preoccupied with mental calculations. The Cheesbroughs looked to each other, and came to a realisation of their own. 'My God, George! Is he the man from the tent we read about in the paper?' They looked to Wilkinson.

'Aye,' he said. 'We have reason to suspect this David Rose for the murder of Margaret Stuart.'

13

WEDNESDAY 4th JANUARY
THE CORONER'S INQUEST RESUMES ...

DAYLESFORD COURT HOUSE SAT halfway up Wombat Hill, at the very head of Albert Street. With two square windows either side of the arched doorway in its Romanesque façade, it presented as a face watching over the township below. If by this design it was the intention of the architect to reassure the good citizens and intimidate the bad, the building was a failure. At least, it had failed Maggie Stuart, whose murder at the very opposite end of Albert Street had been committed under its direct gaze. But justice is the responsibility not of buildings, but of good men, as Coroner William Drummond reminded his jury of twelve when the inquest resumed at nine in the morning. Fifteen witnesses had been called, so the day loomed as a long one.

With a public gallery full to the wood-panelled walls, proceedings began with Louisa Goulding called. Mr Dunne, acting as crown prosecutor, and a father of young children, was considerate of her age, and adopted a conversational approach so that she might talk unfettered by the strictures of questions. After ten minutes in the box, during which she spoke about her friendship with Maggie, and how they sang hymns and told each other stories, Louisa was asked a final question by Dunne.

'Did you ever speak to the man who had the tent?'

'No. I was too frightened of him.'

'Thank you, Louisa. You've been very brave. Maggie would have been proud of you.'

Boxing Day picnickers Johanna Hatson and Elizabeth Shier each gave their testimony about the swarthy man with the unpleasant look they'd seen at Wombat Park, and agreed that he might well have been Italian. Next to be called was Mrs Sarah Hopkins, a small and slightly stooped woman of bony fingers and face.

'Mrs Hopkins,' Dunne said, with a smile, 'you and your husband live in Albert Street, near Mrs Stuart's house?'

'I live near Mrs Stuart's, that is correct, but I'm alone; my husband passed away two year ago.'

'You say you saw a suspicious-looking man?'

'Very suspicious. Very peculiar, too, 'n'all. It was about six in the evening, after the picnic it was. He —'

'Go on, Mrs Hopkins.'

'Sorry, I thought you was going to say something.'

Dunne gestured for her to please continue.

'As I was sayin', he was very peculiar looking. Low set, sallow complexion, and there were colour in his cheeks; pinkish like. Like he'd been out in the wind. He had a very cross look, and dark hair and whiskers, but no moustache. Just here.' Here she used her hands to show where the man was whiskered. 'He had a mahogany-coloured hat, plush I'd say, and he was wearing a dark coat.'

'Might he have been Italian?'

'Well, I thought he was, or some sort of foreigner, but then he spoke real good English, as good as me tellin' you this now.'

'So he spoke to you?'

'Well, he weren't talking to himself!'

Giggles issued from the gallery, and Drummond was prompted to caution the witness.

'Please, Mrs Hopkins, just answer the question.'

'Yes, Your Worship. Sorry, Your Worship.' She turned to Dunne. 'He wanted a drink, but I wouldn't let him in. If you ask me, he'd had too much to drink already.'

'And did he leave?'

'Yes, he did. Without so much as a grumble. He even called me "Madam". Still, I was scared of him, I can tell you. I mean, that face was one only a blind mother could love.'

Sarah Spinks was the next witness, and the fourth female in succession to describe the strange man with the scary face. After her testimony, which by then was sounding much like a repeat of the testimonies that had preceded it, coroner Drummond adjourned for lunch.

SERGEANT TELFORD HAD BEEN standing at the back of the courtroom early on, but slipped away late morning to pay a visit to the police lock-up. Constable Dawson admitted him and stood by outside. The sudden flood of daylight blinded Bonetti for the moment, as did the darkness for Telford.

'Have you moved furniture in yet, Sergeant?' Bonetti said, as if the Telfords' domestic comfort was his chief concern.

'We'll have to buy some first!'

The two men shared a chuckle, a counterfeit gesture that masked their undeclared mutual contempt; for Telford, Bonetti's unforgivable deceit, and for Bonetti, Telford's pitiable failure as a husband. What kind of a man would so neglect his woman? But Telford was certain only he knew the truth, and was enjoying his sport. He remained standing while the prisoner sat knees-up on the bunk.

'Listen,' Telford said. 'This is no place for you, and I'm sure you'd know Mrs Telford is very concerned about you being in here, so please, why not just say where you were on the night of the 28th? Good heavens, whatever it is, surely it can't be as grave as being suspected of murder?'

Bonetti was unpersuaded, and, in the gloom, unreadable. Telford worked hard to conceal his annoyance, and to curb an inclination to throttle the little bastard, tell him he knew what had been going on, and that by God he'd see him in hell! But again, the gloom obliterated the subtle facial flickers revealing of a man's mind.

Telford continued. 'A suspect was arrested in Geelong on Sunday. A James Mason. Fits the description; clothes, face, age. He tells the Geelong police that he's never even been to Daylesford. Maybe he has, maybe he hasn't; all that matters is that he wasn't in Daylesford on the night of the 28th. Got his boss to vouch for him, so he's a free man, just like that. There's a lesson in this for you, I think, Mr Bonetti.'

Each man stared into the shadowy face of the other, neither speaking, both hearing the magpies carolling outside. Telford broke the stalemate with a noisy exhalation. He called Dawson through the grille. The door was unlocked, and heaved open on squealing hinges. Telford looked back at Bonetti, sitting in the angled light, only his face hidden in shadow.

'Do think about what I've said. A sobering thought that you're now the only suspect in custody.' He stepped out and, with squeals, the door was heaved shut.

'Sergeant Telford.' Bonetti was at the grille, his face striped vertically in shadows. Telford turned, the constable preparing to open the outer iron gate.

'I do this for something more important than my freedom,' Bonetti said.

Telford waited, watching the dark eyes looking out at him as if of an animal blinking from its burrow.

'A woman's honour.'

Telford said nothing, but his look gave him away: Bonetti knew the face of jealousy when he saw it.

DETECTIVE WALKER LEFT THE Cheesbroughs at midday on Wednesday, well satisfied that he had wrung them dry of all the useful knowledge they had concerning their recent employee. While they could give him no indication of where Rose was headed after leaving — not even in which direction he turned once he was out the front gate — the times of his comings and goings were precious little nuggets. Trooper Brady was right; even if Rose was still at Cheesbroughs as late as 9.00 p.m. on the evening of the 28th, that left plenty of time for him to be at Margaret Stuart's at ten-thirty. That he was late up on the Thursday morning only deepened the suspicion. The investigation was making fine progress, Walker considered, and he permitted himself a little smugness as he trotted with Constable Mansell back to town. He arrived at the station to news from Melbourne.

'Remember my saying there was a miner on the Melbourne train from Malmsbury?' Constable Tandy said. 'Silly bugger drowned himself in the Yarra. Left his clothes on the bank, all folded, with a train ticket in his trouser pocket.'

'Description?'

Tandy shook his head. 'Let's just say that if he was Italian, I'm a Zulu.'

Walker made no nod to the levity.

'What about the dago in the lock-up? Bonetti,' he said.

'Still hasn't accounted for himself.'

'Too bad for him.'

'His counsel's been making noise.'

'Pearson Thompson, that old coot? Why doesn't he just die!'

'He may well, shacked up with a whore half his age. Mary Foley, you know her?'

'The woman he got off a drunk-and-disorderly?'

'That's her. A week or two with that'd kill any man!'

This was a remark Walker did find amusing, and joined Tandy in a lewd snigger.

AT TWO, THE CORONER'S inquest resumed, and in a short time it was Alice Latham's turn to give evidence. This, the word of the dead woman's mother, was what many in the gallery had been waiting for, and much murmuring and resettling in seats accompanied her amble to the witness box.

In consideration, a chair was provided, and she sat in it with her hands in her lap, one resting in the cup of the other. She seemed tired, disengaged. Certainly her features were steady, and not those of a woman likely at any moment to break down before the court. After the swearing-in, Dunne thanked her for her attendance and made acknowledgement of the ordeal she was enduring. And then it was on to questions, firstly about her family circumstances. She answered, in the main, with her gaze fixed on no particular spot, avoiding the eyes of the jury, the gallery, Dunne, and Drummond.

'I been married eleven or twelve years to my present husband, Joe Latham,' she said. 'I had three children by my first husband, and eight by Joe.'

'And —'

'To my knowledge,' she interrupted, matter-of-factly, 'none of my children from my first husband are still livin'. Margaret was the last.' She looked away, alarmed at her own bluntness. 'She were just seventeen years and two months when she married George Stuart,' she muttered to herself.

'What did Maggie do before she was married?' Dunne said.

Alice straightened her features and faced her questioner.

'She were a waitress and barmaid, and good at it. And she were no tart, unlike some. And when she were home, she helped with the cleanin' and washin' and mindin' the children. She always brought home her pay, too, and gave it to me — five to fifteen shillin's a week when she were workin'.'

'Your husband, Joseph Latham. Tell the court about him.'

'He's a tinsmith, works for himself and up at McKell and Studt's. He were away eight months in New Zealand not long ago, on the gold, but still he sent fifteen pound back while he was there.'

'So, a good husband and father?'

'Of course!'

'And what did he think of Maggie?'

Alice took a few moments to study Dunne's face, as if for an implication of something untoward in his question.

She looked away. 'Joe was very fond of her. At least … at least, until she were married.'

'Your husband didn't want Maggie to marry, did he?'

'Not to George Stuart, he didn't. But I gave my permission.'

'George Stuart has told the police that Joe Latham beat Maggie.'

Alice snapped her head to Dunne, and then up to Drummond. She looked away again.

'Joe did beat her four months ago.'

Noises of disapproval issued from the gallery.

Dunne continued.

'George Stuart said that Maggie told him that Joe Latham threatened to cut her throat if she married Stuart.'

'Well, she never told me that!' Alice huffed, and shifted in her seat as if her underwear was constricting.

'Maggie was frightened of her stepfather?'

'She were a very timid girl, easily frightened by lots of things.'

'Joe was so fiercely opposed to Maggie marrying George Stuart that he couldn't forgive her for it, could he, Mrs Latham?'

'I said as much before!'

'So why did you give permission for her to marry, when your husband was so opposed?'

'Because she were my daughter, not Joe's, and it took all of her wages to clothe and feed her … Anyway, neither of us went to the weddin'. All Joe said was that Maggie would repent it —'

'Marrying Stuart?'

'Yes, but I never heard him threaten her. Never. You know, Joe even built the house Maggie lived in with George Stuart.'

Alice was quite agitated now. Drummond and Dunne exchanged a look, and nodded that it might be time for a change in the line of questioning.

'Mrs Latham, I do understand you must be suffering terribly. For a mother to lose her daughter in such horrible circumstances as these is almost beyond imagination.'

Alice made no response, save for a slight shrug of her shoulders, which brought on a murmur in the gallery.

'Would you like some water?'

Alice nodded to Dunne that she would, and a clerk brought her a glass. When she'd taken a sip, Dunne resumed.

'Tell the court, Mrs Latham, in your own time, where you were on that terrible night.'

'I went to bed, soon after half-past eight. I can't be sure of the exact time, as we don't have a clock in the bedroom.'

'Where was your husband?'

'He were already in bed. He did get up about half-past ten or eleven, and lit his pipe. He were out of bed only a few minutes. He sat up in bed to smoke.'

'Had your husband been drinking that day?'

'He were sober as a judge, he was. And what if he had been drinkin'?'

'Mrs Latham, your husband, by your own admission, had been violent to your daughter, and given his opposition to the marriage, and with drink —'

'I told you. He hadn't been drinkin'.'

'Very well. And were you in bed when the police came?'

'Yes. We'd only just dozed off.'

'And what time was that?'

'About three o'clock.'

A murmur from the gallery revealed minds busy speculating on what Mr and Mrs Latham might have been up to, to be awake at that hour.

'Did Maggie ever mention to you a man who lived in a tent close by her house?'

'No, she never did say anythin' to me. But I had heard there was such a man.'

With no further questions to be put, Alice Latham stepped down, and her husband was called to take the chair, still warm from his wife. Alice was permitted to remain in the courtroom while Joe gave his testimony. He seemed overawed by the occasion — a belligerent man not accustomed to having to constrain his natural disposition.

'Joe Latham,' Dunne said, 'what kind of a girl was your stepdaughter?'

'She was a good girl. And, as far as I know, she never went beyond proper bounds with no man.'

'Please, Mr Latham,' Drummond said, 'would you speak up, for the jury to hear.'

'I beg pardon, Your Worship.'

'You were on good terms with her?

'Yes, we were on very good terms.'

'Did you beat her?'

Many in the public gallery leaned forward; this was the kind of question they had come for.

Latham shook his head elaborately. 'No! Never to hurt her. Only with my hands. I never used a whip or a stick. No, we was a happy family.'

Alice Latham spoke up from her seat. 'If ever he beat her, she deserved it.'

Drummond looked to Dunne and made a decision. 'I'm sorry, Mrs Latham, but I must ask the constable now to remove you from the court. You can wait in the anteroom.'

Alice shrugged, gathered herself, and stood for the policeman now by her seat. She turned away sharply to avoid his offered hand, and walked out. The signal was given and questioning resumed, this time from Harold Kreckler, of the jury.

'Did you threaten to cut your stepdaughter's throat?'

'Never did I threaten her with such a thing.'

Dunne followed up quickly. 'How did you and George Stuart get on?'

There was much of the cornered cat in Latham's demeanour, not so much because of the questions, but that he was being questioned. Had he been able, he might have fled the room, or else leapt at someone. Drummond had to prompt him now.

'Mr Latham, would you answer the question?'

'I — I've known him nine months, and I never had no difference with the man.'

A juryman was quick to interpose, 'You didn't approve of him marrying your stepdaughter.'

'He did come to my house to ask my consent about two months ago, and I did refuse him. I told him she was too young. That was why I didn't approve. And, I'll say this, I never threatened to cut her throat when she did marry him! Never!'

Latham's combative nature had surfaced, and he snapped like a caged beast poked with a stick. Drummond cautioned him, and Latham had sense enough to contain himself.

'Beg pardon, Your Worship.'

'Did you know Mr Stuart's working hours?'

'No.' Latham seemed affronted by the question, or else he was affecting incomprehension at why it was put.

Coroner Drummond was indicating by glances at the clock that the court might have heard enough from this witness, bar final questions from himself, concerning the man in the tent.

'I did see a peculiar-looking man, Your Worship,' Latham said, seemingly glad to have the focus redirected. 'About a month ago it was, near Maggie's house. He wore a black hilly-cock hat, he had black hair, a beard, and no moustache, and he wore a black beaver coat. And cord trousers, definitely.'

'You haven't seen him since?'

'No, but I could swear to him. He was a flash-looking fellow.

He might have been a foreigner, but I couldn't say for certain, seein' as I never had a word with him.'

Latham left the box with the setting sun streaming through the two windows in the court house's west-facing façade. Drummond had made it clear to all concerned that he was determined to complete his inquest before the day was out. This wasn't a trial, after all; all that had to be established was by what means Margaret Stuart had met her death — whether by her own or another's hand.

George Stuart now entered the box. He preferred to stand, and the chair used by the Lathams was removed.

Mr Dunne extended his most profound condolences to the witness. Stuart nodded his appreciation, but curtly, revealing an impatience to be getting on with his testimony. Dunne obliged. His question was put, and George Stuart gave his account of the night of December 28th.

'On Wednesday last, I left for work at twenty minutes past three. I returned very soon after twelve o'clock. The first thing I noticed was the barrel off the chimney top. I thought it must have been the work of the wind. I saw there was a light at Pitman's. It was a very dark night. I went to the front door. It was closed, but unlocked. All was dark. I found a candle and lit it ...'

His head was down. He was trembling. The courtroom was silent, all faces fixed. He touched his brow, and his head came up. 'I carried the candle towards the bedroom door. It was open. I went in, and found my wife dead on the bed.'

That he had said this so straightforwardly seemed to disturb him more than the words themselves, for he uttered the sentence without falter, and only then did he sway on his feet. A quick-thinking Mr Dunne hurried to steady him.

'When you're ready, Mr Stuart,' Drummond said, considerately, though the day had been so long. A glass of water was provided. He drank it all.

'I ran off to Pitman's and gave the alarm. And then with

Pitman and another, I went back to the house.'

'Pitman's your neighbour?'

'Yes, the refreshment rooms. I should say his place is a grog shanty, a brothel.'

'And what did you know of the man whose tent was up by your house?' Drummond said.

'My wife complained about him, on two occasions in all, I think. The first time she said he was making too free with her, asking her questions and telling her he would like her for a wife. On Christmas Eve, he came to the house when she was there. My wife locked the door, but was so scared she called over to Rothery's later for the little girl. My wife complained that he would pass by the house several times, and look in and speak to her whenever he got the chance.'

'Describe this man.'

'Dark complexion, dark hair, dark eyes. He wore a wideawake hat and moleskin trousers.'

'Did you ever speak to him?'

'Once, when me and Maggie were out walking. He said good evening, and I said good evening back. He never gave me his name, and I never gave him mine.'

'You have told the police that your father-in-law, Joe Latham, threatened to cut Maggie's throat. Did she tell you this?

'Yes, she did. She told me so before and after our marriage. She told me that her stepfather threatened to cut her throat when she was twelve years old! My wife also told me that her mother had told her that Latham had threatened her with vengeance, if she married me.' Here he paused, long enough for Dunne to begin a new question, but Stuart was away again, and Dunne and Drummond nodded to each other that he be given his head. He went on, with some fire. 'I married Maggie anyway, without her stepfather's knowledge or consent. Her mother knew we were to be married. I showed her the marriage lines, and she showed them to Latham. Ever since, he has had nothing to do with Maggie, and she has been in great fear of him.'

He stopped. He was spent, yet even in the dimness of the now lamp-lit court, peacefulness and repose could be seen in his countenance. The tension that had set his jaw and gathered his brow through his testimony had dissipated. Some in the gallery were dabbing their eyes and blowing noses. Drummond had suspended his note-taking, and Dunne and the jury their questioning. For several quiet moments, nothing stirred as each man thanked God he had not been dealt a hand such as that dealt the poor man before them.

The silence was broken by Drummond, who, noting that the time was approaching nine o'clock, decided that the inquest had reached its natural conclusion. He thanked George Stuart and bade him step down. And now, Drummond addressed the jury.

'Mr. Foreman and gentlemen of the jury, you have heard and taken part in the examination of the witnesses of this inquest. That a most foul murder has been committed, you can have no doubt. That it was accompanied by violent attempts may be inferred from the position in which the deceased was found, and from the clear and intelligent medical evidence adduced. And hence the motive for the bloody deed would probably arise, either from the unfortunate victim's recognition of her assailant, or his resolve to silence screams that threatened to rouse the neighbours. As the case now stands, I think it would not be advisable to limit the verdict to any one particular individual, while it is possible, though not probable, that proceedings may have to be taken hereafter against some person or persons hitherto unsuspected. And now, gentlemen, as I do not consider it necessary or advisable to make any further remarks, I will request you to retire, and frame your verdict.'

The jury stood and filed out to an anteroom, and after a fifteen-minute deliberation, returned with a verdict of wilful murder against some person or persons unknown.

14

FRIDAY 6th JANUARY
78 ELIZABETH STREET, MELBOURNE

OTTO BERLINER HAD A fine head of hair, black and lustrous, with body enough to hold its form in a breeze. It was in good form now — parted arrow-straight to the side, and newly washed — as he opened today's Victorian *Government Gazette* and read with more than casual interest an announcement at the very top of the front page:

> MURDER OF MRS STUART AT DAYLESFORD
>
> Two hundred pounds reward. Whereas between Ten and Twelve o'clock on the night of Wednesday, the 28th of December last, Margaret Stuart was murdered by some person or persons unknown, at her residence, situated in Albert Street, Daylesford: Notice is hereby given that a reward of Two hundred pounds will be paid by the Government to any person giving such information as shall lead to the apprehension and conviction of the murderer or murderers.

It wasn't the money — though he could always do with it, supporting his mother and sister in Sydney — it was the reference to his former stomping ground, as any reference to Daylesford caught his eye. He'd spent five years there, a long time to a man of twenty-nine, and though almost two had lapsed since he'd last applied his detecting acumen in that crime-bound town, the memory of his tenure there was vivid, if not fond. Rife goldfields lawlessness wasn't the reason for his leaving, nor was it the manifest incompetence of his fellows; in Otto's estimation, and regrettably, crime and police incompetence were characteristic of the entire colony. Rather, it was a peculiarity that had decided his hand.

Unlike the Berlin winters of his early boyhood, a Daylesford winter was not especially cold, not by the standards of his country of birth. Snow was infrequent, and when it did come, was barely thicker than a heavy frost. But a Daylesford winter had a damp all its own. A lurking, dripping, mouldy damp, it was, one which in a frontier town of draughty wooden buildings was no friend to a susceptible pulmonary constitution. So, before the bitter chill of 1863 rolled in and installed itself in his chest, Otto packed up and took his delicate lungs to Melbourne. Although, he did consider that the ineptitude of his colleagues would have seen him leave soon enough.

Otto had read about the murder of poor Maggie Stuart, and could imagine the excitement it provoked — not least among the police, who'd be running hither and thither, rounding up any number of suspects to improve the odds that they had the killer in custody. That oaf Telford would be leading the charge. And now, with this fat reward on the table, no man of swarthy complexion was safe. He might even be arrested himself! Such amateurs they were. There was no system to their detecting, no science, no initiative, no imagination. It was all supposition, speculation, and hope. Little wonder, when a man off the street could be made detective with a month's training; Superintendent of Detectives Nicolson and that twit Chief Commissioner Standish had a lot to answer for. *Well*, Otto thought, looking about the first-floor room that would soon be his office, *wait a few months till these premises are open for business as the country's first ever Private Inquiry Office. Then, right here in the very heart of the city, the public will have a detective service on which they can rely.*

PEARSON THOMPSON ARRIVED AT the lock-up for a second visit to Serafino Bonetti. He wasn't sure whether he admired his client or pitied him. It was something he himself would never countenance, of course — forego his freedom to protect a woman's honour. But then, he conceded, the women of his acquaintance invariably had little honour to protect. Anyway, it was all a bit silly, really, this misplaced chivalry. And it was never a good idea to tempt fate with the law — not in this jurisdiction, at least.

Constable Dawson turned the key, slid the bolt, and heaved open the door to let the lawyer through.

'Good God, it's dark in here. And so dank,' Thompson said, to remind his client, albeit cumbersomely, that life on the other side of the wall was much preferable.

'I get used to it,' Bonetti said, which drew a sigh from his counsel. He presented the bunk as a host would the best chair in the house. 'Please, Mr Thompson, be my guest.'

'I'm happy standing, thank you, Mr Bonetti. Look, just how long do you intend to stay in here? Because you could be out within the hour.'

'There is no hurry. It is too hot outside. I get food here. They will let me go soon. As soon as they find the killer.'

'And what makes you think they're looking? Mr Bonetti, listen to me, you're the one charged with murder. The police searched your lodgings, and found blood on a shirt and a coat. And a vest.'

'I told them, I killed a sheep. Tell me, how can you kill a sheep without spilling blood?'

'They don't believe you.'

'Bah!'

Neither man spoke. Voices carried through on the draught from the vent, their faintness amplifying the isolation. Thompson thanked God it wouldn't be him left alone after this meeting.

'Very peaceful, don't you think?' Bonetti said, as if contemplating taking up permanent residence.

'Serafino, please. At least tell *me* the truth. I might be able to find a way around this that satisfies this most admirable, if misplaced, sense of gallantry of yours. Who was this woman?'

Thompson's eyes were accustomed now to the gloom, and he noticed the brightness in his client's eyes.

'Gallantry,' Bonetti said. 'Yes, gallantry. That is the word. Thank you. You understand me, I think, Pearson.'

'To a degree. So come on, who —'

'Mrs Telford. I was with Mrs Penelope Telford on the evening of December 28th.'

'The sergeant's wife?'

'The sergeant's wife.'

'Lives just here?' Thompson pointed north.

Bonetti nodded like a schoolboy caught stealing biscuits.

'Does Sergeant Telford know?'

'He suspects, like all jealous husbands do.'

Thompson took a moment to resist an urge to applaud the audacity of this man, or even to show his admiration in a sly grin. 'So, is it gallantry or fear that has kept your mouth shut? You know, Serafino, it might occur to you that if your lover cares about you, she ought to come forward now.'

'No! And you must not speak to her. I will stay here until they have caught David Rose.'

'Don't be such a fool. David Rose is just another suspect. If the police reckon he's their man, why are you still in here?'

This logic seemed to come as a rude shock to Bonetti. His face fell with the realisation.

Thompson pressed. 'Who told you about David Rose? Has Mrs Telford been here?'

'Of course not. She sent a message.'

'Don't you see, man, she's told you about Rose to keep you quiet. To give you reassurance. She thinks you might be about to talk.'

'Never!'

Thompson took a deep breath. This was familiar — a client intractably resistant to sound advice. There was nothing to be done, except for Thompson to be satisfied that he had done all he could.

'My dear Serafino, your solicitor, Mr Geake, engaged me to speak on your behalf to the magistrate, to have you released. Yet I come here today, and, despite your revelation, you haven't told me anything with which to plead your case. Am I to assume that you won't tell me anything, ever, upon which I can act?'

'When David Rose is arrested, you will speak to the magistrate. You will not speak to Mrs Telford. Now, I think our business for today is done.'

SUNDAY 8TH JANUARY
78 ELIZABETH STREET, MELBOURNE

THE TELEGRAM WAS DATED that same day, and had been delivered to Otto Berliner within an hour of its sending. Still in the employ of the Detective Department, he'd been tidying up loose ends on yet another forgery case — there were so many these days — when the lad from the Central Telegraph Office had arrived.

Otto took the paper and in a moment read its single line, and in another decided on the response. He looked at the boy. 'Come in, come in. Help yourself to a boiled sweet while I write my reply. In that jar on the desk.'

'Yes, Sir. Thank you, Sir.'

Otto wrote his answer, and handed it and payment for it to his visitor. As soon as the door was closed, Otto began to pack for Daylesford.

SERGEANT LAWRENCE TELFORD HAD been making a study of his wife, watching for changes in her mood. But in the six days of Bonetti's incarceration he could detect none; at least, none that an unhappy woman deprived of her young lover might reveal. She'd commented on and asked questions about Bonetti's predicament with no more than the expected level of concern and frequency a caring woman might have. She expressed the hope that he would be proved innocent of the charge, and disbelief that that lovely young man was a killer. But there were no tears, no yearning, no anger. Married life had continued as before, at least that part of it she shared with her husband. *Strange*, Telford thought, *this absence of passion*. He could almost feel sorry for the dago, bravely protecting the honour of a woman who really didn't give a damn. The man was a fool! And what a poor fool, to be charged with the slaying of Margaret Stuart. To think, his fornicating had put him in gaol for murder. Such justice! Such sweet serendipity!

But was it possible that he and Penelope weren't lovers? Had he condemned the man on an inkling?

THE MAIL TRAIN TO Malmsbury departed from Melbourne's Spencer Street Station at 7.15 p.m. From Malmsbury to Daylesford was by coach. Otto had made the journey to and from Daylesford many times, but never at this hour. Had Nicolson sent his telegram in the morning there would have been time enough to take the 12.15, to arrive in Daylesford at a civilised five o'clock in the afternoon. This later departure wouldn't see him at his destination till one in the morning! And it would take more than an hour longer. Nicolson knew this, of course — Otto was certain. Nicolson would have had to swallow a mountain of ego in making this request. But Otto had replied that, yes, he would lend his expertise and local knowledge to the hunt for the suspect. Forcing him to the later train was Nicolson's way of letting Otto know he wasn't that important. *So insufferably petty was that man!*

How long he would be in Daylesford, Otto didn't know; Nicolson's telegram was like so many telegrams: big on importance, light on detail. At least there was a name included for this 'man with the tent'. If David Rose was still in the district, a day or two ought to suffice. If he was clear of it — and in nine days he could be well clear — only a day or two would be needed to ascertain as much.

Otto closed his suitcase and placed it by the door. It was half-past noon now, which left a good five hours to do some useful research, allowing time to dine early and to pack cheese and bread, and a flask of water, for refreshment en route. It was his intention to arrive in Daylesford clear-eyed and informed. He would read again selected newspaper reports, including those of the coroner's inquest. He would investigate further than any of his colleagues had, and become *the* authority on David Rose.

At seven, Otto boarded his train, and with the sun obliterating the western view of the rail yards, decided the best option was a nap. He felt he'd earned one.

MALMSBURY STATION WAS REACHED at 9.48 p.m., as per the timetable. Otto was impressed; in his book, punctuality and the keeping of promises were standards to live by. He alighted with his suitcase on the bluestone platform. With a thud, a canvas mail sack from the rear carriage joined him there, and the train pulled away, exhaling smoke and steam, and shattering the stillness with whistle blasts and squeals of metal. Imposing bluestone station buildings stood dark and forbidding across the tracks. On this side was a timber shelter for waiting passengers. Behind it, the coach was waiting, its six horses fidgeting and rattling their tack — eager, it seemed, to plunge headlong into the dark tunnel that was the forested road to Daylesford. Otto walked over. He pressed a hand against the rump of the lead bay, and was struck by a thought that the colony's very prosperity depended on the power of that massive and noble muscle; at least where the railway didn't reach.

The driver appeared, and Otto presented his ticket and climbed aboard. A young man had preceded him, and was cushioning his head for sleep with a rolled-up garment pressed against the window frame. Otto took a seat opposite, facing the direction of travel, as he preferred. The night was clear and cool, and the moon bright. Frogs growled from beyond the reach of the station lamps. The coach swayed as the driver loaded the mail, and again as he climbed to his seat. Otto heard him exchange a goodnight with the stationmaster. From the shadows, a police trooper appeared, doing up his flies. He climbed up with the driver, and at ten, with a bark at the team, Cobb & Co began the three-hour drive to Daylesford.

15

MONDAY 9th JANUARY

SERGEANT LAWRENCE TELFORD WAS the first to greet Otto. He found the detective at 7.00 a.m., emerging from the police quarters, his hair and dress impeccable.

'Your accommodation was to your satisfaction?'

'Precisely as expected, Sergeant Telford,' Otto said. 'Where shall I find Superintendent Nicolson? The sooner we get underway, the better.'

If Telford had forgotten why he loathed this pompous little Prussian, this brief reacquaintance had been sufficient to remind him.

'He's on his morning walk. We're to meet at the station at eight. If you come down there now, my wife has boiled some eggs for your breakfast.'

'That's very kind of her,' Otto said, and was amused, for he knew Mrs Telford from Daylesford days, and he could be sure these eggs were not just country hospitality. Penelope was a woman with a wandering eye, and at first blush it might make no sense why the bovine sergeant should be paired with her. For Otto, it was proof of a favourite personal maxim: for everything in this world, however obscure or unlikely, there was an explanation.

What better for such a woman than such a husband?

At first meeting, Superintendent Charles Nicolson was a humourless marriage of dour visage and Scottish brogue, albeit a tall and athletic one. Those in his circle knew him as a policeman of great pluck and zeal. Otto himself had the highest regard for Nicolson's great feat of daring when, as a cadet, he had caught the murderous Van Diemonians O'Connor and Bradley. But like him? Not much.

Otto had only just returned from washing his hands when the man himself entered the room.

'Berliner,' he said, arm extended. 'I'm glad you're here. Pleasant journey?'

They shook hands, the grip desultory. 'As pleasant as midnight coach journeys can be, Sir.'

Nicolson hadn't wanted an answer; he'd already turned away to greet Superintendent Francis Reid and Detective Williams from Castlemaine, and Daylesford officers — Sergeant Telford and Trooper Henry Brady — as they filed in from the yard and took their seats around the table. Otto, like Nicolson, remained standing. A latecomer appeared at the door: Detective Thomas Walker. He caught Otto's eye, and offered no glimmer of recognition, though they had shared the Daylesford posting for six months prior to Otto's leaving. He took a seat, and Nicolson began.

'Gentlemen, I think you will all know Detective Otto Berliner, if not personally from his time here, then surely by repute. Perhaps his best work in Daylesford was solving the Tibbets murder. So, I'm sure you'll agree that his expertise will be of great help in our task.'

Otto acknowledged the tribute with a slight nod of his head. Those seated remained unmoved.

'So,' Nicolson proceeded, 'this wretched David Rose. Where the devil is he? Walker?'

'Chees —' was as far as Walker got, before Otto decided it was time to put his stamp on this meeting, and, he knew, deny Walker the initiative.

'May I remind everyone that we are after a murderer, which may or may not prove to be David Rose.'

All eyes turned to the upstart with the educated diction and impeccable hair, who, with this technicality, had usurped proceedings. Nicolson twitched, and from the exchanged glances among the others, Otto knew he was on his own — territory he found both familiar and reassuring.

'I know it may seem to be stating the obvious, but it is worth reminding ourselves that if we are preoccupied with Rose — and my reading is that there is much preoccupation with Rose — we will blind ourselves to other possible suspects. David Rose is a suspect; we should not presume his guilt or innocence.'

'A good point, Detective Berliner,' Nicolson conceded, 'notwithstanding that we do have a man in custody already. But for now, the business of the day is to find and apprehend Rose, guilty or not.' He turned to Walker. 'Please, Detective, you were saying, where Rose was seen last?'

'Yes, late morning of Thursday the 29th — the morning after the murder — by George Cheesbrough, at his farm, six miles north-east of here. He dismissed Rose, for being late rising that morning.'

'I wonder why,' Telford said with a wry smile, mirrored by Brady.

'Maybe he was ill,' Otto said, to make the point Telford seemed not to have grasped.

Telford scoffed. 'He ought to have been real ill, after what he'd done.'

Here, Nicholson stepped out of the room, which encouraged Telford to speak uninhibitedly to Otto.

'Well, do tell us, Detective Berliner. Who else could it be?'

'Surely, Sergeant, you haven't forgotten the man you put in the lock-up, charged with the same crime? You should be following that up; maybe Bonetti did do it.'

Telford was suddenly speechless.

'They could have been in concert,' Reid said.

'It is possible,' Otto conceded, if only to model open-mindedness.

'As for Rose,' Reid continued, 'I think it reasonable to surmise that he went to Cheesbrough's to give himself an alibi, so that when the body was discovered he could claim he was nowhere near the place.'

'I agree,' Brady said. 'He could have walked into town that night and been back in his bunk at Glenlyon by one or two. Easily.'

Who was this Trooper Brady, Otto wondered, to be so certain of himself? Did he have a personal grievance with Rose? Or was he just an ambitious little tick?

'It's the rising late gives him away,' Telford added, to a hear-hear from Brady.

'Surely you have an opinion, Berliner?' Reid said.

'I do, Superintendent Reid. I say look at what the evidence says, not what you want it to say.'

Nicolson was back in the room as Reid pressed. 'What I mean, Detective Berliner, is do you have an opinion as to Rose's guilt or innocence?'

'Yes, I do, Superintendent.'

'Hallelujah,' Telford muttered. Reid gestured for Otto to explain.

'I think it is important that we apprehend and question Rose, because he may well be Margaret Stuart's killer. But frankly, I would be surprised if he were. Or, to put it another way, I wouldn't be surprised if he weren't.'

'Based on what?' Reid said.

'Experience. And what I have read about David Rose. Of course, I could be wrong. But as the superintendent has just observed, this bloody murder has provoked great passions in this town, and it is natural for good people to want to find and punish the killer, or killers. The danger, in my view — and I am not sorry to labour the point — is that in the desperation to have justice done, objectivity is lost. When objectivity is lost, justice is never done. We decide who killed Mrs Stuart, and we look for confirmation that we are right. This is bad police work. Yes, Trooper Brady, Rose may have had time to walk from Glenlyon to Daylesford and back; this does not mean he did —'

'But he did ask Cheesbrough's wife whether the dog would bark at late-night intruders,' Walker said.

'Yes, so what is your point, Detective?'

Walker made a face to convey a small contempt for the question. 'Well, Detective, it makes you think, doesn't it? Rose was concerned about the dog waking its master when he returned home that night.'

'Or else, Detective Walker, he was simply asking a question about the dog.'

'Sir,' Telford said, 'with the greatest respect to the esteemed Detective Berliner, my experience as a policeman is that the best way to catch a criminal is not to sit around talking, but to get out, town to town, street to street, house to house, if necessary. The more time we take in talking, the further away Rose is. He could be in New South Wales by now.'

'I agree,' Brady said.

Nicolson took charge. 'Rest assured that if Rose is in New South Wales, he will be arrested there —'

'How long has it been since the murder?' Otto said. 'Two weeks? I would think that, had he so chosen, David Rose could be anywhere in Australia by now.'

Otto enjoyed that — enough to add, directing his attention to Telford, 'So, a few minutes sitting in here talking is not so important, I think.'

'Quite,' Nicolson said, sparing Telford further embarrassment. The sergeant looked to the ceiling as Nicolson proceeded.

'Now, gentlemen, I do know you feel the urgency; this murder has shocked and appalled us all, and the entire colony besides. And you are right, Sergeant, sitting in here isn't catching a murderer —'

This, Otto thought, was the kind of nonsense that typified the incompetence of the Victorian police, and it was coming from the top. *Disregard clear thinking and strategy because the men are itching to get out and feel good chasing something. Were they police, or foxhounds?*

A slight, bespectacled man had appeared at the door. Otto knew who it would be. He hastened over, and was handed three sheets of paper. He thanked the man and rejoined the meeting, at a moment of the most perfect timing.

'So, Detective Berliner,' Nicolson said, 'as the sergeant says, we are agreed; David Rose is merely a suspect. Now, your expertise has been called on to help with his apprehension. What do you suggest?'

'May I say, firstly, that I am very pleased that Sergeant Telford and others are so eager to get out into the countryside to join in the search for Mr Rose. And I am eager to join him. But where shall we begin our house-to-house hunt? I shall tell you. Yesterday afternoon, before I had even left Melbourne, I made certain enquiries, via the telegraph — and here I acknowledge my associate at the Electric Telegraph Office for agreeing to accommodate me on a Sunday afternoon, for I have now, here in my hand, responses to those enquiries. And may I say how appreciative we should all be that these replies have been made so promptly, for they will greatly expedite our task.'

Otto was enjoying himself, giving this lesson in first-class detective work. He waved the first sheet aloft.

'This reply tells us that David Rose passed through Daylesford at around four o'clock on the afternoon of December 29th —'

'Who says?' Reid said.

'Sir, good detective work depends on information, and

accordingly I make it my business to cultivate mutually trusting relationships with certain reliable persons in the community. You would understand, I'm sure, why I would not breach a confidence.'

Reid seemed a little put out. Otto held up a second sheet.

'This attests to David Rose being camped at Blanket Flat that same night, and that the next morning he left to seek work, so he is meant to have said, around Mount Prospect.'

Otto stepped forward to the table and the map thereon. 'Therefore, I suggest, Sir, that we confine our search between this side of Creswick and Smeaton.'

Nicolson nodded. 'Fine work, Berliner, and I agree.'

Otto acknowledged the compliment with a nod. He pocketed the telegraph replies. The third, he hadn't read out — for now, in his judgement, was not the right time.

Nicolson assigned officers in pairs to roads to be searched within the designated area, and by ten-thirty the men had mounted and were riding west down Albert Street. Bystanders watched the procession; some clapped and offered words of encouragement. In the public's mind, these men were off to bring in the murderer.

Otto was with Detective Williams, a man whose silence that morning he'd noted. Such men, Otto usually liked; they thought before they spoke, and said nothing if they had nothing to say. To Otto, equability was a fine quality in a detective, and Williams, with his calm manner and thoughtful countenance, seemed to have it. The greying temples inspired confidence in Otto that this was a man of experience and judgement, a man he could rely on. And this assessment was only reinforced when Williams suggested to Otto that he ought to see the murder scene. It showed respect and courtesy, and more; it demonstrated a commitment to the detecting profession, for every crime scene is an opportunity to learn and improve.

'The husband hasn't stayed here since the night it happened,' Williams said, dismounting and hitching his horse to a fence railing. 'Who can be surprised? A house is not just a house once you know murder has gone on.'

Otto looked up the short rise to the humblest of domiciles. A shed it was, practically, sitting there among the tree stumps. With a window either side of the door, it seemed to be looking back at him, like a dumb animal, or as if to say *Nothing ever happened here that is of any import.* Indeed, it was like so many other worker's residences of the town, with their simple façades masking God knows what complicated lives within.

They walked over the rough ground to the front door. Williams pushed it open and led the way in.

'The vultures have been,' he said, 'and taken all the clothing, the crockery. There was even a crinoline in the bedroom. To think, some witch is wearing that beneath her skirts, bloodstained and all.' He shook his head. 'No shame.'

Otto ran his practised eye over the walls and floor.

'There was a meat safe here,' Williams said, standing in the spot. 'Walker first saw the pipe on top of it.'

'What pipe?'

'The pipe he thought belonged to George Stuart. It turns out Stuart had never seen it before.'

'So it's a vital piece of evidence.'

'Yes. I came here on the fourth and took possession of it.'

'The same pipe, was it, sitting here on the meat safe, unattended for a week?'

'Walker said it was the same pipe.'

'Of course. And where is it now?'

'I gave it to Detective Walker.'

Williams was unsettled by his colleague's tone. But Otto was now examining the whitewashed walls of the fireplace.

'These are supposed to be the marks of the corded trousers, I presume?'

Williams came over to see.

'I suppose. I can't be sure.'

'And there would have been soot all over the floor, a man having come down the chimney.' Otto bent to brush his fingertips over the boards. He examined them. 'No sign of any now. It's all a bit late, of course.' A feeling of some despair was taking hold in Otto's chest as his suspicion grew that this investigation was not being conducted with the standards of diligence the crime warranted — the standards that he lived by. God knew what detail had been overlooked, misread, misconstrued, contaminated. For the likes of Walker and Telford, as long as they had something to chase, they could tell themselves they were making progress. But this Williams fellow seemed to know what he was doing. Yes, Otto reminded himself, he did have a tendency to take personal responsibility for everything. This wasn't his case; he was in Daylesford for a specific task, and by the day's end he might well have completed it. He couldn't and shouldn't try covering for the inadequacies of his colleagues. That way, crushing disappointment lay.

He walked through into the bedroom. The bed stood stripped and askew.

'These boards were pulled up?'

'Walker did, I believe, looking for a knife. No luck.'

'They drained the cess pit?'

'There is none; the Stuarts used an old shaft a hundred yards off. I haven't heard that it's been searched.'

Murder's not important enough to get covered in shit for, Otto thought to say, but held his tongue. He saw the rent in the wallpaper at the head of the bed. A frenzied assault it must have been, for such a wild stab —

Williams came in. 'Gives you a chill, doesn't it?'

Otto looked at his colleague. 'I think you're probably a good detective, Williams, but some advice: eliminate the subjective. It'll make you see things that aren't there, and overlook things that are. It will lead you to false conclusions. It may well give you a chill to be in a room where a young woman met a violent and bloody death, but you're a detective, not a poet.'

Williams nodded, but Otto saw only puzzlement in his colleague's eyes.

'We should go, Williams. I've seen enough.'

16

10.00 A.M. TUESDAY 10th JANUARY
DAYLESFORD COURT HOUSE

DAVID ROSE STOOD IN the dock under the gaze of a crowd that had come to see a killer. Those not early enough to have made the opening-time dash for gallery seats remained outside, jostling and craning to watch the prisoner being escorted the fifty yards from the lock-up. They stared, as if at a fantastic ape captured from the wilds. But what they saw was a man: stout and thickset, with long and dense black hair and beard. His moustache was strangely formed of two patches either side of his shaved top lip, from which two teeth protruded just a little. He wore a coat of a dark imitation sealskin, with brown-braid binding, duck trousers, a belt with a large brass buckle, and a billycock-hat with ventilators. He walked round-shouldered in heavy, lace-up shoes. He was agitated, looking around him, this way and that, as he was still when Magistrate Drummond called order for proceedings to get underway.

Superintendent Reid rose to inform the court that the prisoner had been apprehended the day before, on Monday the 9th, and asked for a remand of seven days.

'The arrest was made by Trooper Henry Brady?'

'Yes, Your Worship.'

Drummond directed Brady to stand and give an account of the arrest.

Otto Berliner watched the young constable rise with a triumphal swagger. He was proud, all right, but what had he done other than follow orders arising out of timely telegrams? The gallery wouldn't know this, of course, nor much care, probably. To them, the capture of the murderous Rose was largely due to the resourcefulness and persistence of this fine, brave young policeman. Action was something the layman could understand and applaud; the subtle strategy behind it was never so appreciated. It was a disheartening reality that made Otto only too glad to be leaving for Melbourne on the four o'clock coach.

'I arrested the prisoner at about two o'clock yesterday afternoon in the neighbourhood of Kingston, sixteen or eighteen miles from here.'

So, Otto thought, *no mention of his partner, Wilkinson*. It spoke to character whether or not a man acknowledged his partners, Otto believed.

'You've been in pursuit of the prisoner since when?' Stanbridge asked.

'Since December 29th, Your Worship.'

That would be nearly two weeks, then, Otto calculated. *And how long after the arrival of Detective Berliner did you apprehend Mr Rose?* he thought the magistrate might ask, though he could work that out for himself. Otto reckoned twelve hours, maybe even eleven. But Brady was now describing the arrest, and, in Otto's opinion, in rather more detail than was necessary.

'The place was a mile or three miles off the road, about a mile south of Hepburn's lagoon, in a paddock full of scrub. He was sitting on a log, though he removed from that whilst I was crossing a creek. When I got up to him, I jumped off my horse and caught hold of him. I passed my hand round his throat.' Brady here demonstrated the hold on himself. 'I said, "I have been looking a long time for you." I said, "I arrest you on a charge of murdering Mrs Stuart, of Daylesford." I told him not to say anything that would be brought against him.'

'And how did the prisoner respond?'

'He seemed astonished at the charge. He said, "Do I look like a murderer?"'

Otto looked at Rose. What does the prisoner think a murderer might look like, he wondered? No one in the gallery would have had any doubt. Yes, the man in the dock looked like a murderer: unkempt, unrefined, brutish, not one of them. They would be blind to the childlike incomprehension in his face, the sheer incomprehension that he should find himself standing there.

Brady continued '... he had a large swag with him. Inside I found a butcher's knife and a razor. I remarked that there was a stain on the razor, and he said it had got wet in the swag. I found the following things in his swag: some bedding, a tent, a quantity of tattered garments, trousers, shirt, a frying pan, a billy can, three pipes, and £5 7s. 6d. in cash, including a five-pound note.'

'And on his person?'

'In his pocket he had a pocket knife and another pipe.'

'And he admitted that he was the man who lived in the tent near the deceased woman's cottage?'

'He did, Your Worship. And that he had spoken to her.'

Drummond indicated to Brady to stand down. 'Remand is granted for seven days. Return the prisoner to the cell.'

Otto Berliner watched Rose, and saw a man at the edge of his very limited wits, unable even to ask a question that might bring him some degree of understanding of how he had come to be in such a predicament. Except perhaps that he had found himself in such predicaments throughout his life. He was an ex-convict, after all, as the reply to the third telegram had confirmed, transported to Van Diemen's Land at sixteen for house-breaking. But this was murder, and the punishment was to be sent on a journey a good deal shorter: a drop at the end of a rope. Otto had sympathy for the fellow. Murderer or not, no evidence had been presented; he'd just pitched a tent near the deceased's home, and had spoken to her shortly before her demise. Remand was simply at the convenience of the police, to keep the man handy while evidence could be gathered. But if smiles and laughter were an indication, this was good enough for the gallery. Its tiered rows of citizens were filing out now, certain that Daylesford was a safer town with David Rose locked away. Had everyone forgotten about Serafino Bonetti?

Otto stood. It was approaching noon, and lunch presented as the best idea. Across the room he saw Drummond still seated at the bench, and talking with Nicolson and a familiar face of old acquaintance: that carunculated relic, Pearson Thompson. *My God*, Otto thought, *he's still got a shingle out*. He wondered whether he should go over and shake hands with his old adversary. The man had been gentleman enough to congratulate him on the guilty verdict for the Tibbets murder, after all. Thompson had put up a reasonably stiff defence for his client, but really, his strong suit was drunken prostitutes and petty thieves, for whom over the years he had spared much time behind bars. It was too late for handshakes now, anyway; Nicolson had joined them, and all three promptly repaired to the magistrate's room, whereupon the door was shut behind them.

THE ALBERT HOTEL ACROSS the street had been a favourite lunch venue of Otto's on the occasions when he appeared in court. It was also a regular haunt of Pearson Thompson's, so Otto's decision to dine there this day wasn't entirely without design. He ordered corned beef and salad, and found a table by a window overlooking the Court House. He didn't see Thompson emerge from his meeting, but the man was true to his habits anyway, and came in.

The dining area was too small for patrons to escape the notice of their fellows, and the detective and lawyer nodded to each other in mutual recognition. Otto stayed busy with his food; Thompson, with a waitress. He was chatting easily with her, encouraged by her coquettish looks and chuckles. As was the barrister's predilection, she was young, and with the kind of innocent muliebrity to which vain men of mature years readily fall captive. They finished their intercourse with what looked like Thompson's relating of an amusing anecdote before she disappeared through to the kitchen, and he looked about for a free table. Catching his eye, Otto invited him to his. Thompson came over.

'Berliner,' he said, offering his hand.

'Thompson.' They shook, Thompson as limp-wristed as Otto remembered.

Thompson sat and smoothed his moustache with a parting of thumb and forefinger.

'I didn't expect to see you up here. I thought you were going private?'

'I am, but until the office opens I remain a public servant.'

'Well, old man, public or private, Nicolson tells me your sleuthing came through.'

Otto affected not to be appreciative of the compliment, lest it appear he was surprised by it.

'Not that it did my client any good,' Thompson added.

The purpose of the meeting with the magistrate and superintendent was now clear to Otto.

'Drummond turned your application down?'

'Only because Nicolson objected to it.'

'This is no surprise.'

'No, Nicolson wants to keep both suspects detained because he has nothing but circumstantial evidence against Rose, and Bonetti has not explained himself — neither his whereabouts on the night, nor the blood on his clothing, though he did say it was sheep's blood. But how can anyone tell?'

'Bonetti has no alibi?'

'He has, but won't say. The man's a fool.'

'A married woman, then.'

'Of course. And no, Bonetti does not want her to come forward.'

'Once more, this is no surprise; her husband will be embarrassed, and she will be disgraced and without means.'

'That's about the size of it.'

'Does Sergeant Telford know what his wife's been doing?'

'Good God! How do you know — ?'

'Bonetti built the new extension to Telford's quarters at the Police Camp, and it is not unknown that very red blood flows through Mrs Telford's veins. So it seems to me the man had what I call motive and opportunity. And, by the way, I didn't know — until you just confirmed it.'

Thompson seemed impressed, if not irritated. 'Well, I didn't actually tell you.' His sausage and mash was set down by the woman he'd been speaking to earlier. He smiled at her. 'Thank you, my dear,' he said, with a light touch on her forearm. She smiled and left.

'Lola,' Thompson said, leaving it for Otto to interpret in whichever direction he chose. He loaded his fork. 'With Rose remanded, Bonetti was assuming he'd be a free man. And I think it's a reasonable assumption; they can't both be guilty. It's an indictment of police competence and an affront to justice. But I'm wasting my breath telling you.' Thompson's mood had soured. Otto resented the implication; he had his own differences with his colleagues, but he wasn't about to sympathise with a defence counsel's beef. He watched Thompson chew, reload his fork, and then point it at him as he spoke.

'Bonetti's innocent, Berliner. That's undeniable. The irony is, I think I want him released more than he does!'

'So you can represent Rose, I take it.'

Thompson paused his eating.

'I really hadn't thought of that. It has some appeal to a man at the twilight of a long career. Straightforward, undemanding —'

'Payment government-guaranteed.'

'No expectation of victory.'

'You think Rose is guilty?'

Thompson chuckled. He shrugged.

'Let's say that if he hangs, no one's going to be surprised, or grieved!'

'What shall you do about Bonetti?'

Thompson smiled. 'Goodness me, Berliner, I thought that would have been obvious. I shall have a little chat with Mrs Telford, of course.'

WITH AN HOUR AND a half to while away before the coach, Otto thought to take himself on a walk through town, to see who was about — in particular, a fellow who had arrived in Daylesford well after he himself had left, and whose involvement in the murder investigation was to Otto as fascinating as it was revolutionary. At the bottom of Albert Street, in Burke Square, just past Doctor Doolittle's consulting rooms and Tognini's Hotel, Otto found the man's premises: The London Portrait Gallery. He entered to a tinkling of a bell and a warm greeting from the proprietor. On first impression, he was a man of disarming manner.

'Good afternoon, Sir. Thomas Chuck,' he said, and offered his hand.

Otto accepted it and they shook. 'Otto Berliner,' he said.

'Detective Otto Berliner?'

'Yes.'

'I had heard one of Daylesford's finest was returning,' the photographer said.

'Only for a day, Mr Chuck.'

'And it proved that a day was all that was required.'

Otto smiled. How gratifying it was to hear that one's abilities were appreciated, admired even.

'I saw your photographs, Mr Chuck. Who would have thought that Daylesford, of all places, would be at the forefront of crime photography? An exciting future, I think.'

'Maybe, but I think I shall keep to landscapes and portraits.'

'No challenge when your subject keeps so still, I suppose.'

Chuck forced a faint smile, and Otto was immediately appalled at his making light. He hastened to atone.

'Tell me, Mr Chuck, you took two photographs?'

'I was asked to take two.'

'By whom?'

'Detective Walker. He wanted one of the deceased on her bed, and one of the locality.'

'Well, you're clearly a master of the craft.'

'Thank you. I wonder, though, Detective, how much use they are.'

'To which side: prosecution or defence?'

'To the side of justice.'

The answer took Otto by surprise, and agreeably so. Here was a fellow he could grow to like very much.

'Quite right. Anyway, I'm no longer part of the investigation; it's back to Melbourne for me now. I plan to leave the police department this year, to begin my own practice.'

'In that case, may I ask what you think of David Rose?'

Otto thought a moment. A glib reply would be an insult to this man of manifest compassion and integrity. 'I think only that he's a man, and a man no less deserving of justice than any other.'

'And you think he will get justice?'

'It pains me to say, Mr Chuck, that from what I've seen so far, I don't know. It was a horrible crime, and people want to unleash their anger over it. It would be easy to believe that whoever killed Mrs Stuart is a creature not like the rest of us.'

In the softening of his face, Chuck conveyed his acknowledgement of the honesty of the observation. And then he hung his head.

'I'm sorry. That scene at Stuart's. It was … the smell, the flies. So many flies. I'll never forget it.'

'No. Dreadful.'

'I keep imagining that poor woman's last thoughts.' He pressed fingertips into his forehead and made his scalp white. He looked up, and Otto saw that his eyes had reddened. 'I saw David Rose yesterday, when he was brought in. I had to go, to see for myself what kind of a man would do that to a beautiful young woman. I shouldn't have gone. It was horrifying, shameful, to be one of the mob.'

'Rose might well be the murderer, Mr Chuck. People are angry.'

'Yes, but do they want revenge more than they want justice?'

The two men were silent in a moment of mutual understanding. The tension in Chuck's face eased.

'I'm glad to have met you, Detective Berliner.'

Otto smiled and turned for the door, and then thought of something. 'If you were so inclined to share your thoughts further, you might write to me. Or if ever you're in Melbourne, we may meet over lunch perhaps. I'd be delighted to learn more about photography. It would seem to have great application in my profession. You do come to Melbourne?'

'On occasion. And thank you, Detective Berliner, I shall certainly write.'

'Please, it's Otto.'

'Tom.'

THE FORESTS TO THE east of Daylesford flashed by in shadows and shafts of light. A crowded coach of ten passengers it was for the return journey to Malmsbury, and on a trying road Otto was glad of a window seat for the support the chassis afforded. He had expected also to be glad to be heading home; instead, he was troubled. Why had he accepted Nicolson's request, he wondered?

He had nothing to prove; his record of achievement was already legendary: the Tibbets and La Franchi murders, the forgeries, the burglaries ... so many crimes, so many plaudits in the press, and official reports for 'skill and zeal' in bringing perpetrators to book. That Nicolson made the request ought to have been ample affirmation. What need was there to demonstrate to former colleagues his prowess yet again? None, of course, and now he was left with an uneasiness that he been compromised. Yes, thanks to him, a man had been apprehended, but Otto had simply been a bloodhound, brought in to sniff out a suspect and then to be sent home to his kennel. This wasn't how a good detective worked! It certainly wasn't how he worked. Alas, he despaired that his colleagues, however inept, did not share his assiduity, nor even subscribe to it.

What evidence was there against this David Rose? Against Serafino Bonetti? What evidence had been missed, contaminated, destroyed? What other suspects had been overlooked? What investigations were underway? It was an indictment of his fellows that he should have so little confidence in their abilities — but worse, he feared, an indictment of himself that he would suspend his standards for cheap vanity.

On the upside of the ledger, and there usually was an upside if he cared to look for one, was making the acquaintance of Tom Chuck. Yes, Otto thought, it had been a brief meeting, but he was sure he'd met a man of like mind there, a man of integrity, a man he could trust.

17

THURSDAY 26th JANUARY

BUSH FLIES WERE AT their summer height. They rose in clouds from street dung, and dispersed to lips, eyes, sweaty backs, and sugar bowls. A month before, they had gathered on Maggie Stuart's corpse, animating it with their ceaseless scuttling and swirling. For nearly two days they feasted and reproduced on her bloating body, until it was denied them. And then, when the police turned their backs, the human scavengers arrived in their stead.

Daylesford remained excited by December's tragedy but on edge no longer, now that David Rose was locked away. No one had seriously considered Serafino Bonetti to be the killer; he was that attractive and polite young man who worked at Colanchini's Bakery in Vincent Street, who did the odd bit of carpentry and repairs on the side. And if he was the killer, why would the police have been expending so much effort in finding this other fellow? Even Detective Berliner had been called up from Melbourne to assist in the hunt; that's how determined they were to bring Rose in, so the thinking went. And the reports from those who'd actually seen the man were hardly favourable — and most damning were the testimonies at the inquest, widely reported in the press and on the street.

All this, Pearson Thompson gathered, explained why Bonetti was in a quietly optimistic humour on this morning that he'd come to visit his client. But after his protracted resistance to sound advice, it was time the young fornicator sobered up.

'Mr Bonetti. Serafino, my friend, surely enough is enough. He…' Thompson pointed a finger over his shoulder to the adjoining cell, 'has been there for more than two weeks now, yet you're still here. Why? Because they have nothing on him but hearsay and prejudice. You, however, have blood-soaked clothes and no alibi. Except of course, you do have an alibi, and I have been remiss in my obligation to you not to reveal it to the police. Remember, your welfare is my concern — the honour of a lady is not.'

'You've told the police?' Thompson detected no particular note of annoyance in Bonetti's tone. He supposed the poor fellow really had had enough of all this silly gallantry.

'No, I haven't. But I've taken it upon myself to let your lady friend know my views. So you can either tell the magistrate yourself, or leave it to her. Of course, I made it clear to her that, unlike yours, her word wouldn't be doubted.'

Melbourne Argus
Telegraphic Despatches
Daylesford, 27th January

Serafino Bonetti, the suspected murderer of Mrs Stuart, was brought up at the Police Court this morning and discharged. Superintendent Reid explained that his detention had arisen from the untruthful and unsatisfactory nature of the alibi set up by the prisoner. It appears that the prisoner, on the night of the murder, was engaged in an intrigue, and had prevaricated in his answers to police in order to shield the woman's reputation.

Otto Berliner put down his newspaper and considered the implications of this report. Bonetti had been in custody for over two weeks since Rose's apprehension. The case against Rose was weak, of course, and remained just as weak now; Bonetti's release not being due to evidence against Rose. The difference that Bonetti's release made was the urgent need now for the police to make the case against Rose strong, to find evidence that was substantial, beyond the circumstantial case that had put him in gaol and kept him there almost a month. This ought not be enough for him to be held any longer, let alone for him to be hanged. Otto intended, was determined — compelled — to stay *au courant* with developments in Daylesford. He was, after all, entitled to regard himself as part of the ongoing investigation, even if his talents were currently and officially being applied to solving city crime. He thought to write to Tom Chuck, if only to let the man know that he'd been sincere in his wish to correspond.

18

TUESDAY 7th FEBRUARY

SOLICITOR JAMES GEAKE WAS all smiles and reassurances. Clients, he reckoned, particularly those on remand in dark cells, wanted counsel that raised their hopes. Dashing hopes was the prerogative of judges. With his loose-fitting suit and untidy brown hair, his physical presentation wasn't the key in inspiring confidence — it was all in the talk.

Constable Dawson opened the cell door and let the lawyer through.

'Mr Rose — James Geake.' He extended his right hand, which Rose took for the duration of a single shake. 'Thank you, Mr Rose, for taking the opportunity to speak with me ... my God, isn't it dark in here!'

Rose wasn't in the mood for chit-chat, that was clear, so Geake suspended it.

'Look, Mr Rose. David. The police have had you in here for, what, four weeks now? Three remands, and still no trial date has been set. It really is most unsatisfactory. But on the bright side, it tells me the case against you is built on the flimsiest of foundations. And what's more heartening is that you've considerable support in the local community, and further afield — a lot of sympathy.

People are saying, if there's evidence, Mr Magistrate, for pity's sake, put the poor man on trial. If not, let him go!'

Geake shook his head and threw his hands up in disbelief at the manifestly unjust treatment of his client. When Rose sat there, indifferent to all this brightness and buoyancy, Geake's eyes faltered. They swept about the cell, and back to the dark and brooding face looking back.

'I'm sure you're hoping that this time the magistrate sees sense.'

David Rose made no remark, and gave no expression.

'Nonetheless, Mr Rose, as I've just said, you've had three remand hearings so far for no good result, so my advice is that you need legal representation.'

'I didn't kill the woman.'

'That's what you say, and I don't doubt your word is true. But if, heaven forbid, you are committed for trial today, you will need a barrister in court. My firm recommendation is Mr Pearson Thompson, a man who once worked in chambers at Lincoln's Inn. That's in London. And, I hasten to add, if you are not in a position to pay, the government has funds set aside for such cases as yours.'

David Rose made no response. There had been times like this in his life, times when he had been locked up at the pleasure of authority, and he had found there was nothing to be done about it. He would get what the judge decided he would get, whatever the likes of this James Geake and his barrister friend said.

'If things don't go well for you today, Mr Rose — and I mean if — and you are committed for trial, Mr Thompson and I would do our utmost as your legal counsel. I say that to give you some comfort in this difficult time.'

Rose remained unmoved. They gazed at each other, both men seeming to understand that what would give comfort right now was Geake's departure.

The solicitor rapped his knuckles on the door.

'So, Mr Rose, do think about what I've said, and I wish you very well for this afternoon.'

DAYLESFORD COURT HOUSE
DAVID ROSE COMMITTAL HEARING

AT THE CONCLUSION OF the previous case — a dispute over wandering goats — spare gallery seats were promptly filled for David Rose's committal hearing. The prisoner was brought to the dock, and superintendents Reid and Nicolson took their places on the prosecution side. Coroner William Drummond, now acting in the office of Magistrate, resumed the chair, alongside Mayor George Patterson.

'You're not represented, Mr Rose?'

The prisoner shrugged.

'Then, Mr Rose, I advise you to listen attentively to the evidence; it will be of great importance to you that you do so.'

Rose was suddenly anxious. He felt the glare of the gallery, and saw the whispering among the rows.

'You understand, Mr Rose?'

'I am a little nervous, Your Worship. I'm a man of weak understanding, you see. I only wish that my innocence be proved to the utmost.'

'You may wish to take notes of the evidence. You can write?'

'No, Your Worship. Please, may I be seated? I feel faint.'

Drummond indicated for Constable Dawson to procure a chair, and called for Reid to begin.

'The prisoner, David Rose, is charged with murdering Margaret Stuart on December 28th last. It is germane to state that Mr Rose was transported from England in 1849 to Port Arthur in Van Diemen's Land for seven years, having been convicted of burglary, stealing £8. Since arriving in this colony in 1858 on a conditional pardon, he has been twice convicted of larceny — once at Kilmore, and once at Portland.'

Drummond addressed the prisoner.

'You admit to this account?'

Rose nodded.

Reid continued, reading from prepared notes. 'Ever since the murder of the unfortunate Mrs Stuart, the police have been unremitting in our exertions to bring the murderer to justice. And now, we, the police, are ready to proceed with this case; we submit that the evidence presented today be grounds for committing the prisoner to trial.'

'Thank you, Mr Superintendent. Please continue.'

George Stuart was called and sworn. Reid offered the witness a limp smile, and put his questions. When asked about the man in the dock, Stuart answered with measured certainty.

'Yes, the man my wife complained of being too familiar with her is the prisoner.'

Drummond turned to Rose. 'Do you wish to ask a question?'

Rose got to his feet. 'I only spoke as I passed him one evening, a Friday. I said, "Good evening."'

He fidgeted nervously and sat down.

Reid was handed a clay pipe by Sergeant Telford.

'I want you to tell me if you have seen this pipe before, Mr Stuart.' Reid held it out for him.

'No, Sir, I never saw that pipe before.'

'Not in your house?'

'No. I'm sure it was never in my house.'

Telford showed the pipe to Rose.

'I have never had this pipe in my possession,' Rose said. He shrugged, and grimaced, as if to convey that he had no understanding of why he was there.

Detective Walker was called. He seemed to have come in some haste, for his brow was sweaty and face florid. He, too, was questioned about the pipe that had been found.

Walker blew out his cheeks, coughed, and began, reading from notes. 'I was at the house at about ten minutes before two o'clock, on the morning of December the 29th. I found the pipe ...' Reid picked up the pipe and handed it to the magistrate and mayor, who gave it cursory inspection. 'It was on the top of the meat safe in the first room.'

The hearing proceeded, with Reid calling, in turn, Louisa Goulding, Joseph Mounsey, and the Cheesbroughs, who all attested to the prisoner being the man of whom they had spoken.

Then Sarah Spinks was called, and the first hiccup appeared in the prosecution's case.

'Is the man you saw outside Maggie Stuart's house on the night of the murder the prisoner?' Reid asked.

She looked to the dock. She had taken her seat with an air of equanimity, and answered Reid's question with certainty of mind.

'The prisoner appears too stout. It might have been him. I only know him by report.'

'You have seen the prisoner before?'

'Yes. Once playing with my children, twice passing my place. On the evening of the 28th. At the time, and since, I fancied the prisoner was the man outside the Stuarts' house, but, as I said, he seems now too stout.'

The witness was thanked and asked to stand down. Glances were exchanged between Reid and other police, perhaps to acknowledge Mrs Spinks' confident delivery, or more likely to share their irritation at her doubts.

Reid called Thomas Hathaway, a slight man of ruddy complexion whose bandy legs predisposed him to clamber, rather than step, into the box. He stood now, Bible in hand, with an air of nervous impatience about him.

'I'm a livery stable keeper, and the prisoner was in my employ last September and October, for about two weeks.'

'Did you see the prisoner smoke a pipe?'

'Yes, often. He seemed always to be smoking.'

'Was it any of these pipes?' The clerk held out the tray. Hathaway selected one of the two curved ones.

'This one. The bowl is broken inside. I remember well because he had left it alight one day in the stable. A wind got up, and I saw sparks being blown across the hay. I picked up the pipe and told him I would break it.'

'What did the prisoner say?'

'He said, "For God's sake, don't break it. I would rather give a sovereign than it should be broken."'

The chair in the dock squealed as Rose was to his feet and glaring at the witness. Looks of delighted alarm registered on the faces in the gallery, in anticipation of confrontation.

'Are you not afraid that the devil will come and take you away out of that box?' Rose said, his hands gripping the railing such that it flexed and creaked.

Drummond was measured. 'Mr Rose, please remain calm. You will have your opportunity to address the witness.' Rose sat down and looked to the ceiling. His lips were moving, as if in prayer.

Hathaway had kept his gaze to the bench and not once returned the prisoner's stare.

Reid spoke. 'I have no further questions, Your Worship.'

'Thank you, Mr Reid. Now, Mr Rose, the floor is yours. Do you have any questions for the witness?'

Rose sat forward, forearms on thighs, and exhaled. He dropped his head a moment and lifted it.

'No, he has told too many lies already.'

Murmurs issued from the gallery, and died away under a glare from the bench. Drummond glanced up at the clock, and then turned to Patterson to indicate that, with the time at four-twenty, proceedings would now be brought to a close.

'Mr Rose, you have heard the evidence presented. Is there anything you wish to say before the bench hands down its decision?'

Rose looked as if he might have very much to say, yet had no idea where to begin. He threw his hands up and shook his head in the frustration of the moment. And then he was still.

Drummond exchanged a brief glance with Mayor Patterson, as if to ask, *Have I not given him every opportunity?*

He then addressed the court. 'Very well, as much as this case is a tragic one, it is indeed a very peculiar and mysterious one. The evidence, as presented against you, Mr Rose, though it be purely circumstantial, is nonetheless sufficient for this court to commit you to stand trial for the murder of Mrs Margaret Stuart. This will take place at Castlemaine Circuit Court on the 21st of February. Constable Dawson, return the prisoner to his cell.'

SATURDAY 11th FEBRUARY, MELBOURNE

OTTO BERLINER DELIGHTED IN his monthly forty minutes in the chair at Linden's Gentlemen's Salon of Collins Street. The rake of the comb across his scalp he counted among the great pleasures in life, and privately attributed much of his capacity for clear-headedness to its stimulation of cranial blood flow. The trim and shave were for presentation, but the combing was positively therapeutic. Otto preferred a clean-shaven face; elaborate sideburns and broom-head moustaches he didn't care for, and, for the purposes of disguise, a whisker-free face was as a blank canvas onto which any of the widest range of false pieces could be affixed.

Newly tended, Otto liked to find a seat in the coffee house next door, and there he would open his newspaper to round out the hour over a brew. And as he read, he would make annotations, as prompts for later reference or simply to record his comments. Today, he read that David Rose had been transferred to Castlemaine gaol to await trial. In anticipation, he had his sharpened pencil at the ready:

> Rose, under a mask of stolidity and nervousness, really conceals great self-possession and cunning. Though he appeared agitated and anxious during portions of the police court examination, there is reason to believe he was perfectly

cool. While in the dock, his face wore the expression becoming one whose life was at stake; but during an interval in the proceedings, when removed from the court, his assumed decorum gave way to laughter. It is well known here that Rose is an old hand, and quite capable of committing violence. That he is also a man of strong passions can likewise be proved. It is understood that the police have other evidence than that made public. However, there is only too much reason to fear that the testimony will fail to insure a conviction. The pipe identified by the witness Hathaway as Rose's, and which Detective Walker found on a meat safe in the murdered woman's house, will be sworn to by others. Still their evidence may well be doubted. It is all but incredible that the murderer should have descended the chimney with such an article in his mouth, or have used it in the house either before or after killing his victim.

Otto folded his paper and sat in quiet contemplation. Such opinionated reportage really was to be deplored. Only the final sentence could be said to have made a reasonable inference; though it was a wonder that the author hadn't construed an explanation commensurate with the judgemental tenor of the rest of his piece, now decorated in pencil by lines, circles, and exclamation marks.

Otto sighed. He felt the bristly grain of the nape of his neck, and the smoothness of his jowl. In the window he saw his wraith-like reflection, stationary amid the flow of pedestrians seemingly passing right on through it. He had a very bad feeling about this Rose case: the unprepossessing illiterate with a criminal past and a slight overbite already had a noose around his neck.

PART II

19

WEDNESDAY 15th MARCH 1865
DAYLESFORD COURT HOUSE

JOSEPH LATHAM STOOD IN the dock, resentment swelling his collar. He had been in the lock-up since Friday, and it was George Stuart who'd put him there, on a charge of stealing. In the witness box stood his wife, Alice. Their eyes met, and quickly she turned away as she heard Magistrate Drummond put his question.

'Yes, Your Worship,' she said. 'The dresses and jewellery do belong to my late daughter, and these items are at my house.'

'The charge brought by Mr George Stuart against your husband is that some time on New Year's Day, three days after the murder of your daughter, he unlawfully removed these items — to the value of £10 — from Mr Stuart's house.'

'They weren't stolen. They were my daughter's, and, yes, they are in my possession. I admit it.'

Drummond considered a moment. 'The charge is not sustained. Case dismissed. You're free to leave, Mr Latham.'

TUESDAY 25th APRIL, CASTLEMAINE COURT HOUSE
THE PROSECUTION APPLIES FOR A POSTPONEMENT

AT SEVENTY, PEARSON THOMPSON wasn't in the best of health, with a gouty foot and an unreliable bladder being particularly bothersome ailments in his general state of decrepitude. Eliza's tracking him down to his new address in Castlemaine hadn't made his situation any less onerous; but as long as he had income enough, he could keep her at bay. That Mary Foley was expecting his child was not of immediate concern, and he wasn't expecting that it would be; she was a woman with some capacity for self-restraint. Besides, he was fond of her; he liked to come home to her. Her willingness to please he took as reward for speaking up all day for those of her ilk: the ill-educated, coarse-mannered of the world.

At ten in the morning, he hobbled into the court and saw his client already in the dock, clad in prison garb, and no less unfavourably presented for it. The barrister signalled that the accused might like to sweep the hair off his face, if only so the court might see that there was a human being before it, albeit an uncommonly hirsute one. Rose complied, to a degree, and Thompson proceeded to his place. He nodded a good morning to Smyth, the crown prosecutor, whose growing reputation Thompson would acknowledge were it not the case that the man was half his age. Smyth smiled back, but Thompson discerned no respect in it. But when was a young Irishman respectful to an ageing Englishman anyway? Judge Williams was presiding, and opened proceedings by taking a submission from Smyth, for a postponement.

'Your Honour, in support of this application, I have here an affidavit from Detective Constable Thomas Walker of Daylesford, to the effect that since the last postponement, he and Detective Williams have discovered a certain article of clothing, which they believe would be important evidence against the prisoner. But yet their case is not ready for trial, and that, if postponed till the next Circuit Court he — that is, Detective Walker — believes that additional and important evidence would be forthcoming against the prisoner.'

Thompson was having none of this. He rose abruptly, to signal the import of what he was about to say. 'Your Honour, on behalf of the prisoner, I must strenuously oppose the application. Mr Rose was committed on February 7th to stand trial on February 21st. That date lapsed, and since then there has been yet another postponement, because there was not a tittle of evidence against him, although fourteen detectives had been getting up the case. It would be a denial of justice to keep the prisoner in custody any longer.' He sat down as emphatically as he had jumped up.

Judge Williams suggested a possible concession. 'He may, perhaps, be admitted to bail.'

Thompson was shaking his head in the manner of a man confident he had moral right on his side. He stood again, slowly this time, and spoke with commensurate measure.

'Your Honour, with respect, how can a man like the prisoner get bail? His character and reputation have been so maligned that at Daylesford the police were obliged to bring him by a circuitous route to the court, or he would have been torn to pieces by the crowd. And how certain are the police of the prisoner's guilt, when two other men were taken into custody for the same offence? And, I might add, one of them, Bonetti, shared a lock-up with the prisoner for a period of weeks! No, the fact is there is not a particle of evidence against the prisoner. The husband of the murdered woman says he is not the man who committed the murder; the police know he is not the man; and there is not the slightest evidence against him.'

Judge Williams watched Thompson's performance impassively. The repetition was not helpful to the barrister's argument. When it was done, he looked to Smyth, unhurriedly rising in his place and conveying in his unruffled manner that reason was on his side.

'I would point out to my learned colleague, Your Honour, that there is, in fact, a great deal of evidence; and it is believed that other evidence will be obtained.'

Smyth eased back into his chair as Thompson stood to counter: 'If my learned colleague is referring to an item of clothing found in a log near Cheesbrough's farm, I say that it is not known that this item belongs to the prisoner.'

Smyth let this go by with a grimace, as if to say he really had no idea what Thompson was talking about.

'Your Honour, defence counsel may be suggesting that the prisoner has been unreasonably detained. Well, I don't need to remind him that murder is a very serious charge, and I point out that the prisoner was only committed on the 7th of February. So, the prisoner has not been in gaol more than two months and a half.'

Thompson was quick to rebut. 'But he was in the Daylesford lock-up for four weeks before that!'

Williams waggled both hands for the two gentlemen to be silent while he considered his decision.

With a glance to Rose, he gave it. 'I will remand the prisoner; but the trial must be proceeded with at the next Circuit Court.'

Smyth gestured that this was a decision he was happy to comply with. Not so Thompson, however. He stood, and with an arm extended towards the dock, said, 'Does Your Honour think the prisoner ought to be remanded? Two other men were brought up for this murder, and the prosecutor himself doesn't really believe that the prisoner is the man!' Smyth rolled his eyes, and shrugged to the bench in bewilderment. Thompson went on. 'There have been fourteen detectives, *fourteen*, getting up evidence against the prisoner, and they have done everything they can do.'

Thompson seemed to have stepped across the line that separates argument from complaint, and Williams was having none of that. 'Fourteen, you say, Mr Thompson? Perhaps they want sixteen.'

The judge suppressed a smile, though Smyth did little to conceal his amusement at the quip.

Thompson would not be discouraged. 'The police don't know what they want. The prisoner is made a victim to appease the popular clamour —'

Smyth was indicating that Rose was wanting a word. Thompson took a moment to consult, and returned to say, 'The prisoner informs me that they won't allow him to shave his beard.'

Smyth shrugged.

Williams was similarly disposed to the grievance. 'Prison regulations. I cannot interfere in the matter.'

Thompson began to speak, but was hushed by the judge, who by his weary tone manifestly had had enough.

'I've considered the application, and heard the objections to it. The prisoner will be remanded until the next Circuit Court, in July, it being understood that he would then be discharged if the Crown was not ready to proceed with the trial.'

That, it seemed, was the end of the matter. Not for Pearson Thompson.

'Then might I ask upon what recognisances Your Honour would admit the prisoner to bail?'

Williams replied without calculation, the bluntness of it surely intended to dissuade Thompson from protest.

'Two hundred and fifty pounds himself, and two sureties of £250 each.' *So*, Thompson calculated, *that's Rose and two others each to stump up twice a constable's yearly pay.* The impossibility of bail was thus made clear, and Thompson could do nothing but slump in his chair. But as if the impossible was not enough, Smyth put in the boot.

'Your Honour, I ask that a week's notice be given to the law officers of the Crown of the intended sureties before they are accepted.'

'Certainly, Mr Smyth, and I might add that my promise to discharge the prisoner at the next sittings, if the Crown was not ready to go on with the trial, would not be binding if the prisoner were admitted to bail.'

Smyth nodded his acceptance of the conditions. Thompson sighed, and capitulated. 'I have not the slightest reason to believe that the prisoner will be able to find sureties.'

Smyth knew as much, and made no remark. The court rose as Judge Williams made his exit and David Rose was escorted from the dock.

20

FRIDAY 10th JULY
78 ELIZABETH STREET MELBOURNE

SIX MONTHS HAD ELAPSED since Otto had met Tom Chuck. Despite their good intentions, no correspondence had passed between them. This was no surprise to Otto — eighty miles was bound to test an embryonic friendship — but it did weigh on his mind from time to time how he would readily put work ahead of attending to personal matters, such as writing to a friend. His plans for a future in private inquiry enthused and excited him, but at twenty-nine, there were other things to consider; namely, marriage, and having a family. As for Chuck, inattention to a promising acquaintance was a matter Otto intended to redress before too much longer. And then, as fate would have it, he was beaten to the punch by the man himself.

Chuck's letter arrived with the morning's post, and Otto felt as excited as he had as a child with an unopened Christmas gift. He made himself a pot of tea, settled behind his newly arrived desk, and opened the envelope. Along with a brief letter, a newspaper cutting was enclosed. The handwriting was beautiful, on the best-quality paper. He put the cutting to one side and began to read:

Dear Otto,

I hope this letter finds you well.

If by the unlikely possibility it had escaped your renowned hawk-eyed notice, herewith a letter to the editor from Pearson Thompson, barrister, in *The Argus* on July 3rd. I send it because it brought so sharply to mind our conversation in January. Alas, it would seem to me that far from allaying the fears we expressed at that time, Mr Thompson's letter only confirms and deepens them. If David Rose is guilty, then well and good. The police seem so sure of it, but such is the apparent sparsity of evidence against him, and consequently so long has he been in custody without trial, is there not doubt enough to be concerned that the real assassin may still be free? But maybe I should not be so troubled by this, not at a time when my dear wife Adeline has been gravely ill after losing the child. If there is a silver lining to the cloud that has hung heavily over us these past months, it is that our young Henry has shown himself to be equal to the challenge. His support is more than a father could ever demand from a lad of his tender years. I'm truly blessed.

I trust all is well with you and that your progress towards private practice proceeds apace.

Yours,
Tom

Otto let the letter lie on his desk while he took a moment to gaze idly out over Elizabeth Street, so busy with Friday commerce. *The poor fellow. His poor wife.* What a man of compassion Tom Chuck really was, he thought, to wear his heart so openly upon his sleeve, and for a man he barely knew. Was this a virtue, Otto wondered? It was unusual, certainly, in his experience. He supposed he ought to feel honoured to be so trusted with such private revelation. He did feel honoured. He picked up the enclosed cutting. No, he hadn't seen it before; the Rose case had receded somewhat in his priorities. He began to read, as usual, with pencil poised:

Melbourne Argus,
Friday 3rd July

Sir,
Now that the public press has at last given its opinion of the gross injustice that has been done the prisoner David Rose, charged with the murder of Margaret Stuart, by his lengthened imprisonment of nearly six months, and his having been remanded twice upon the most flimsy evidence — or rather no evidence at all — as counsel for that deeply injured man, I am induced to give the public some information on that subject, which I believe they are ignorant of.

He was prior to his committal to Castlemaine Gaol confined for four weeks in the lock-up of this township (Daylesford), and subsequently brought before the judge at the next Castlemaine Assizes, in February last, and remanded at the instance of the Crown prosecutor. His confinement was then continued till the following Castlemaine Assizes, in April last, when, as his counsel, I made a special application to the judge (Williams) that he should either then be tried or be immediately discharged. My application was strenuously resisted by Crown prosecutor Smyth, who had no additional evidence to bring forward against the prisoner. Judge Williams refused then to discharge the prisoner, but made a peremptory order that he should be either tried at Castlemaine in July next, or be then discharged. Conceiving, as I did, that the conduct of the Crown prosecutor was utterly repugnant to the English law, and a cruel oppression against the prisoner, I did not hesitate to give public expression of my opinion that such was the case. Indeed, it is monstrous that the Crown prosecutor should thus be empowered to put any prisoner on his trial when he pleases, and to refuse to have him tried until the time when it is convenient for him to do so.

It will thus appear that David Rose will have been imprisoned nearly seven months before he will be brought up before the judge for the third time, and then to be discharged, as no evidence has been, or can be, procured upon which the Crown prosecutor can file an information against him.

Will the Government compensate David Rose for this cruel incarceration, and if so, to what amount? The English Parliament compensated Baxter to the extent of £15,000 for his illegal imprisonment; and the Legislative Assembly of this colony compensated Windsor (£1500) for the illegal sentence he underwent. These compensations for cruel wrongs on these individuals will form precedents for a proper remuneration to which David Rose will be entitled.

Such an injustice could not have been committed in England against any prisoner, as the Grand Jury of that country would long ago have either found a true bill against David Rose, and put him on his trial, or ignored it, upon which he would have been entitled to his discharge.

This being the case, let me ask why the criminal laws of this colony are not assimilated to those in England? The former were passed expressly to keep down the convict population of New South Wales; and are they to be perpetuated in this colony, thereby realising in regard to Victoria the never to-be-forgotten expression of Lord Redesdale, when Lord Chancellor of Ireland, that he found in that country 'one law for the rich, and another for the poor'.

Is it just that the Government should provide counsel and pay witnesses for the prosecutor, and leave the prisoner (generally without money and without friends) to defend himself against such an adversary, with his hand allowed to any extent in the public purse?

Trusting that these remarks may make some impression on the public mind in regard to the injustice done the prisoner David Rose.

I am, Sir, your obedient servant,
Pearson Thompson
Counsel for David Rose.
Castlemaine, June 28th.

P.S. — The husband of the late Margaret Stuart wholly acquits the prisoner, and points to a different person as the murderer of his deceased wife. — P. T.

Otto looked at the newsprint, now nigh unreadable with annotations. Good God in heaven, he thought, what was silly old Pearson hoping to achieve by such shrill public bleating? It was all very well to set out the facts of his client's circumstances, but to aver that there would be and could be no evidence brought against him, and further, that the accused would not only be discharged but would also be entitled to mountains of compensation was such unsubstantiated pre-empting that it could not possibly prompt a mote of public sympathy. The only impression on the public mind that Pearson was likely to make was that he, as the detained man's counsel, was not competent to contest the charge in a court of law, given that he considered the proper processes of the law ought to be subordinate to the opinion of the bereaved husband!

The old man had done his client no good service with this bewailing of procedure, and if on seeing it in print he hadn't been just a little embarrassed by his words, then heaven help David Rose. Still, Otto thought, Thompson had at least reminded him of the feebleness of the police case, which to their shame seemed no less feeble than it had been back in January when Rose had first been arrested. What were they doing up there in Daylesford? Surely, he thought, unless evidence was found, or a more likely suspect apprehended, the charge would have to be dropped. That would almost be a pity, for a trial might be just what was needed to bring police incompetence to public attention, at last and spectacularly. Now that would be something to relish!

Otto folded the pages and returned them to the envelope. He was glad to have received Chuck's letter, not as much for its content as for its having been sent; it was a thoughtful act, and composed at a time of great personal tribulation. He took a sheet of paper, and ink from his drawer, and penned his reply.

My Dear Tom,

Thank you for your letter, and Thompson's lament, which I had not seen. But I must declare that I am quite distressed to learn of your loss. In a time of such personal trial, that you remain troubled by a concern that justice be done for a man unknown to you, speaks to me of a rare selflessness. You truly are a man of courage and conviction, and your beloved Adeline could not be in better, more attentive care. I send her my earnest wish that her recovery will not be long in coming.

My own circumstances, while hardly comparable, will, for the next two or three weeks, take my attention from that sorry case. In a few days I shall be sailing for Auckland, there to explore opportunities for my new private-inquiry office. I know you also will be busy, but perhaps, if circumstances allow, you might keep me informed of the course of the trial? I would greatly look forward to hearing your observations upon my return.

Yours,
Otto.

21

WEDNESDAY 26th JULY, CASTLEMAINE COURT HOUSE THE TRIAL, THE QUEEN V DAVID ROSE, BEGINS ...

HIS HONOUR SIR REDMOND Barry sat wigged and gowned in his lofty chair, and waited with imperious forbearance for those below to be seated for the nine o'clock start. Tom Chuck was among them, third row back in a full public gallery. He'd been informed by the police that he might be called as a witness, just to attest to the photographs. But he had come the twenty-five miles anyway, for a reason of his own: simply, to know that a monster was not still at large, that the creator of the horror in the cottage was the man in the dock. He'd been watching David Rose closely, but saw no snarl, no angry gesture — just a stooped and impotent figure who'd shuffled to his place, where now he sat, blinking like a frightened child. He was as unshaven and as rudely garbed as Tom remembered him from January, but back then his face was coloured and full, not leached and drawn from having spent six-and-a-half months in the shadows and damp of a stone cell.

The crime and the man charged with its commission never seemed more at odds with each other, and Tom needed to see that the processes of justice would reconcile the two. Adeline, now with health restored, and being the understanding wife that she was, had given her blessing for him to set aside these few days; she'd suffered his nightmares, seen the lack of joy in his work, and wanted her husband's melancholy done with. And he was honoured that Otto Berliner should suggest he be his eyes and ears in court. So now Tom took out his pencil and notebook, ready to record his observations.

To the left of the gallery sat a forbidding phalanx of policemen, Superintendent Nicolson the most notable among them in the uniform of his rank. To the right, the jury; save for their Sunday-best attire, they formed an unremarkable double row of twelve local men of various age. Two publicans, a blacksmith, a tinsmith, a boot-maker, a storekeeper, a gardener, a butcher, a fruiterer, a carpenter, a miner, and a puddler from the ironworks comprised the collective brain that would decide David Rose's fate.

If appearances were to count in the jurors' calculations, the Crown had more than a head start. Prosecutor Charles Alexander Smyth and his colleague, Butler Cole Aspinall, were bright men in their thirties, crisply dressed in fabric finer than was usually seen in Castlemaine. Even beneath their wigs, their hair was bouncingly clean, their eyes clear and wide, their postures assured and certain. And if by chance their youth and swagger might have irritated some, sober gravitas was lent to the team by the staid and grey-templed Crown Solicitor, Henry Gurner. This was a prosecution that looked ready for the contest, one that commanded respect and inspired confidence.

In opposition, at law and in look, was the defence. Led by the oldest man in the room — senior to Judge Barry by twenty years — stooped and deliberate of movement, was learned counsel Pearson Thompson. His suit was smart, if a little old, and of a cut superior to the crumpled tweed worn by his colleague, the lean-bodied Daylesford solicitor James Geake.

On the call of the clerk, Watkins, the respective teams broke from their huddles, allowing proceedings to begin.

Into the silence rose Smyth. He gazed about the room, as if to familiarise himself with the architecture, then, thrusting his right hand towards the dock, turned to address the jury.

'The prisoner at the bar stands charged with the wilful murder of Margaret Stuart, the wife of a miner at Daylesford, on the night of the 28th of December 1864. I am well aware that the public has given great attention to this case and that the press has commented upon it on several occasions; and such being the case, it is almost impossible but that most persons have already arrived at some conclusion respecting it. I mention this because I want to impress upon you good gentlemen of the jury the necessity of banishing all foregone conclusions, if you have any, and rest your convictions on the evidence, and that alone. I hope you will consider the particulars, which will be elicited carefully and dispassionately, and discard all reports and comments. I believe you will do your duty both to the Crown and the public. And now, to the particulars of the case.'

He paused to consult his notes, then told a tale of innocence and evil.

'The woman at the time of her death was seventeen years of age. She lived with her husband at Albert Street, Daylesford. The house was situated on the brow of a hill, and was a small wooden erection containing two rooms. The husband used to go to work at different periods of time; sometimes he was engaged at night, and at other times in the day. When engaged in the night shift, he usually left home at 4.00 p.m. and returned at midnight. I draw your attention now to this model of the house ...'

JOE LATHAM'S LEFT ARM corralled a bowl of porridge, his right loading spoonfuls into his mouth. His wife bustled in, bearing lengths of wood for the fire.

'I said I'd do that,' he said.

'Don't trouble yourself; it's done now.'

Alice Latham emptied the pieces onto the hearth and brushed down her apron. She stood and sighed. She wanted to know nothing of the Rose trial until its conclusion, and even then she'd wait for word rather than seek it. She prayed only that it would all be over quickly and that no more would ever be said.

Behind her, Joe blew out a long breath. He stood, sending his chair squealing across the boards and his bowl wobbling like a coin. Alice turned.

'What is it?'

A vein had filled in his neck; another bulged across his forehead. 'This house. You. This fucking life. I'm sick of it!'

Two young daughters appeared at the door. On their father's glare, they withdrew. Alice retreated to the trough to begin the dishes.

He was behind her now, cooing. 'I'm sorry, love.' She felt his hands at her buttocks, fingers kneading. His breath was in her ears now, his tongue at her neck.

'Come on, Alice,' he breathed. She closed her eyes and gripped the dishcloth as her dress was gathered and lifted. 'God, you smell good. I've missed your smell.' His breathing was hard; any appeal to desist was now futile. Her drawers were torn to the floor, and all she could do was brace herself and endure.

CROWN PROSECUTOR SMYTH HANDED a photograph to Frederick Beard, the foreman of the jury.

'I want each of you now to study this photograph, taken of the victim as she lay, near nude and mutilated.' The shocking image was passed along the two rows, variously to winces and frowns and faces that gave nothing away.

'The question arises as to how you gentlemen of the jury are to connect the prisoner at the bar with the individual who so cruelly butchered this woman; and I say butchered, because it is the only word that seems to convey an idea of the manner in which the unfortunate victim was murdered.'

Smyth paused for silence to press his words deep into the

jurors' minds. He closed his eyes as if to lead them to picture the horrific scene for themselves ... and then he resumed. 'On the day following the murder, Dr Doolittle made a post-mortem examination of the body, and arrived at the conclusion that the deceased had been violated. If, gentlemen, you entertain this idea, you would, no doubt, come to the conclusion that the perpetrator of this dreadful act had entered the house with lustful intentions.'

Up to this point, Smyth had barely looked at the man in the dock. Now, he focussed his attention squarely on him, daring the jurors to examine the wretch before them and not believe what was being laid to his charge.

Smyth proceeded to give his account of the police investigation — Rose's conversations with Maggie as reported by Louisa Goulding, the discovery of the pipe, the condition of the house — all of which Tom had heard before, albeit by less eloquent, and less persuasive, speakers. And so, he put his notebook away for now and sat there as a juror might, harkening to this clever salesman before him. When Smyth came to Rose's movements after the murder, Tom resumed his note-taking.

'Such precaution this stranger took on leaving the township,' Smyth said with haughty disdain, 'that he baffled the police, and evaded detection for upwards of a fortnight, although every exertion was made to track him out and arrest him. The Tuesday night prior to the murder, this man engaged with a farmer named Cheesbrough. The very next night, the murder took place. The prisoner had a conversation on the farm with respect to a dog, when he asked if the dog was accustomed to bark much at people at night; in fact, he took such precautions as a man would take who intended to commit a crime; every precaution he could take to evade detection, this man took. The day after the murder, on Thursday December 29th, the prisoner was more than an hour late in starting work, and he was subsequently on that forenoon dismissed.'

A picture of a devious scoundrel, a skulking fox, was thus

being painted by Smyth, though it did come at the cost of characterising the police as dull-witted, to have been fooled by a man so unrefined. Tom wondered if it hadn't occurred to anyone that evading detection might most effectively be achieved by leaving the district.

Tom had been watching the jury for clues as to how they were receiving Smyth's version of events. From time to time, one juror or another would look away to the prisoner, as if to square the man with what Smyth was saying about him, to take David Rose's physical appearance as corroboration. Smyth pressed on, describing Rose's movements after his dismissal from Cheesbrough's.

'He next engaged with Dr Coates, at whose farm at Kingston, a distance of some twenty-five miles, he arrived at about four o'clock on the Friday evening, having apparently camped out and travelled through the bush in the interval ...' *At Kingston*, Tom thought. *That would require him to walk through Daylesford, which is hardly the action of a man wishing to evade arrest*. '... On the same day, while conversing with a man named Wolf, a fellow labourer at Coates' farm, Rose pulled out a razor, and said to Wolf, "This razor cut a person's throat."'

Smyth paused here for the gallery to gasp and murmur at this horrific revelation. Tom sat up in his seat. Could this be the evidence, he wondered, which pointed undeniably to the man's guilt, which ensured that justice would be done? He looked at Rose, and had to resist seeing the prisoner rendered differently by Wolf's words. But if they proved true, Tom knew he would readily believe the man in the dock capable of such a monstrous crime.

Smyth pressed on.

'Now, I might be told that a man who had cut a woman's throat would avoid making such remarks, but it is just possible that the crime was so impressed upon his mind that he would willingly converse with any person, so long as he thought he did not go too far, in order to lighten his over-burdened mind.'

Tom scribbled a note. Otto would know about these things, how the mind of a murderer worked. His own layman's understanding was telling him that this was not what a killer would do. And if Rose was guilty, why *was* he still in the district? Smyth was pacing the space before the jury box, the jurors watching him, which Tom supposed was the point of the pacing ... He put down his notebook and pencil; a feeling of nausea had suddenly reasserted itself in his stomach. It had been inchoate on the coach ride over that morning, but now in this stuffy courtroom it had seemingly fully gestated. There was nothing for it but to take a few minutes' respite in fresh air.

MARIA MOLESWORTH SAT AT her window and stared into Pitman's yard through water-blurred panes. She felt the draught on her ankles, and heard the blasts of wind-driven rain against the glass. So bleak a day it was, but not so bleak as she felt. What was she doing with her life, she wondered? What kind of person had she become? She knew the answers, and hated both. There was only one course opén to her: she had to get out of Daylesford, and so she would, within the month.

TOM HAD RETURNED TO his seat to find that Smyth was describing events three months after the murder, and investigations not known at the time of David Rose's committal hearing.

'On April 9th, Detective Williams, with three black trackers, found a blue guernsey shirt, which was also found to be the property of the prisoner. There was blood on this shirt, too, and shown to have all the characteristics of human blood. This shirt was found rolled up and stowed away in the hollow of a tree, in a paddock adjoining that of Mr Cheesbrough, in whose employ, of course, the prisoner was engaged. Gentlemen of the jury, the prisoner was seen in the vicinity of that very tree on the morning after the murder, before his dismissal by Mr Cheesbrough.'

The significance of this evidence was not immediately apparent to Tom. Wouldn't many a labouring man have blood on his shirt? He looked at the jury, seemingly comprehending everything behind their expressionless faces. Maybe as much of the weight of the prosecution was in the presentation as it was in the substance. He saw Pearson Thompson, jotting notes and wearing a face of incredulity, no doubt exaggerated for the jury. So, was this the jury's challenge, to separate fact from performance? He looked back to Smyth, who, with his thumbs planted in his vest and rocking on his heels, was bringing his opening remarks to a close.

'Here we have a man, who before the murder was known to have been making advances to the deceased; who made inquiries as to when her husband would be absent; whose pipe was found in the house of the murdered woman an hour after the murder; who was seen by Mrs Sarah Spinks hovering about Stuart's house on the night of the murder about the very hour when, according to the medical testimony, it was committed. A man who was able to give minute particulars of the crime to Michael Wolf on the Saturday — before any news reached the Coates farm — who was seen in the morning after the murder in a paddock, where his business did not lead him and where his shirt was found hidden, clotted with blood, bearing all the characteristics of human blood …'

Tom let his eyes settle on a juror, perhaps the youngest of the twelve, and saw in his face how obliged he was to Smyth for this summation. Tom imagined himself to be that juror — who no doubt had more pressing things to be doing — and how readily he might be persuaded by its simplicity and by the authority of the man delivering it. Yes, if Tom were that young fellow, he well might not see the art in Smyth's work …

A change in Smyth's oratorial tone brought Tom's attention back to the prosecutor.

'Now, complaints have been made that the prisoner had been kept an unnecessary time in custody, but I contend that it is far better that the whole of the facts of the case should be collected before the prisoner was put upon his trial. Nay, it is even fairer to the prisoner, because if the inquiries which have been continued to the last moment had been favourable to him, he would have got the benefit of them ...'

Was this brilliant or ludicrous, Tom wondered, to aver that David Rose had been done a great service in being locked up for almost seven months?

'... If, when you hear the evidence, you have upon your minds a reasonable, a rational, doubt, it will be your duty to give the benefit of that doubt to the prisoner at the bar.' Smyth made a sweep of his hand in the direction of the dock and held it there a moment, challenging anyone to entertain that there could be any doubt. Then, with a rise in volume, he delivered his climax.

'But if, on the other hand, the evidence I will call is such as to leave upon your minds no such doubt, then I trust that, unmindful of consequences, you will do your duty to yourselves and the country, and however painful it might be, return a verdict of guilty!'

JOYCE PITMAN STOOD AT her stove, turning a wooden spoon through the thick beef and vegetable stew she would sell to patrons. She'd been thinking often of George Stuart, lately — and today in particular, him being away in Castlemaine, having to relive that horrific night of eight months past. It had her wondering what she could do to help her neighbour in his time of trial. And lo, here was the answer, literally right under her nose! She was not one for superstition, or all that much for religion, but was this not a sign?

CONSTABLE IRWIN TOOK THE stand, his uniform and hair clean and sharp, his bearing and voice assured, as he answered Smyth's question.

'I made a search for a weapon and found none. I saw marks of blood on the pillow, bolster, door, and on the outside of the door, and on the bedroom door at the edges. I examined the chimney. There were marks in the whitening, like they could have been made by corded trousers of a man sliding down.'

Irwin's manner inspired confidence in Tom, and, he imagined, in all those in attendance. He was sure of himself, and thorough in his observations.

Pearson Thompson rose now to test how attentive he was to a detail of particular import to his client.

'Did you, Constable Irwin, see a pipe in your search?'

'I did not see a pipe. I searched the safe, and did not see a pipe there. I removed the plates from the inside of the safe. I did not see a pipe, or any plates on the safe — none were there.'

Thompson smiled, nodded, and sat down as Smyth was promptly back on his feet with unforeseen supplementary questions for his witness.

'Constable Irwin, what were you looking for on the top of the safe? A pipe?'

'I was looking not for a pipe, but an instrument, a murder weapon.'

This seemed to satisfy Smyth and he made to sit, but Irwin hadn't finished.

'The pipe could not have been lying on the safe without my seeing it.'

Detective Thomas Walker was next in the box. He was a plain man, Tom thought, of a quality that would only be magnified in a photographic portrait. He seemed nervous standing there, as if facing a promotions committee, or a disciplinary hearing. But when he spoke, he gave a confident account of events as he saw them that fateful evening. He saw blood on the walls and the doors, and none on the key in the lock. He sounded particularly certain of himself when questioned by Smyth about the pipe.

'I noticed the meat safe. There were a quantity of eggs, a pudding, a kettle, and sundry items inside. On the top of the meat safe was the pipe, and out of it had fallen the ash.'

At the direction of Smyth, clerk Watkins showed the witness a pipe.

'I believe that to be the same pipe,' Walker said. 'I later picked up the pipe in the presence of Alice Latham. She said it could have been George's, the deceased's husband. So I left it on the meat safe. On January 3rd, Detective Williams brought me the pipe. I had seen it on the meat safe at Stuart's frequently in the interval. When I first saw the pipe, I never knew of Rose, or that such a man was in existence.'

And then it was Pearson Thompson's turn to cross-examine, and Walker's mood soon turned testy.

'You didn't give testimony at the inquest, did you, Detective Walker?'

'No.'

'Though your evidence is presented as critical to the case.'

Smyth was quickly to his feet in protest here, but Thompson cut him off with an airy, 'It wasn't a question, Your Honour — just thinking out loud.'

It seemed to Tom that Pearson Thompson was feeling in fine fettle, and enjoying his work.

'No witness today, until you, Detective Walker, has testified to having seen a pipe on the meat safe at Stuart's cottage. Constable Irwin even stressed there was none to be seen. Do you have superior powers of observation, Detective?'

Walker seemed to bristle at this derision. His lips tightened, and he exhaled noisily before giving his reply.

'I have heard Irwin's evidence. He was there before I was there. He is not in a position, after saying there were no plates on the top, to say no pipe was there.'

Walker looked to Smyth, who acknowledged with a nod a point well made.

Thompson continued. 'You suspected the prisoner of the crime, based on your belief that the pipe was his?'

'As I said, I didn't even know the prisoner existed. An Italian was locked up for this crime for more than two weeks after the pipe was found. I never was looking for a pipe; when I saw it, I was looking to see if any knives were missing. It was after I was told that the prisoner worked with Hathaway the stableman that I went to see Hathaway. He described the pipe as I'd seen it. Only then did I form the opinion the pipe belonged to the prisoner.'

At three, as Louisa Goulding was being called, Tom decided he'd had enough for the day, and when Walker stood down, he took the opportunity to make a discreet exit. He stood for a few moments on the courthouse steps, watching the bustle, and thinking how Maggie Stuart had also once been another face in the street. Not David Rose, though; Tom couldn't place him in that busy scene.

22

THURSDAY 27th JULY
THE SECOND DAY OF THE TRIAL

TOM WAS CALLED WITHIN ten minutes of proceedings recommencing at nine o'clock. He had to attest to nothing more than being the photographic artist who had produced the two photographs: one of the deceased on the 29th of December, and one of the house with neighbouring properties on the 30th. His time in the box was brief, but his discomfort at being called for the prosecution was no less intense. He had simply made the visual record; it was for others to interpret what they saw.

Tom stepped down, and Detective Walker was called.

Perhaps recalling Walker's nervous start of yesterday, Smyth first settled his witness with a smile and a pause, before beginning with a simple question.

'Is it possible, Detective, in your estimation, for a man to walk from Cheesbrough's to Stuart's undetected?'

'Yes.'

Smyth sat, and Thompson was quickly to his feet.

'Detective Walker, how many public houses are there between Cheesbrough's and Stuart's, do you think?'

'I believe there are eleven, in all, though I would need to —'

'So, to avoid detection, a man walking from Cheesbrough's to

Stuart's would have to avoid the road, would he not?'

Walker remained composed. 'A man going from one to the other could make a short cut without going by the public houses at all.'

But at night? Tom willed Thompson to ask. *Why doesn't he ask!*

Sarah Spinks was called.

Tom watched her, and promptly decided that this was a woman of character. Here, in this masculine enclave, she stood unfazed and proud. And so much rode on what she had to say, for hers was the only testimony that could possibly place David Rose at the scene of the murder. It would have suited the prosecution no end had she let the impression stand that it was David Rose she had seen outside Stuart's the night of the murder. But she wouldn't allow that. When Smyth, in his opening address, had drawn firm conclusions from inconclusive evidence — the blood on the shirt, the inquiry about the dog, the questions asked of Maggie Stuart, and so on — Mrs Spinks' integrity and adherence to the facts stood as a lesson to all and a challenge to any juror who had bought Smyth's version.

'The man I saw on the night of the murder was by a stump 160 yards from Stuart's house. Detective Walker and I stepped it out,' she said. 'I was nervous after dark because there had been some garrotting, but I was with a gentleman friend. The man passed by me ten feet away, but I couldn't see his face. From his dress, the man I saw that night was very like the man I saw with my children. I didn't think anything about it at the time, but when I heard the police were looking for Mr Rose, it struck me that the man I saw might have been him.'

Smyth didn't disguise that he was unhappy with the imprecision from his witness, and asked a question to draw a categorical answer. 'The man who offered your children lollies at his tent a few days prior to the murder — is he the prisoner?'

'Yes, the prisoner is the man I saw with my children.'

Smyth was happy to have established this much, and sat down.

Pearson Thompson approached the witness box.

'To be clear: the prisoner is the man you saw with your children, but you cannot be certain he is the man you saw the night of the murder?'

'That is right, Sir. When I saw the prisoner in the dock at Daylesford in February, I said I thought he appeared much stouter than the man I had seen the night I was coming home from the theatre.'

Thompson now called for the depositions made by Mrs Spinks at the coroner's inquest on 4th January and before the police magistrate on 7th February to be read to the jury. 'This will make clear the consistency of the witness's recollection of events,' he said, with a condescending shake of the head for Smyth.

And so the depositions were read by clerk Watkins. When he had finished, Smyth was ready with a question and written notes from which he would quote.

'Mrs Spinks, we have all just heard in your deposition to the coroner that, in reference to the man you saw on the night of the murder, you are, to use your words, "confident from the hat and coat that it was the man I have described before". And "I believe that to be the same man I saw playing with my children."'

Smyth held out his arms to the jury as if to say 'Is my point not proven?'

He sat down, to nods of approbation from his associates, Aspinall and Gurner.

Sarah Spinks was clearly frustrated that Smyth should use her words as his playthings. Thompson stood and gave her the opportunity to respond. She did so in full measure.

'It must be a mistake if it is down in the coroner's deposition that I swore to the man. I did say in that deposition that I could not swear to him. There was no moon that night. It got dark quickly, and I didn't turn around to look at the man. When I saw the prisoner in the dock, I said he appeared stouter than the man I saw that night. Looking at the prisoner now, I can't say that he is the man I saw that night. I could only notice the figure, not the face. All I can say is that the hat and the coat worn by that man were like those worn by the man I saw with my children.'

Smyth was to his feet. 'The prisoner being that man?'

'Yes —'

'Thank you, Mrs Spinks. That is all.'

PENELOPE TELFORD HAD NOTICED Serafino Bonetti delivering bread to the Albert Hotel on several occasions these past few months. She saw him there now, from her veranda: that beautiful young man. He really had been such a dear, gallant fool to keep their secret safe for two whole weeks in that ghastly lock-up, and how unappreciated he may have felt that since the end of his imprisonment she should neglect to express her gratitude. Now, she thought, on this dreary day, with Lawrence away for the week in Castlemaine, was the opportune time to make amends.

She hurried down past the Court House and onto Camp Street, shopping basket in hand, to contrive a chance meeting as Serafino exited the building. The door opened, and there he was in the shadows of the hotel interior. She quickened her step. He was on the threshold, and then she saw him turn, and steal a surreptitious kiss and a fleeting caress from the pretty young barmaid there.

Penelope looked away and hurried on downhill, the dread feeling of advancing age rising within her.

IT STRUCK TOM JUST how much he was drawn to strong women. There was Sarah Spinks, for one, and Adeline, of course: women who knew their own minds and weren't afraid to express them. Here was another, Jane Cheesbrough. Yes, she told Smyth, the prisoner did ask about the dog, but she heard no barking that night, as she would had a stranger been about — or, Tom guessed, at whatever time David Rose was supposed to have returned from butchering Maggie Stuart. And neither did she notice anything strange about the prisoner's behaviour the morning after the murder. She remarked that he was a good deal dirtier then than now — an observation that drew a few indiscreet chuckles.

Detective Williams described how Tommy, one of the black trackers, discovered the blue shirt in the paddock adjacent to Cheesbrough's. He explained that as there were stains on the shirt, he took it to Melbourne on the 13th April and gave it to John Kruse, a chemist, for analysis.

After lunch, Kruse himself was in the box. Smyth asked him whether the stains on the shirt were of human blood. Kruse seemed much accustomed to giving evidence, and, for Tom, his German accent lent him an air of authority and great credibility in these matters of science.

Smyth smiled at his witness, and it seemed that much was expected by the prosecution of this testimony.

'You analysed the stains?' Smyth said.

'Yes, and I found that the spot on the shoulder was blood.'

'Human blood?'

'The corpuscles of this blood were similar to those of human blood, yes.'

Thompson was slow to his feet. Whether this was due to his age, or because he was unsure of his line of questioning, or even for deliberate effect, Tom couldn't be sure. Perhaps it didn't matter, though the barrister's unhurried state did contrast with the crisp, certain movements of the prosecutor, if that made a difference in the minds of the jurors. At last, Thompson put his first question, which Kruse answered with no hint of taking affront.

'I am not a duly qualified medical man, Sir, but an analytical chemist. Here, my diploma from Hanover.' He handed Watkins a sheet of paper, who passed it to Thompson, thence to Judge Barry.

'Does this qualify you to give an opinion on blood stains?' Thompson said.

'I am aware that in certain cases no one but a competent medical man should be allowed to give an opinion upon blood stains, and also that there is no direct medical process by which blood can be identified as human blood.'

'Can you positively identify the blood stain you examined as human blood?'

'No, I cannot swear that the stains I examined are not of the blood of an ox or a dog, as the corpuscles of these animals present the same appearance as those found in human blood.'

Smyth next called Sydney Gibbons, a man as slender as his namesake, but not remotely so lithe. He spoke assuredly, in a monotone — as if, like Kruse, he had given forensic testimony before.

'I am an analyst, chemist, and microscopist. On 2nd January I received a parcel from Constable Irwin containing two fragments of hairs from the hand of the deceased, and a parcel of hair from her head ...'

He continued to list a total of five samples of hair he had been given for analysis; from the sheets, the blue shirt found hidden in the log, and from the head and whiskers of David Rose. The results of his microscopic analysis were inconclusive. Some hairs from the sheets were male; some, female; some, of indeterminate origin. One curly hair from the bed sheets could have been from the husband or the prisoner, but he couldn't be certain which.

Gibbons delivered his findings with such clinical detachment that he might have been reading a shopping list. For Tom, there was no separating the items from the scene, images of which were sickeningly vivid — none more so than the image he himself had captured for all to see.

'I also received from Constable Irwin two preparations of matter taken from the body of Mrs Stuart. From examining them, I judge coition had taken place by more than usual force shortly before death.'

This was an image that Smyth was happy to leave for the

minds of the jury. He sat down as Pearson Thompson rose.

'Mr Gibbons, this forceful coition you mention shortly before death. Just how long before death, in your opinion, might this have occurred?'

'It may have been up to eight or ten hours.'

'Eight or ten hours? I put it to you that this is hardly "shortly before death". Before you examined the vaginal matter on the glass slides, had you heard that George Stuart has attested that coition had occurred between him and his wife in the early afternoon on the day of her death, some eight to ten hours before her death?'

'I had heard that, yes.'

Thompson looked at the witness with exaggerated incredulity. 'Are you a qualified physician, Mr Gibbons?'

'No.'

Thompson raised an eyebrow and held it there for effect, before continuing.

'Would you say that connection with the deceased was forced?'

'I will not say the woman was raped, no.'

Thompson nodded, his expression serious, though he was surely very pleased with Gibbons' inept performance.

'Regarding the hairs you examined, you don't seem confident in being able to identify each of these.'

'If I were to shake the hairs together, I don't pretend to say I could identify every one. In some cases I may be able tell the male from the female hairs. There is one hair I speak to with certainty: a perfectly straight hair twelve inches long, very coarse. It was found on the sheet. Another, very fine and eleven inches long, taken from the pillow, resembles that taken from the deceased's grasp.'

'Could that hair have come from the head of George Stuart?"

'I couldn't swear to that. I have not examined his hair.'

A murmur rolled through the courtroom. Surely this was a significant omission. A monumental dereliction, even. Thompson feigned astonishment, but was no doubt delighted that a body of evidence had proved so inconclusive as to lend no weight to the prosecution's case. He certainly seemed delighted as he exchanged a word with Geake.

'No further questions,' he said.

The bandy-legged livery stable keeper, Thomas Hathaway, took the stand next, to repeat the testimony he'd given at the committal hearing back in February. David Rose listened this time without protest as Hathaway swore again that the pipe presented was the pipe David Rose was smoking the day he nearly set fire to the hay.

He glanced at Rose as he completed his account, remembering the protest from the dock the last time he gave it.

'What did you do with the pipe?' Smyth said.

'I dipped it in a bucket of water. And I had to turn out three trusses of hay into the yard.

'You could recognise the pipe?'

'I had that pipe in my hand for a quarter-hour, so I had good knowledge of it.'

A pipe was handed to the witness.

'This is the pipe I saw the prisoner smoking,' he said.

'And then what did you do?'

'I gave the pipe to the prisoner, and told him not to smoke about the stable.'

'Quite so.' Smyth nodded in a manner, Tom considered, meant to convey that a witness so responsible would have to be commensurately trustworthy. Hathaway beamed, as if unaccustomed to such reverence.

'One last question, Mr Hathaway,' Smyth said. 'Did the prisoner have a knife?'

'Yes. He had two or three. One was a tobacco knife and a clasp knife with a broken point. It would close up, the blade folding to the handle.'

And so the second day concluded, with Hathaway leaving the box, blushing at Smyth's nodding to him for a job well done.

23

FRIDAY 28th JULY
THE THIRD AND FINAL DAY OF THE TRIAL

IF DAVID ROSE WERE to be hanged, so it seemed to Tom, it would be for a pipe. Every witness who testified to have seen the prisoner smoking was asked to identify a pipe from a selection offered. And so the theme continued on this, the third day. Trooper Brady, Sergeant Telford, and Constables Mansell and Dawson each declared — some for the second time — that the pipe identified was not his and that it wasn't he who had placed it on the meat safe. Nor had any of them seen it on the meat safe — a point Tom still found curious. Only Detective Walker had noticed it there, at least until Detective Williams took possession of it a week after the murder.

The outstanding matter of the identification of the hairs on the marital sheets was clarified mid-morning when Sydney Gibbons, the analytical chemist, and Detective Walker were recalled.

Walker informed the court that at ten past eight o'clock the night before he had taken four hairs from George Stuart's head and four from his beard. With Stuart in Daylesford, this had necessitated considerable travel, and trouble in finding the man.

'Yes,' Gibbons said in reply to Smyth, 'I received the hairs from Detective Walker.'

'And on examining them, what could you conclude?'

'Only that the curly hair found on the sheets might be the husband's, or the prisoner's.'

The anti-climax was farcical, and Pearson Thompson, with a broad, incredulous grin and much head-shaking, indicated that he had no questions for the witness.

Tom could understand why the prosecution should posit the pipe as the key link between David Rose and the murder scene, but the stowed shirt? What did it matter if it was Rose's, and if he chose to hide it? The bloodstains on it were mere specks, and could not even be verified as human. Still, the prosecution called two further witnesses to describe in detail the attire they had seen the prisoner wear in the time they had associated with him in various employments. But now the prosecution unwrapped something bigger: the foreshadowed testimony of Mr Michael Wolf, the man with whom Rose had worked at Dr Coates's farm after he left Cheesbrough's. There was glee in Smyth's demeanour now, like that of a poker player about to lay before all a winning hand. Tom recalled Smyth's preview of Wolf's testimony in his opening remarks, and how the gallery had been horrified by a mere taster of what might come.

Tom watched this witness settle himself in the box, legs slightly apart, his hands before him holding a peaked cap. If there was anything lupine about him, it wasn't apparent; the man was slender, with darting eyes and a wary manner. *Fox* would be apt, Tom thought. The man even had red hair.

'On Sunday, we were together in the hut,' Wolf began in answer to Smyth. 'I was lying on the top bunk. The prisoner asked me to hold a neck-tie — a black silk one.'

'What time was this?' Smyth said, as much to raise the suspense as for clarity.

'This was eleven o'clock. I was stretched in the bunk, reading a newspaper. He wanted me to hold the tie so he could sharpen a razor. I did so, lying on my bunk. He commenced sharpening and

I said, "It is a good razor." He said, "Yes, it is a good razor, that it cut a person's throat."'

It was the second time the jury had heard this, but there was no diminution of the horror of it. Tom wondered whether Wolf's testimony was being rendered all the more believable because it was familiar. Was this a clever ploy by Smyth? He looked at the jurors, and wondered just how wise this assembly of country shopkeepers could be to the wiles of a sharp lawyer.

'How did you react to this horrifying revelation?' Smyth said.

'I said, "Whose throat did it cut?" And he said, "It would not be right for you to know everything." I told Rose I would break it into pieces sooner than use such a razor!' Wolf thumped the railing. Smyth let a moment pass, before proceeding.

'What did you do?'

'I continued lying in my bunk.'

At this, Tom's eyebrows rose; it seemed that Wolf's indignation had escalated considerably over the intervening months.

'Did you have other conversations with the prisoner?' Smyth said.

'I did. The morning before, on the Saturday, he asked me if I knew anything of the Daylesford murder. I said no, and he said, "A person came down the chimney and cut the deceased's throat when her husband was on night-shift." He said that her throat was cut, and "he likely got his will of her", and that it was "just the price of her or of any other person who served a man as she did."'

The court was suddenly alive with the sounds of sudden inhalations, of groans, of mumblings and whispers. Jurors shifted uncomfortably in their seats, and all — Tom included — cast looks to the man in the dock. It seemed necessary to put a face to the crime, as if doing so would make it comprehensible.

Smyth pressed on.

'Tell us, Mr Wolf; did the prisoner speak about this most grave matter on other occasions?'

'He did, several times over a few days. He seemed very excited about it. When he spoke to me, he asked what I thought of it. He asked me, "Supposing a man done it by himself, could they bring any evidence against him, or he be found guilty of it?" I said I knew nothing at all about that.'

'And how long was the prisoner at Coates'?'

'Eight days. He left on Sunday afternoon, the 8th of January, after an altercation with Doctor Coates.'

Pearson Thompson had been busy taking notes throughout this testimony, and was quickly to his feet when Smyth resumed his seat. Wolf seemed immediately on his guard, as if steeling himself for questions he would rather not answer. Thompson offered no reassuring smile; instead, a disbelieving smirk.

'Mr Wolf, tell the court a little about yourself — what work you do, how long you've been in this colony ...'

'I'm a labouring man, from Limerick, Ireland. I've been a year in this colony. I was in the constabulary, but left of my own free will.'

'Well, a policeman's salary is not all that grand, is it?'

'I was paid two pound thirteen shillings a month. It was sufficient.'

'You would have heard of the £200 reward posted for the apprehension of Mrs Stuart's killer, no doubt?'

'I did. Though I don't expect to get any of it.'

'Really? After that testimony you just gave to my learned friend? Was there a witness to the conversation you had with the prisoner?'

'No.'

'When did you hear about the murder?'

'People were talking of it on Saturday.'

'And when did you read about the murder?'

'I read it in the paper on Sunday, and the conversation was on Saturday.'

'Saturday the 31st December?'

'Yes.'

'Which paper?'

'The *Argus*, but an account of the murder wasn't in Saturday's *Argus*. That was the paper I was reading, and the paper the prisoner saw. I saw the account of the murder on Sunday, and the conversation with the prisoner about the murder was on Saturday.'

'But people were talking about the murder on the Saturday.'

'Yes, but I didn't get to hear of it. I had heard nothing of the murder on Saturday, when the prisoner was speaking to me at work. He told me he had come from Daylesford.'

'Maybe the prisoner read about the murder in the paper, or heard about it from someone.'

'He didn't say he'd read the paper or heard any rumours. He had not been in Kingston, and the hotels were closed.'

Tom was confused. Wolf seemed to be making suppositions he was not entitled to make. Surely the jury would see that. Or were they less concerned with examining precisely what Wolf had said than impressed by the sense he conveyed of something being not quite right? Any juror not paying full attention — and there seemed to be a few, if vacant looks could be so interpreted — might simply defer to others when considering testimony. They didn't want to have to think; they wanted to be told, to be reassured, that their verdict was the right verdict. If this were the case, the prosecution would win the day, for Smyth's performance was polished and assured. Thompson's, though it had its lucid moments and minor victories, was patchy, and at times bewildering with opportunities not taken to ask important questions. Nevertheless, weren't the facts on the side of acquittal, Tom wondered? If only Otto could be here to offer an expert assessment.

Smyth's recalling of Doctor Doolittle elicited puzzled looks, even among the staid-faced jurors, for what could he add that hadn't been said before?

'Doctor Doolittle,' Smyth said, 'thank you for your attendance again.'

Doolittle nodded. He seemed to Tom a gentleman, a man of thoroughness and integrity. Maybe this was behind Smyth's calling him.

'Doctor, you've examined the knife found in the prisoner's swag?'

'I have.'

'Would you say that the murder may have been committed with it?'

'It may have, yes.'

'Thank you, Doctor. Oh, one last thing. This pipe, found on the meat safe …' Smyth held up the pipe. 'Did you put it there?'

'No. And neither is it my pipe.'

'Thank you. No further questions, Your Honour. That concludes the case for the prosecution.'

Smyth sat down and shared a nod with Aspinall at a job well done.

Judge Barry made a note or two, and looked to the clock.

'We'll adjourn now for lunch, and resume with the statement for the defence at two. Mr Thompson?'

Thompson acknowledged this with a curt nod.

'All rise,' Watkins directed.

Tom left promptly in search of a quiet tearoom or the like, where he could collect his thoughts and be away from the speculations that were already the subject of every conversation.

GEORGE STUART STEPPED OFF the bucket at the top of the New Wombat shaft to find Joyce Pitman standing there, beaming at him like a proud mother. *Is she here for me?* he wondered. She was on her way over.

'Mr Stuart,' she said. 'I thought you might be at the trial.'

'No, I'm not. As you can see. I've said my piece there, and it's best I set my mind now to other matters.' He began to walk off. She hesitated, then caught him up.

She lifted a small billycan. 'Perhaps you'd care for some hearty stew? It's hot, if you'd like some now. I brought a spoon.' She held it out.

George looked at her, perplexed by this unprecedented attention. But then he thought, what man would turn down such an offer? Not his kind.

He took the spoon. 'Thank you, Mrs Pitman. I will. It's very thoughtful of you.'

WHEN ALL WERE SEATED and quiet, Pearson Thompson rose slowly to his feet. He steadied himself a moment, as though lunch had been a little hard to digest. Judge Barry looked over his spectacles to indicate that everyone was waiting. The barrister began, with a disclosure that stilled the room.

'Your Honour, I have been taken very unwell this afternoon, and I'm not sure that I can go on with this case, but I will try.'

'Very well,' Judge Barry said, in a tone which suggested that Thompson might have to die before an adjournment would be considered.

Thompson read the judge's mood correctly. He coughed gently into his handkerchief, took a sip of water from a glass, and, after a moment where it seemed he was riding out a headache, looked up at the twelve men and began his petition.

'Members of the jury, this case is one of the greatest importance, one upon which the life or death of a fellow human being hangs.' He pointed to Rose, as if anyone needed the clarification. 'You will see that the prisoner stands in the dock at a great disadvantage, as arrayed against him are two eminent counsel, a perfect army of police, and, in fact, such an amount of collective talent as has ever been witnessed in this court, while I am his only advocate. The Crown contends against him with a golden shield, while the unfortunate man is without money or scrip.'

He swept his gaze across the jurors, perhaps for a sign that his plea for their sympathy had registered. He coughed and resumed.

'I charge you, good gentlemen of the jury, to dismiss from your minds any preconceived notions as to the presumed guilt of the prisoner. His alleged crime has been the talk of the whole country, and the entire press had been in arms against him. You are trying a case of murder, the most horrible that has ever come under my notice, for if there ever was a deed that exceeded all others in atrocity, the killing of Margaret Stuart is such a one.'

Here he paused, a little longer than he might have intended as he riffled through his notes. Coughs from the gallery and one from the judge drew attention to the delay. At last, with the sought page at hand, he continued, with great dramatic vigour — his supposed ill-health apparently no longer of concern.

'No one has a greater abhorrence than I of the crime of murder, but I will tell you that there is another description of murder which is not less atrocious, and that is called judicial murder — the hanging of an innocent man.' He looked at his client, and so encouraged the jury's eyes in that direction. Rose lowered his gaze, maybe through shyness, or shame and guilt.

'I will now proceed to review the evidence, but before doing so I have a serious complaint to make, which is that this case has been got up in a manner the reverse of creditable to the authorities. Things were not managed this way in England, and having practised as an English barrister, as well as an English magistrate, I can affirm that fair play has not been shown to the accused. I recall the trial of Palmer there, for the poisoning of John Parsons Cooke. In that case, the venue had been changed to London on account of the prejudice that existed against the prisoner in his own county …'

Tom Chuck had been jotting some notes to this point, but now his hand was still. He had no knowledge of the workings of court — save for these two-and-a-half days — but this argument of Thompson's surely was missing the mark, and spectacularly!

How was citing cases from England a help to his client? What did these Castlemaine jurors care of legal intricacies? Yet Thompson carried on with an air of supreme belief in the import of what he was saying, while glazed eyes began to blur the vision of juror and public visitor alike.

And what was all that about feeling ill? Was Thompson's heart in his work? Oh, if only Otto could be there to hear it for himself! Tom wondered how he was getting on in New Zealand, whether he might be back yet ...

At last, the old barrister returned from his bizarre detour, back to the specifics of the case.

'Now, may I say from the outset that, notwithstanding the exertions of the Crown, the evidence against the prisoner is of a very slight character. It does not appear that he had ever taken any liberties with the deceased woman, and the remarks he made to her amounted to mere civilities.' A wave of his hand was meant to underline just how trifling Rose's words had been. 'The evidence showed that the prisoner was a hard-working man, always seeking work when he was not in employment. With reference to connecting the prisoner to the pipe said to have been found on the meat safe, no reliance can be placed on the testimony of any of the witnesses. Does anyone believe the evidence of Hathaway? Was it at all likely that he, not being a smoker himself, would have kept the pipe in his hand for a quarter of an hour while his stable was threatened with destruction by fire? And how would it be possible for that man to have removed heavy bundles of hay with a pipe in his hand? You must remember, gentlemen of the jury, that a reward of £200 has been offered for the discovery of the murderer, and my own impression is that the pipe had been placed on the meat safe designedly with the object of securing the prize. As for the evidence of Hathaway, I believe the man perjured himself.'

This was a comment to raise eyebrows and elicit muttering in the gallery, and an exaggerated open-mouthed expression of mocking disbelief from the prosecution. Judge Barry kept his features tidy, and simply wrote a note. Thompson proceeded confidently.

'I refer now to the evidence of Mrs Spinks as to the man who was standing at the stump on the night of the murder. She said herself that it was impossible to see him clearly enough on that dark night to be sure of his identity. As for the attempt to prove that the prisoner had walked from Cheesbrough's place within the time that he was last seen there and the hour at which the murder was supposed to have been committed, I say it is not only improbable but impossible! The prosecution didn't tell you that the short route from Daylesford to that farm is across paddocks covered with ripening corn, and it is impossible that anyone could have made his way through this within the time.'

Tom shifted in his seat; he was finding Thompson's performance ever more frustrating. Improbable, impossible; it was a matter of opinion. Why not point out the vital fact that Rose would have had to cover the journey in the dark? And what kind of man would walk so far in the dark of a moonless night with murder his objective, all the while smoking a pipe? Tom had stopped writing, to think, and to remind himself that the defendant's guilt or innocence wasn't his prime concern; rather, that Rose be fairly tried. This, Tom assumed, would necessitate being rigorously defended.

'The morning after the murder, the prisoner was not found in an excited condition,' Thompson said. 'I presume it is beyond question that whoever had murdered the woman had come down the chimney, and though the Crown produced a shirt said to belong to the prisoner, there was no attempt to show that there were any marks of soot or whitewash on it. In fact, there were no such marks. Again, if a man had come down the chimney, it would have been impossible for him to have ravished and murdered Mrs Stuart without leaving sooty marks on her person, which, by the evidence of Dr Doolittle, we know is not the case ...'

This, Tom thought, was much better; challenging the jury to weigh some key points.

'... The medical evidence negates the assertion that the deceased had been violated, and there is a total absence of motive on the part of the prisoner for the commission of the crime. You, good gentlemen, must consider that no reason was assigned for the committal of this murder. I appeal to you all, and even to the learned judge himself, whether any of you have ever heard of a murder being committed without some reason being assigned. Let us even go back to the beginning of the world. Did Cain commit a murder without a reason? Did St. Paul, when he murdered the martyr Stephen, was he not persecuting the Christians? Again, did King David commit a murder without assigning a reason? No, he did not, nor had there ever been a murder committed without some reason having been given.'

Tom could scarcely believe what he was hearing. He looked about the room to see Smyth and Aspinall exchange looks; they appeared supremely comfortable — maybe even amused. The judge sat impassively, as did the jurors, perhaps taking their lead from the bench. One or two in the gallery nodded, as if Thompson had struck a rich vein of powerful argument. If he saw this as support, it was enough to encourage him, and on he went, confidently and expressively.

'If the prisoner had committed this murder, he must have had some reason, as it was hardly probable that he could go to that house and effect his escape without being recognised by some person or other, seeing that he was well known in the district.'

Tom let this go by; like so much of what both Thompson and Smyth had said, the logic eluded him.

'The evidence with regard to the hairs examined by the analyst is undeserving of attention, and that of Michael Wolf highly questionable. Murderers are usually remarkable for their taciturnity, and how foolish he would be to say he had in his possession a weapon with which he had committed murder. I think that, like Mr Hathaway, Mr Wolf has played loose with the truth.'

Thompson raised his voice over the provoked murmur, and it promptly died away.

'Gentlemen of the jury, I put it to you that all the evidence brought by the Crown is of a purely circumstantial kind. I contend this whole charge was one trumped up for the sake of fixing the guilt on the prisoner, and is scarcely in any respect reliable. There is nothing in the case but supposition, inferences, and arguments; there is nothing conclusive, and if there is a doubt, that doubt must be given in favour of the prisoner. I now leave the case in your hands, believing you will give it your most judicious, impartial, and serious consideration.' He fixed his eyes in turn on several of the jury, straightened his suit, and resumed his seat. He hadn't noticed until then that Smyth had leapt to his feet. Thompson was immediately back to his, speaking as he rose.

'Your Honour, I must object. The prosecution has no right —'

'Your Honour,' Smyth cut in, 'the Crown does indeed have the right of reply. The defence put in and read the depositions by Mrs Spinks —'

Judge Barry was already nodding. 'Quite correct, Mr Smyth, this does indeed entitle you to a reply.'

Thompson did his best to look dumbfounded, but it seemed he knew the procedure perfectly well. He sat down without further protest, as Smyth began.

'Gentlemen of the jury, the prisoner's counsel here has attempted to create an idea that the police, or other persons, had designedly placed the pipe on the safe. Such a statement is totally unsupported! The evidence called for the Crown fully substantiates all I have said in my opening statement, and I simply ask the jury to weigh well the evidence before acquitting the prisoner.'

'That pipe is not mine.'

The sudden interruption from the dock caught everyone's attention. All faces turned to David Rose, standing at the rail with his jaw set and gaze fixed on Smyth. Thompson looked unsure whether to be pleased or not. He glanced at the jurors for their reaction, but Smyth had already reclaimed their attention.

'Gentlemen, we are not assembled here to convict David Rose of murder, but to ascertain if he is guilty of the fearful crime laid to his charge. The prisoner's mouth is not sealed; he is entitled to make a statement.'

Smyth sat down, beneath a halo of magnanimity.

And now the prisoner did speak.

'Your Honour, gentlemen of the jury,' David Rose said, still standing. He was manifestly agitated, and held the railing to steady himself as his feet shuffled. 'I have been in prison so long I feel too weak to give a full account of matters in support of my case.' He hung his head, and slumped back into his chair. It was a moment in which Tom felt a great welling of sympathy for the poor man. Murderer or not, the human tragedy of Rose's situation was impossible to deny. He was on his own here. Not one witness had been called on his behalf, and, as far as Tom could ascertain, there was not one friend or relative in the gallery. What a grim state of affairs, he thought, to have Pearson Thompson as one's only support.

And now Smyth was moving in.

'We, the court, have to expect from the prisoner an explanation of the many circumstances upon which the Crown relies for a conviction, but nothing whatsoever has been brought forward to disprove the statements of the Crown's witnesses. It cannot be denied that the pipe has been fully and clearly identified as the property of the prisoner, and I do not think that you good gentlemen of the jury can come to any conclusion other than that he had left it in Stuart's house within half an hour of the time at which the murder had been committed …'

This pipe again. Tom was struggling with its significance. Rose denied ownership, though several witnesses attested to it being his. And only Detective Walker saw the pipe on the meat safe. Could so many people have missed it? And even if it was there, *and* even if it was David Rose's, did that make him a murderer?

Rose was standing, though he seemed barely capable of it. Smyth motioned to Judge Barry that he had made his point and was happy to let the prisoner speak. And he did, with a denial that was passionate, and of unexpected sophistication.

'Your Honour, hasn't a man conscience? And is there not a God? Has not Almighty God put conscience into men? If I was standing on the gallows now, in the presence of my Maker, I'd swear that pipe was never between my lips. Where is conscience? And where is God? Money and gold are the champions of this colony. It has been proved that this is so. I am weak and poor, and so tired I have hardly the power left me to speak for myself.' He gazed around the room, for want of knowing what else to say or do, and then sat down and buried his face in his hands.

Tom watched with a blank face and an ache in his chest. Could there be anyone in that room who did not feel the slightest shred of compassion for this wretch? Smyth sensed the mood, and was promptly on the offensive, as if there really was a chance the jury might be swayed by pity.

'I might add, Your Honour, while we are addressing this point, that the charge by learned counsel that the police had placed the pipe on the meat safe in order to convict an innocent man is curious, for does it not mount to an admission that the pipe was the prisoner's? I would call now for the defence to confirm this, or withdraw.'

All eyes turned to Thompson. After a whisper in his ear from Geake, he stood and made the best fist of an embarrassing back-down.

'As it cannot be proved, I withdraw.'

Smyth made the shallowest bow, taking care not to appear smug. Thompson sighed with irritation at this false nobility, and Smyth returned to his speculations.

'I do not believe the razor was the instrument with which the murder was committed. I am inclined to believe the deed was done with the missing clasp-knife, sworn to have been in the possession of the prisoner, and a man of the prisoner's thrifty habits was not likely to have thrown away a knife without some reason.'

Tom looked to Pearson Thompson. Could the man not object here? On what grounds could Smyth assert that a murder had been committed with a knife he had not seen and could not prove the prisoner had even had in his possession? And if Rose ever had it, he may simply have lost it, or discarded it. Maybe the handle had broken, or it was blunt beyond restoration. And if Smyth believed it was a knife, did that not render Wolf's testimony invalid? Tom shifted in his seat and sighed heavily, drawing a cross look from the man next to him. And then, on this shaky foundation, Smyth built an even flimsier construction.

'If the prisoner had a reason for getting rid of the knife,' he said, 'it was an article which could be easily disposed of.' So, Tom paraphrased to himself, as if it might clarify matters: Rose was said to have a particular knife, which he could have used to commit a murder, which would be the reason he would dispose of the knife, and this would be easy to do, it being a knife. 'Jesus Christ Almighty,' he muttered. Smyth was treating the jury as children; but then, they seemed to be believing his performance as children. Seemingly lest his whole confection be examined, Smyth moved on promptly, with some remark or two about treating the prisoner fairly, and then, after a small bow to the jury, straightened his gown and resumed his seat.

The moments of silence following rendered the air colder, now that the distraction of the contest was finally ended. Muffled conversations broke out and filled the void. Tom kept his own company, preferring not to speculate over Rose's fate; there was enough of that going on already all around him. He watched Judge Barry, busy collating his notes. He looked at Rose, sitting motionless on his chair, elbows on his knees and face to the floor. There had to be too much doubt, surely, to find him guilty, let alone to send the man to his death. Tom considered he might even leave now; it was too late for the coach, but he could get an early night and be back with Adeline for breakfast. How fortunate he was to have such a wife, a woman so loving to accept without question that he had to be here. He wanted nothing more now than to be with her.

Barry had put down his pen, and was looking up over his spectacles. He nodded to Watkins, who called for order. Tom decided it was best to stay, to hear what the learned man made of what had transpired these past three days.

'Gentlemen of the jury, I have observed that the evidence upon which the Crown relies is to a certain extent direct evidence, and to a certain extent presumptive, or circumstantial, evidence. Most crimes of this nature are decided upon circumstantial evidence, inasmuch as it rarely happens that witnesses are found who were present at the commission of a deliberate murder, and that kind of testimony is frequently thought to afford the best proof. With respect to the comparative weight due to direct and presumptive evidence, it has been said by a high authority that circumstances are in many cases of greater force, and more to be depended on, than the testimony of living witnesses; for witnesses might be mistaken themselves, or be wickedly disposed to deceive others, whereas circumstances and presumptions, naturally arising from facts proved, could not err.'

Tom didn't know where to begin to even write a brief summary of this reasoning. He would have liked to, for digestion with Otto later. Alas, it was lost on him. Maybe it didn't matter; maybe this was a judge's standard opening at a murder trial. Still Barry kept on, and for as long as Tom heard mention of 'circumstantial evidence' and 'juries drawing hasty conclusions' and 'fallacious inferences', he let the words flow by his ears on the close courtroom air. But he remained alert enough to know, when the judge had left the theoretical and general for the practical and specific, to be again attentive.

'The evidence against the accused to justify conviction should be such as to exclude to a moral certainty every hypothesis which does not point to his guilt. You must be of the opinion that it is not merely consistent with the prisoner's guilt, but inconsistent with his innocence, bearing in mind that the first great presumption was the innocence of the accused until he be proved guilty.'

Barry here paused for a sip of water from a glass, a cough, and a minor two-handed adjustment to his wig. With a glance to the jury, he proceeded.

'If it were necessary to search for motives in this case, many could be found. If this woman were violated before death, the motive to take away her life was, perhaps, the strongest that could have actuated the man who violated her, for if she survived the dishonour his life would be in peril. But if she were not violated, and I am inclined to the opinion that she was not, there were two equally strong motives for the taking of her life. One: the attempt at violence is a crime of great enormity, punishable with a severe sentence. Two: the man, disappointed by meeting with the resistance of a powerful and virtuous woman, might have been actuated by the cruel impulse of disappointed lust, and thus have taken her life. This latter motive is the stronger of the two.'

Judge Barry referred to the matter of Rose's inquiry about Cheesbrough's dog, and to the mode of entry by the killer into Stuart's cottage. For each, he left the jury to decide the import. He was similarly disposed to the evidence of the hidden shirt, and the blood and hair analyses. He acknowledged the inconclusiveness of Sarah Spinks' evidence, too. And then he came to the words exchanged between the prisoner and his alleged victim.

'The remark made by the prisoner in the conversation he had with the deceased woman a few days before her death might be considered as merely rude compliments, or familiar expressions of admiration, but there is a significance in his inquiry about the time at which Mrs Stuart's husband went to work, and in his asking where the little girl Louisa Goulding lived, as by that means he became aware that the woman was alone at night when her husband was absent.'

Which doesn't mean he acted on it, Tom thought the judge might add. *And how reliable is the recollection of a girl of such tender years?*

'The medical evidence fixes the time of the woman's death at about eleven o'clock, and supposing the prisoner to have left Cheesbrough's at nine o'clock on the night of the murder, he would have had two hours to travel six miles and eleven chains. That time is ample, as it was proved by the apprehending constable that he himself walked that distance at the ordinary pace in one hour and thirty-five minutes.' *Yes, he did, Judge Barry, during daylight hours!* Tom exhaled in exasperation. Was he the only man in the room who thought this significant?

And then came the pipe, the item central to the prosecution. What would the judge make of this, Tom wondered. Presumably, that Hathaway's evidence was strong and remarkable, and the varying testimonies taken together were contrary to any suggestion that the police had concocted a story to implicate the prisoner. Well, Tom thought, Pearson Thompson had already, humiliatingly, conceded this point.

Barry advised the jurors that the mode of entry to the Stuart house had not been proved as being by the chimney, and then he came to the testimony of Michael Wolf. He cautioned the jury that they had to be assured that the words reported as being by the prisoner were in fact used by the prisoner, and meant by the prisoner in the way they were reported. On hearing this sage advice, Tom looked in turn to Rose and Thompson for their reception of it. Rose seemed utterly indifferent, and perhaps wasn't even listening. Thompson nodded his concurrence, and exchanged a tiny smile with Geake. And then followed a statement from the judge that so astonished Tom for its lack of sagacity that he made sure to scribble it down verbatim so that he might share it with Otto at the first opportunity.

Some closing remarks from the judge passed Tom by as being

of the kind made at the end of all such cases, and then came Barry's final words of all, addressed to the jury: 'It is now half-past nine o'clock. I charge you now to retire to consider your verdict.'

Tom stood with the rest of the court as the judge stood and left for his room. Despite the hour and the many hours already endured, the public gallery had remained full throughout. The dock was already vacated; Rose had been promptly taken to his cell, where Pearson Thompson would now be headed. How long the jury would take, Tom couldn't guess, not being familiar with such things. Would a long deliberation indicate uncertainty in their thinking? Did they know already, delaying their verdict merely to give the appearance of giving due consideration? If the jury shared his thinking, though, there'd be a finding of not guilty, and his own confusion would make sense.

Tom went out to the rear yard, where twenty or more men stood around in small groups, stamping their feet and lighting pipes to keep out the chill; others were taking the opportunity to empty their bladders in the trough mounted for the purpose in a small shed. The mood was light, with laughter and discussions taking place about all manner of things, from the trial itself to current affairs and domestic trivia. They might have been theatregoers at interval. Tom could detect no mood of uncertainty here, no concern that the verdict would not be the right one; that is, that Rose was the killer. But maybe they knew this before the case even began.

At twenty past ten o'clock, the jury filed in. The prisoner was led to the dock. All rose as Judge Barry entered. He took his seat, and the court settled. On the judge's nod, Watkins stood and read the names of the jury, and then addressed them collectively, 'Gentlemen, have you agreed upon your verdict?'

Foreman Beard, the oldest of the twelve, stood, as stiff as a guardsman. 'We have.' One juror let his head fall forward; another looked to the ceiling.

'How say you? Is the prisoner at the bar, David Rose, guilty or not guilty?'

'Guilty,' Beard said, and sat down, eyes steady and jaw set.

Watkins nodded. 'Gentlemen of the jury, hearken to your verdict, as the court records it: The Queen against David Rose, for murder. Verdict: Guilty! So say you all?'

A resounding chorus of 'Aye,' was given, and Watkins turned to the box.

'Prisoner at the bar, David Rose, you have been found guilty of the wilful murder of Margaret Stuart. Do you know, or have you anything to say, why sentence of death should not be passed upon you, according to law?'

David Rose had remained seated during the verdict, sitting forward, his head down, denying the gallery. At the clerk's invitation, he looked up and rose to his feet. He seemed suddenly faint, and grasped the railing in front of him. And though he was shaking, when he spoke it was with certainty.

'I am not the man who committed the murder.'

From behind Tom came a scoff; a few heads shook in contempt. Someone muttered, 'Liar.'

Rose looked about the room. With so many faces turned in his direction, he may have crumbled. Instead, he found his voice and used it to plead.

'The words I spoke to the woman were words of friendship. I went to camp on the Friday evening, and the dead woman, who was gathering sticks, came to me. She walked up to me and looked me in the eye, as though she had some strange suspecting of what I was going to do there. I bid her good evening, and she nodded her head. I said to her, "I am going to camp here until the Christmas holidays are over," and she nodded her head again. I had been harvesting up the country and I had been digging. I said, "You are a nice-looking girl, and it is a pity you have not a sweetheart." She smiled and said, "I am a married woman." I answered her, "I will say no more, or perhaps I shall get my nose broke." I went into the township. I afterwards met her husband, who by his look seemed to challenge me. He wished me good evening. This is all what passed. This is all what I am guilty of. These are all the words I said. I said all this to the policemen, when they took me. This is all I know about it.'

He looked to the jury, then to his counsel. Thompson looked back, and could offer only a wince. Rose retreated to his chair, and slumped there.

Clerk Watkins was already to his feet. 'I call now for silence while the sentence of death is pronounced.' He sat down.

Tom felt the pulse knock in his ears. His breathing had quickened, and a light-headedness dulled his hearing. He swallowed to suppress a rising nausea, and closed his eyes to the thought that a man not ten yards from where he sat would now hear that the state was going to put him to death. Tom looked to the jury — ordinary men much like him. Yet they were so sure of their decision. How?

Redmond Barry cleared his throat. Tom was on the brink of throwing up. He gripped the bench under him with both hands, and swallowed hard as Barry began, prompted by notes to which he referred.

'David Rose, you have been indicted for the murder of Margaret Stuart, a young and apparently well-behaved and virtuous woman. You have been found guilty of that atrocious crime, after careful inquiry, which has occupied the attention of the jury for three days. The crime was committed under circumstances that can find but few parallels in any country. It was attended by circumstances which show remarkable daring in the commission of the offence, and it has required marked intelligence and continued perseverance to bring you to the bar of justice.' He looked up now, and waited a moment for Rose to lift his own head.

'I believe you must feel convinced you have been fairly tried.'

Rose saw that all eyes were upon him. He looked to the bench and spoke, his voice wavering.

'Your Honour, I am an innocent man, and I beg for life. I did not do that dreadful deed. Let me appear what I may, I am not the man who did it, and I know no more about it that the angels in heaven or the innocent, unborn child. If I'm spared, I will do all to produce the murderer.'

A man behind Tom muttered, 'Squeal, you fucking animal.' Someone shooshed him.

Judge Barry allowed a moment to pass before speaking, lest Rose had not finished.

'The case has been conducted in a manner which shows that no pains have been spared to give you every opportunity of establishing your innocence. It is rare to find a case where so many witnesses have been called in which there has been so little variance between the statements.'

To this, David Rose replied with newfound certainty. 'Yes, Your Honour, witnesses are witnesses and conscience is conscience, but my word, of course, would not be believed. My conscience is clear, and if there were twice as many witnesses, I shall leave this world as an innocent man, and, perhaps, you will find it all out in time.'

Judge Barry seemed a little discomfited by the prisoner's unexpected eloquence; his tone became terse, impatient. 'The fact of so many witnesses having been called shows the difficulties the Crown have had to contend with, and it is known to all acquainted with the conduct of criminal prosecutions that it is more difficult to support a charge when witnesses are numerous than when they are few in number. Every source of information seems to have been exhausted. There are now but few remarks which I feel called upon to make ...'

David Rose fell to his knees. He bowed his head and clasped his hands as in prayer. Barry continued, somewhat triumphantly, Tom considered. 'The result of this trial will show those who have recourse to such extremes in crime that, however safe from detection they may believe themselves to be, they are not beyond the reach of the law. It gives me severe pain to be obliged to tell you that I am not justified in holding out any hopes of mercy. That prerogative does not rest with me. My duty will be simply to report upon the trial as it has occurred —'

Rose stood. He could barely find the breath to speak. 'I am an innocent man, Your Honour, an innocent man.'

'— but I cannot hold out to you any hope that the extreme penalty of the law will not be carried into effect.'

Rose tried to speak again, but his throat wouldn't permit it. Even standing seemed beyond his capacity. A glass of water was handed to him — a gesture as much in consideration for the man as it was for the discomfort of the court. He took it, and was able to say, 'Is there no chance my innocence being proved now?'

Judge Barry pressed on.

'A trial of this kind affords to the whole community a great social and moral lesson, more especially to those persons who will not control their evil passions. It is not my intention to weaken the effect of these impressive proceedings by addressing you at greater length. I have now only to entreat you earnestly to employ your remaining time in preparing for eternity. You have appealed to the Supreme Being —'

'Is it possible I am to die an innocent man, Your Honour?'

'— and I entreat you to prepare to appear at the Judgement Seat.' Barry removed his spectacles, and considered the condemned man's further interruption.

'Human tribunals may err; the Lord's judgement cannot. And if you are an innocent man and suffer unjustly in this world, you may be sure of justice and mercy in the next.'

'Jesus Christ,' Tom muttered.

'I am not the murderer!'

Barry put on his spectacles, not to read through but to look over. He spoke now as a gentleman gives directions to his butler.

'The sentence of the court is that you, David Rose, be taken back to the place whence you came, and at such time and at such place as His Excellency the Governor may direct, you then and there be hanged by the neck until you be dead, and that your body when dead be taken down and buried within the precincts of the gaol where you were last confined before this sentence of execution is carried into effect. And may the Lord have mercy on your soul.'

24

TUESDAY 15th AUGUST

DAVID ROSE SAT IN a corner of the exercise yard at Castlemaine Gaol, lobbing stones at a weed. Archdeacon Archibald Crawford approached, and stopped at the prisoner's feet. He lowered himself to his haunches and balanced there, forearms on thighs.

'Good morning, David. How are you today?'

Rose looked up. 'Is it in?'

Crawford pulled a newspaper from his coat pocket. He nodded and handed it over. 'Yes. Your letter's there.' Rose scanned the print. He recognised his name and various other words he'd said, taken down by Crawford the day before. He got to his feet.

'I've thought of more,' he said.

Crawford was reluctant. He stood. 'David, you have given an account of yourself, and the newspaper was good enough to publish it. I don't think they will want more. In any case, writing more will only …'

'Will only what?'

'Will only make people wonder why you didn't say all of this at the trial. They will think you have been making things up.'

'I'm not making things up!' Rose's voice was loud; Crawford looked about and held up his hands for calm.

'David, please.'

Rose turned away, and pressed his forehead against the sandstone wall. Crawford came up by his shoulder and placed a hand on it.

'David, many people will read your letter. But now I implore you — I beg you — please, you must prepare for the hereafter —'

Rose turned. His face was hard, his eyes wide and restless. Crawford shrunk back.

'Why, padre? There is no day named for hanging.'

'No, but it will come.'

'No! I want to say more. I want them to know the lies of Michael Wolf.'

Crawford looked into the eyes of a desperate, deluded man. He weighed the situation, and relented.

'Very well, David. I will take another letter today, but it will be the last. So mind you take care to say all you wish to say.'

78 ELIZABETH STREET, MELBOURNE

OTTO BERLINER RETURNED HOME, feeling more than a little self-congratulatory. In fact, given how pleased he was with his progress in Auckland, he made a mental note that some humility ought to attend any reporting of developments, lest he be seen as smug. Still, there was no denying he'd been well received across the Tasman Sea, and this could only encourage the view among potential clients that the service he would be offering had broad appeal and imprimatur. There could be no doubt that he had made the right decision, that his Private Inquiry Office should not solely be a Melbourne — or Victorian — enterprise; it should have, right from its inception, agencies far and wide. A branch office would open in Sydney within months, and soon thereafter, agencies in all Australian colonies, and New Zealand of course. In time, he had no doubt, connections would be made in the largest cities of the world. Even sooner, though, would be his retirement from the Detective Department. That day was fast approaching, as the demands of establishing a fledgling business were growing.

Right now though, he was in the mood for celebrating, but not in the fashionable way. For Otto, celebration meant sitting and reading or taking a bath. He might go out for coffee and cake, or take a walk through the Botanic Gardens, or see a play. To Otto, there was no greater reward than the freedom to enjoy solitary pursuits. Nonetheless, even this didn't come simply to him; it was always easier to get back to work, to tell himself he hadn't quite done enough to earn his treat. He was sure he cherished his visits to Linden's Gentlemen's Salon in large part because he had no choice but to submit to the pleasure of the enforced hiatus in the barber's chair.

Some time after three, Otto entered his rooms on the first floor to find that the mail box which hung on the inside of the door was full. Among various items of official correspondence was a letter from his sister, Helga, and another from Tom Chuck. Otto hadn't forgotten the David Rose case; word of the verdict had reached him in New Zealand. As for the details, it was to be his recreation to catch up on newspaper reports just as soon as he was settled at home. But now these letters, of course, took precedence.

First, his sister. Helga was his junior by a year, and lived in Sydney, as she had since the family came out in 1848. She was widowed, and a homebody who, in Otto's opinion, seemed to have redirected her frustrated wifely instincts to the care of their frail mother, and thank heaven for it, because that would be no easy assignment. Sending money each month was Otto's side of the contract, and he never once failed to honour it. This made it all the more irritating to him that Helga should still be soliciting — however subtly — his return to Sydney. 'Mother misses you,' was a regular example, and there it was again, an unnecessary remark in a letter of otherwise welcome news and gossip. Perhaps, though, he was being too harsh; once the office was up and running, and the Sydney branch open, it would be a good time to pay a visit. He put Helga's letter aside and opened Chuck's, which had arrived almost a month ago. It was brief, no more than a paragraph, which made finding out the subject of it all the more tantalising.

July 28th 1865

Dear Otto,
I have this very minute come from court to my hotel room in Castlemaine. If you are returned from New Zealand I expect you will have learned of the probable fate of David Rose and if so, you may be assuming that evidence was forthcoming that precluded any verdict other than guilty. However, in all good conscience, and despite my ignorance in court matters, I am deeply troubled that an innocent man may be sent to his death. I take some courage that I am not alone in my view. Some comment in the press has pointed to inadequacies in the prosecution's case. That said, I feel that I should very much like to share my concerns with you.

Tom

Otto walked to his window. Rain was herding Elizabeth Street pedestrians to the shelter of verandas, leaving the roadway to horses and carriages, and to caped drivers perched glumly on their seats. In a matter of days, surely, David Rose would be dead. Otto remembered reading the grim news of the guilty verdict and casually assuming, as Tom's letter suggested he would, that evidence must have been presented which put the matter beyond doubt. It was the easiest, most convenient conclusion. But now, this letter. Tom Chuck was no fool. If Tom had misgivings, they wouldn't be baseless. Could it really be that a pipe had condemned

Rose? Otto recalled mention of the police finding a shirt —

He glanced up at the clock. Four p.m. It was too late now, but yes, tomorrow he would go to Daylesford. This matter, he decided, simply could not be ignored, not for another day; the execution order from the governor could not be far off. Of course, he gave himself a mild rebuke for thinking it, but an opportunity was not to be missed to demonstrate the superior detective skills his private inquiry office would bring to bear, should he be successful in saving Rose from the gallows. And yet there was another reason — one that was suddenly barking on the periphery of his thinking, like a dog at a fence. He wanted to ignore it, but it was real: a feeling of guilt and perhaps worse, of self-doubt, that it was he who had brought in the wrong man.

WEDNESDAY 16th AUGUST

DAVID ROSE SNATCHED THE newspaper as soon as Crawford entered the cell.

'It's in here?'

'Yes, David. They published your letter. Your second letter in two days. I was surprised they —' Crawford checked himself, but Rose's attention was with the page, scanning the print for familiar words. He let out a chuckle and began to pant, excited, as if the printed word leant his words an authority that could not be denied. He looked up from the page, listening for an angry populace at the gates demanding his release. He turned a demanding gaze on Crawford.

'It's all here, as I spoke it?'

'Every word. David —'

'That I heard about the murder when I was at Blanket Flat, that I never told Michael Wolf that a razor cut the woman's throat, that I didn't say that was the price of her?'

'Yes, David. Everything you told me.' *Everything your counsel should have made clear at the trial but didn't*, he thought to say.

Rose settled. He nodded. With a deep breath and a swallow, he brought his breathing down. He seemed satisfied, at last. Crawford was relieved, for he had grave news. He seized his chance to break it.

'David, please, can you look at me?' Rose obliged, and Crawford sensed that the man had more than an inkling of what he was about to be told. However slightly, it eased the burden. He could not have been more mistaken. 'David, it falls to me, this solemn duty, to tell you that Governor Darling yesterday signed your death warrant —'

'No! No! No!' The news set Rose alight with rage. He hammered his fists against the wall and bawled to the ceiling. Crawford decided to press on; there was no imparting this gently, for Rose or for himself. 'You are to be hanged next Monday morning, the 21st of August, at ten o'clock. David, I am deeply sorry to bring you such word. I do entreat you to calm yourself.' This was a forlorn hope. David Rose was in a world of demons: distressed, outraged, unreachable.

'They cannot fucking hang me! I want to see the governor! I fucking *will* see the governor!'

'Come, David, let us pray together.' Crawford held out a hand and ventured towards the condemned man. Rose snarled and turned away.

'David, let us pray to God to give you strength, so that you may come to Him with your conscience unburdened.'

Rose was tearing at his hair and beard. He screeched. The flap opened; Crawford waved the turnkey away.

'I implore you, David. Your letters have spoken to the people. Now is the time to speak to God. Let his everlasting love comfort you and bring you strength … Please, David, let us pray together.'

Rose stopped his pacing. For the moment, he was composed. 'There is no need to pray. Don't you see?' He held up the newspaper. 'God has already answered.'

OTTO ALIGHTED FROM THE coach in front of Jamison's Hotel in Wills Square at 5.00 p.m. 'My God, this weather!' he muttered as he was reminded of how miserable a Daylesford winter's day could be. And it wasn't just the bite of the windblown mist, or the murky air, that affronted him: there was the mud, too. The rich volcanic soil that summer winds whipped up in eddies of red dust had been transformed by winter's heavy rain to a wet plaster that bespattered hems and horses, and caked the undersides of vehicles. It so clumped to itself, and to anything that might come in contact with it, that crossing the street turned a man's shoes into clods.

Fortunately, Otto had no need to venture from the kerb — not for now, at least — for he would be staying at the Albert Hotel, on this side of the road. This did, however, necessitate a walk of two hundred yards through the rain along a densely puddled footpath. He drew his scarf up across his face and set out for what he expected would be a warm room, a hot meal, and, after reading the newspaper reports he had brought with him, a sound sleep. Tomorrow, there was much to be done.

25

THURSDAY 17th AUGUST
FOUR DAYS BEFORE THE DAY OF EXECUTION

DAVID ROSE STOOD AGAINST the wall outside his cell. Gaol governor John McEwen took a few moments to run a narrow eye over his prisoner. A turnkey stood by with Archdeacon Crawford.

'You've been very disruptive, prisoner Rose,' McEwen said, his voice soft, his manner unruffled. 'Making all your demands. Well, you wanted to see the governor, so here I am.'

A lengthy look was exchanged between McEwen and his charge, each knowing that of course it was the governor of the colony Rose had meant, and each knowing that this was a demand that wouldn't be met.

'I want more food,' Rose said. 'And I want brandy. Or wine.'

McEwen wore a wry grin at the temerity.

'I'm not indifferent to your circumstances, prisoner Rose. Nor am I heartless. I will grant you additional food, on the condition that you conduct yourself with good behaviour. There will be no grog. In the few days you have remaining, I suggest you turn your mind to preparing to meet your maker. Any further disruption from you will not be tolerated. Good day to you.'

EIGHT O'CLOCK TO OTTO didn't seem too early in the morning to arrive unannounced at the London Portrait Gallery. As it happened, given the warmth of Tom Chuck's reception, he might have turned up before daybreak and been just as welcome. The man was positively effervescent at Otto's appearance, and all the more so coming hard upon the news yesterday of Rose's execution date.

'He has been so troubled,' Adeline confided when her husband stepped out of the sitting room to hang the 'closed' sign in the front window. 'He saw that poor woman, lying there horribly mutilated, but when he saw that wretched man brought in, he felt not angry, only desperately sorry for him. He had hoped the trial would prove the arrest correct, that the monster had been caught —'

Otto was nodding. 'Now he's sure that David Rose is an innocent man — or, at least, a man who has not had justice.'

'Yes. Yes, this is why he is so glad you've come. He trusts you, Mr Berliner. He knows you understand the ways of the law.'

Otto nodded, sagely. 'He's a very compassionate man, your husband, but he must know that he is not responsible for the shortcomings and inadequacies of others.'

'But he does have such doubt about his own judgement. He asks, surely the jury and the judge and the police can't all be wrong? Surely, they must know better than he?'

'The short answer, Mrs Chuck, is yes, they can be wrong; so, yes, Tom may well know better. I tell you with no false modesty, Mrs Chuck, that I am often right when my colleagues are wrong.'

Adeline looked at him in a way that had him wondering whether he might have sounded a little too self-assured. Quickly, he added, 'In seeking justice for Mrs Stuart, many have been blind to injustice to Mr Rose. Not Tom, which is to his eternal credit.'

Tom was in the doorway. 'I'm not so wise, Otto. Besides, there is no small degree of public opinion, expressed in the street as much as in the press, that Rose should not have been found guilty on purely circumstantial evidence. That, at the very least, he should not hang.' He came in and sat. Adeline smiled, touched her husband's shoulder, and left the men alone.

Otto waited for Tom to speak. He took a few moments, not sure where to start, then opted for an expression of misgiving.

'I am indebted to you coming all this way, Otto. I confess to wondering whether my letter had reached you, and then when I learned that you were still in New Zealand, I — and then yesterday, hearing the execution day — well, I thought all hope was lost. Still, you're here now! But surely we don't have enough time?'

'We have the time we have, Tom. By my reckoning, four days and one hour.'

'I only hope my belief about the wrongness of the verdict is based on sound reasoning —'

'Tom, I have no doubt of it. I have doubts about the police, and about Pearson Thompson. I've worked with these people; I know the way they think. Oftentimes, they don't think at all. What you have told me is not inconsistent with my experience. And as you said just now to your wife, you — we — are not alone in our concerns.' He grasped Tom's forearm and gave it a quick shake. 'Now, tell me what you know.'

Tom was cheered by Otto's vote of confidence in him. He opened a notebook.

'I've written down the main points where I think the evidence was poor, or at least where I couldn't follow the argument.'

'Good.'

'And I did make notes several times where I thought Pearson Thompson was derelict, or plain incomprehensible. But I may have read him wrongly, or, for that matter, the evidence as well, so —'

'That's all right. I've read numerous trial reports in the press. Just tell me what you have.'

'Very well. I can say, without doubt, that no one item of

evidence proves David Rose murdered Mrs Stuart. The judge even said as much himself. But he said that because there were so many such pieces of evidence —'

'It pointed to his guilt?'

'Yes.'

'I've heard that argument before, and to my mind it is deeply flawed. Many times it's been said in court, and out, that it behoves the accused to rebut such circumstantial evidence, and if he doesn't, or can't, the evidence is lent further weight, or worse, that it is an admission of guilt. It's preposterous! All sorts of wild accusations can be thrown about and ... Anyway, do please continue. What about the pipe?'

'Yes, the pipe. Detective Walker was the only one to see it that night —'

'Yet, he left it there on the meat safe for a week — assuming, of course, that it was there in the first place to be left.'

'That's what Pearson Thompson implied, that Walker placed it there, but when Smyth said that that would be an admission that it was Rose's pipe, Thompson withdrew. In any case, Rose swore it wasn't his pipe, just as he did at his committal in February. But against him, several witnesses said they were certain they saw him smoking it.'

'And the jury believed the witnesses.'

'And so, too, the judge. So they believe Rose was lying, because they would never believe there was a terrible conspiracy.'

'Of course, Tom, it really doesn't matter whether or not the pipe was Rose's.'

'It doesn't?'

'Not at all. Let us say, for the moment, it was Rose's pipe, and it was there on the safe, just as Walker said it was. Does this mean it was David Rose who put it there?'

'No, I suppose not. But George Stuart said he didn't see it when he went to work.'

'Yes, and like everyone else, except Walker, he just missed it.'

'You're right. Judge Barry said if you were looking for a knife, you might not notice a pipe.'

'Or it really wasn't there when he went to work. That was at four o'clock, or just before. What if Margaret Stuart herself found the pipe that very afternoon, and *she* put it on the safe, thinking her husband might like it, or that it had been dropped by a friend of his, or even that it was his?'

'Yes. Yes, that is possible. So why didn't Thompson —?'

'Because he's old and careless. He might not even believe, for all his huffing and puffing in the paper, that Rose is innocent. You might even argue that even if it was David Rose who put the pipe on the safe, that doesn't prove it was he who killed Mrs Stuart.'

'It's the conclusion of the court.'

'Yes, a court that believes David Rose, having walked six miles in the dark, came down the chimney, puffing away on his pipe, and his first thought was to place it on the meat safe before going into the bedroom to cut the lady's throat. He just forgot to retrieve his pipe on the way out.'

'A pipe Rose said he wouldn't give up for a sovereign, if you believe Hathaway.'

'What else do you have?'

Tom turned the page.

'Um ... the Cheesbrough dog. The prisoner enquired whether it was a good watch-dog, and the prosecution contended this meant that he wanted to be sure that when he returned late at night, after killing Mrs Stuart, the dog wouldn't wake the household.'

'Of course.'

'Trooper Brady said that Rose could easily have walked into Daylesford from Cheesbrough's farm in the time available, and without being seen.'

'Even though Brady walked the route in daylight.'

'Pearson Thompson made nothing of that!'

'Tell me about the shirt.'

'The judge didn't think it was as important as the pipe. But you know, if it was Rose's shirt, and he'd hidden it to hide evidence, as the prosecution charged, there was scarcely any blood on it — and maybe not even human blood. And there was no soot or whitewash from the chimney. Thompson did make mention of this, but in the end the shirt wasn't important, and neither were the hairs.'

Tom scanned further along his notes.

'Witnesses said Mrs Stuart was frightened of David Rose.'

'That wouldn't have helped.'

'And Sarah Spinks said she saw a man near Stuart's around eleven on that night, but she wouldn't swear that it was Rose. It was too dark.' He looked up. 'But this was good enough for the prosecution, and the jury.'

He flicked through the last few pages of his notebook, and his face suddenly lit up. 'Goodness me, Michael Wolf. He was working with Rose at Coates' farm. He said Rose told him his razor had cut a person's throat.' Tom looked at Otto. 'Now, why would Rose say such a thing to a stranger? Anyway, Doolittle said the murder weapon was a knife, and Smyth agreed with him! So why even call Wolf?'

'Not for the detail, Tom, but for the story.'

'Oh, and then Judge Barry said ...' Tom searched again, for the words he'd copied verbatim, '... here we are, he said it was strange that, if Rose were innocent and knew of the murder, why he didn't tell Dr Coates as soon as he arrived there, as — this is what Barry actually said — "bearers of startling news were usually well received out in the country".' Tom twisted his face. 'Is that right?'

'Well, every time I'm in the country and in want of hospitality, I make sure I have some startling news to tell. Don't you?'

Tom looked at Otto. The detective had not impressed him as the kind of man who made jokes. Perhaps it was because Otto had always seemed so conscientious. Whatever it was, there could not have been a better lifter of spirits.

Tom continued, his confidence in Otto all the greater.

'Earlier, Smyth had said that it was remarkable that Rose was able to give such minute particulars of the crime to Wolf on the Saturday, before any news had reached Coates' farm.'

'So, he said too little to Coates, and too much to Wolf.'

'Judge Barry said Rose may have told Wolf all he did to ease his conscience. I think, Otto, that if I'd just murdered a woman in her bed, I might keep quiet about it.'

'Maybe you would, Tom, but you're no murderer.'

'No, but if I were ever charged, I would not want Pearson Thompson to defend me. Otto, there were so many, many questions he should have asked. So many witnesses, and none of them rebutted. He didn't even put Rose in the dock so he could explain how he came to know about the murder. There was not the slightest attempt to establish an alibi. Which makes me wonder whether there was one. And where were the witnesses for Rose?'

'Pearson Thompson should have retired long ago.'

'It really is too bad, Otto, this whole business. What's to be done? Can evidence be found to prove Rose is not guilty? Or guilty even? I could be reconciled to that if the evidence showed it to be so.' He fixed a look on Otto. 'Do you think Rose is innocent? Or is it a case of the right man being convicted on insufficient evidence?'

'Tom, if I had murdered Margaret Stuart, I would have left the district within the hour, not loitered outside to be seen by Mrs Spinks. I certainly wouldn't walk back through Daylesford a day and a half later on my way to find work on the other side of town. And how determined, how enraged, would I have to be, to walk six miles into town, in the dark, to brutally murder a woman I did not know, who had done me no wrong? But like you, Tom, I'm not a murderer. David Rose is a strange man — a man I would not care to know, a man I would not like. He's a convict, a loner, transported from his home at sixteen years of age. Who knows what demons he has in his head? You ask me if I think he is innocent. I think the question is, does the evidence prove that he is guilty, and I say no, it does not. At the very best, it shows that David Rose *could* have killed Mrs Stuart, and, sadly for Mr Rose, that was enough for the police, the jury, the judge, most of the press, and much of the general public.'

'So —?'

Otto held up a hand. 'If evidence couldn't be found after all this time, with so many men investigating, that Rose killed Mrs Stuart, then I say there is no such evidence to find. And I say that, knowing full well the local police force's ineptitude.'

'So we prove the evidence wrong?'

Otto was shaking his head. 'Prove it wasn't possible to walk to Daylesford from Glenlyon in the dark in under two hours, that burying a shirt doesn't mean a man is a killer, that making enquiries about a dog doesn't mean one is planning a murder? You see what I mean, Tom. Such evidence of this circumstantial kind can't be disproved.'

'What do we do, then?'

'Find the killer, of course!'

26

OTTO LEFT THE LONDON Portrait Gallery late morning, comprehending all too well what a colossal ambition it was to overturn a murder conviction, never mind that he had yet to find a killer and prove the case — and that he had just four days in which to do it. And who, apart from Tom Chuck, would help him? Not the police, not the judiciary, not the government. Powerful men in authority, with their delicate egos, could never countenance the thought that they might be wrong, and though they would profess loudly to be defenders of justice, what they most feared was embarrassment. And anyway, what kind of an upstart would dare presume to know better than they? Well, an upstart like himself, of course!

So, yes, Otto conceded, the odds weren't attractive, but great risk was worth taking for great reward. It presented a magnificent opportunity. Imagine, one man — well, two — taking on the machinery, and winning! Could there be a greater recommendation, a more convincing testimony, for the Private Inquiry Office?

Otto's wont wasn't to ponder the immutable, but he did wonder at the timing of his return to Melbourne from New Zealand. How many days would be too few? Five, he reckoned — if he counted since yesterday, and even with one a Sunday —

was too many not to take up the challenge. He fully expected spiteful interference and non-cooperation by Daylesford police; but obstacles, as Otto reminded himself, were for overcoming. He would carry out his investigations alone — as was his usual, and preferred, practice — with Tom running errands from time to time as required.

It was fortunate that he had been granted these three weeks' leave, a favour not usually so readily granted. He wondered whether the government had ever considered that his new agency might prove to be a very economically advantageous alternative to maintaining a costly stable of its own detectives for investigations of fraud, unpaid debts, and the like. Would it understand that salaried detectives were paid whether they solved a case or not, and whether they took a month to do a week's work? His Private Inquiry Office, on the other hand, would depend for its very existence on getting the job done, and promptly. In any case, had leave not been granted, he was ready to resign, and he was sure the Detective Department knew that.

But now he had a job to do.

And what an opportune start to his investigations it was to catch sight of the familiarly gaunt form of Pearson Thompson, leaving the office of solicitor Thomas Geake, a few doors down from Chuck's. As the old barrister was a man he had to speak to, Otto might also have taken this coincidence as auspicious, but he was a man of science, and confident in his judgement, so he knew already that he was on the right track. He quickened his step and caught up with Thompson, taking the old man by surprise.

'Berliner! When the devil are you finally leaving this town? It seems every time I'm here, your neatly trimmed head pops up.'

'You know, Pearson, I was just thinking that very thought about you. Let me buy you a cup of tea.'

Thompson took out his watch. 'Too late for a spot of breakfast? At the Vic?'

It *was* too late for Otto, actually, but if breakfast was the price of a conversation with the man, he was sure he could manage some bread and jam.

No more was spoken until they'd ordered at the counter and taken their seats by the window at the Victoria Hotel, one hundred yards up Vincent Street.

'I always thought you'd be a sausage man, Berliner,' Thompson said with a grin.

My God, the fellow was in a pert mood, and so soon after losing a murder case. Perhaps it was his way of compensating for the disappointment.

Thompson abruptly turned serious.

'You see that fellow leading the horse by us just now, down Chancery Lane? To the livery stables out the back?'

'Hathaway, wasn't it?'

Thompson nodded. 'He'd be expecting a slice of the reward for the Rose case, knowing so very much about that pipe. Walker's up for a slice himself, and Williams, and that cocky little trooper Brady. You, too, no doubt, for bringing the fugitive in.' He shook his head and grimaced. 'Is it right, Berliner — morally, that is — that police should have their pockets lined with reward money?'

Otto was spared the requirement to give the obvious answer, for Thompson's omelette had just arrived.

The barrister's face lit up. 'Ah!' He held his fork over it a moment, and then stabbed it through the heart.

'You were disappointed by the verdict, I expect?' Otto said.

Thompson thought for a moment. 'Well, yes, of course I was!' He took a forkful and loaded his mouth.

'Then you did believe your client was innocent?' Otto said, with Thompson masticating like a machine. He swallowed.

'I didn't say that. He shouldn't have been found guilty. There's a difference. I strongly object to sloppy application of the law — no, actually, it is the law I object to. Seven months, Rose was in custody. Seven! It's an outrage. Anyway, I've just come over today to tidy up with Geake, so we both get our dues; salvage something from the wreckage.' He took another forkful. 'So, Berliner,' he said, 'why are you here in Daylesford? Private enterprise not your cup of tea after all?' A fleck of egg clung to the fringe of Thompson's moustache, defying the threshing jaw beneath. Otto wouldn't be steered from the topic.

'I agree with you, Pearson. Rose should not have been found guilty, on the evidence.'

Thompson dabbed his lips with finger and thumb, and smoothed his moustache. 'You know a lot about the trial, for a man who wasn't there.'

'My associate was. I read the papers.'

'Associate?' The implication seemed to amuse Thompson, or irritate him. 'Well, well. And who might that be?'

'That's not important. What he told me is, because it leads me to want to ask you some questions.'

Thompson sat back sharply in his seat; the defence counsel was suddenly in a defensive mood. He wiped his chin and looked out onto the street for a few moments. Otto saw his larynx rise and fall, and his eyes dart. He faced Otto again, this time with a mien of forced indifference.

'So, Detective, by all means ask away.'

'You didn't challenge the assertion that Rose could, or would, walk all the way into town, and at night, for example.'

'I didn't see the point. It was an assertion self-evidently preposterous. Go on.'

'Maybe you should have pointed that out, nonetheless. But let's not dwell on that now —'

'Is that all?'

Otto was quickly on to his next point.

'You didn't put the suggestion that maybe it was Margaret Stuart who put the pipe on the meat safe. She may well have found it that afternoon.'

'She may well have, though I preferred to disprove that the pipe was Rose's. I maintain still that the Crown didn't prove that it was, despite what Judge Barry said. I mean, Hathaway would say anything if there was a reward for his words. Any more?'

'You didn't mention George Stuart's report of Joe Latham's threats to his stepdaughter. In fact, you called no witnesses for the defence, didn't even put up the three pounds that would have secured at least one, went on at length about the law of England — as if a jury of country shop-keepers and blacksmiths is interested — and, perhaps most important, didn't invite your client to rebut any of the claims made against him, including offering an alibi.'

'Good God, Berliner, that's quite a barrage!'

Otto sat, stony-faced. Perhaps he'd come on a little stronger than he should have; he didn't want Thompson to clam up, or walk out. Fortunately, he did neither. After a moment or two, Thompson spoke, and calmly.

'Just what is your interest, Berliner? I know you brought Rose in. I thought you, as a policeman, would be satisfied, if not delighted, with the verdict. Or is there some guilt you're carrying around under that fine head of hair?'

'I've already said, Pearson, I agree with you that Rose shouldn't have been found guilty on the evidence —'

'Quite so.'

'So why was he? Do you take any responsibility? Could you have conducted the defence differently? Perhaps you could have reminded the court that it was a knife, not a razor, that killed Maggie Stuart. But then Smyth did that for you, didn't he?'

Thompson sputtered like a lit fuse.

'Listen to me, Berliner. You dare presume to tell me my job? I took the case because no one else would — the man was damned from the beginning.' He leant forward and slapped the tabletop. 'He's a convict for heaven's sake, from Van Diemen's Land, the worst of the worst. Sent to Port Arthur, did you know —?'

'I do, but to Point Puer boys' prison nearby. He was sixteen, Pearson.'

Thompson waved this away as mere detail, and resumed his rebuttal. 'And, Berliner, since coming to Victoria he's been arrested — thrice that I know of — for molesting women up around Echuca, and elsewhere. Any hope I had of securing his release lay in the law. It was the law and its application that failed Rose. The police — your colleagues, mind you — had no proof.'

'I see. Rose was destined for the gallows, whatever you said?'

Thompson considered this before answering.

'No. I was naïve in thinking that the police case wasn't enough to convict on; if I made a mistake, it was in overestimating the integrity of the legal system in this colony.'

Otto made a quick study of Thompson's tone and manner. He'd heard himself several times being criticised as pompous; well, surely these detractors had never met this man!

'Loath as I am to defend the police, Pearson, I am inclined to believe there was no direct evidence against David Rose because there was none to find.'

Thompson smiled. 'Still a grain of loyalty there, I see.'

'Hardly. My former colleagues made a case on hot air, and got away with it. Do you think there is evidence to be found against Rose?'

'That's not for me to say. In the end it didn't matter, because we had a judge who prattled on about the circumstantial evidence being as valid as direct evidence — or even *more* valid — so the jury had all the justification it needed. And just as well; imagine the compensation Rose could claim should he have been acquitted. I mean, seven months' incarceration of an innocent man would cost the government several thousand, I can tell you.'

In a brief lull, Otto watched Thompson look distractedly about the room, and then leant forward, his eyes fixed on Otto's. He spoke softly, drawing Otto closer.

'Look, we all know Rose had it coming. His record is a veritable catalogue of iniquity. I'd go as far to say he probably did kill her — but whatever the jury's verdict, the prosecution simply did not prove that he did.'

So there it was, the odious confirmation that even Rose's own counsel didn't believe him. Otto was speechless. He leant back on his chair and watched Thompson clean up the last of his omelette, seemingly unconcerned by his admission. Thompson looked up and dabbed his mouth with his handkerchief.

'So, Berliner, all these questions. What are you up to?'

'I don't agree with you, Pearson. At all. I believe Mrs Stuart's killer is still at large, and I intend to bring him in.'

Thompson raised his eyebrows, incredulous.

'Well, if you do bring him in, you can tell him I'm unavailable. I've got my own cross to bear; I'm to be a father, again, in a few weeks. God help me, at my time of life.'

ALICE LATHAM WAS STRETCHING a linen sheet on a line when Otto found her. A grubby-faced barefoot girl in pigtails alerted her mother to the visitor's arrival.

'Mrs Latham?' he said.

She swept aside a curtain of tablecloth, and eyed Otto as she might a hawker of health tonic.

Otto lifted his hat, a new bowler he suspected looked a little out of place away from the city. 'Detective Otto Berliner, ma'am,' he said. 'May I have a brief word?'

'Berliner? I've heard that name. You were workin' in Daylesford, but you left.'

'Yes, I did leave, two years ago now.'

'But weren't you in the search for my daughter's murderer?'

'That I was.'

'Then I should thank you, Mr Berliner.'

'A cup of tea would suffice.'

The woman seemed a little taken aback by the suggestion, but then nodded that a cup of tea was as good an idea as any.

'If you could finish these, Detective, I'll make a pot.' She bustled inside, leaving Otto with a basket of laundry, a bag of pegs, and the girl staring at him from the back porch. He bent and fetched out a tablecloth. It suddenly amused him that his murder investigation should begin with the hanging of washing in a Daylesford backyard, under the supervision of a child. The day itself had much to do with his good humour; the sky was clear and, in the sunshine, wattles across Wombat Hill were a blaze of the brightest yellow amid the dour green of the eucalypts and leafless branches of young oak, ash, and elm. He finished the basket and took it inside. The girl had gone.

The Latham house was small and spare. They were in the tiny kitchen and sitting-room just inside the back door, his host bent over, stoking the stove firebox. Otto took the opportunity to study her. She couldn't have been more than forty, yet she had the waddle of a woman half her age again. Her hair was lank and unbrushed; her hands were coarse and raw. Here was a stranger to the finer things in life.

'How many children do you and Mr Latham have?' Otto said, pouring himself tea into a chipped china cup and finding a chair. There was a pause, and it seemed to Otto she was a little reluctant to reply. She closed the firebox and stood.

'Mr Berliner, I have much laundry to do today while the sun is out, so I prefer you come quickly to your business. If you don't mind.'

'Of course not, Mrs Latham.' There was definitely a change in her mood, as if she had had second thoughts about offering hospitality to a detective. If he was to glean anything, he knew he would have to tread carefully.

'I'll come straight to the point, Mrs Latham.' She was making it plain with her attending to various domestic chores that this cup of tea wasn't going to be a shared, much less convivial, one. This, Otto found irritating — he did always prefer to have the full attention of his interlocutor than not — but he pressed on, confident that what he was about to say would rectify this.

'I am concerned, as others are, that the man condemned to hang for the murder of your daughter is innocent of the crime, and —'

Mrs Latham was staring at him.

'And, so before a terrible injustice is done —'

'You can bloody well think what you like, Detective, but the way I see it, my Maggie is dead, and a man is goin' to pay for makin' her so.'

'Will that be a comfort if there is the slightest possibility that it's the wrong man? To discover that the real murderer is still at large?'

The girl was back, with three sisters. For Otto, the timing was perfect. Mrs Latham smiled at them and wiped the face of the smallest. They each took a carrot from a basket and skipped back into the yard.

'It is not for me to decide who killed my Maggie. That is for police and judges.'

'I agree with you, Mrs Latham, but I think they may have made a mistake.'

Mrs Latham stared at her visitor, her face crinkling as anger and sadness vied. The latter prevailed; she looked away, her eyes reddening.

'Mrs Latham, I am most terribly sorry. I know you may have found some peace in the verdict, but I urge you to —'

'Please, Detective Berliner, just listen to me!' The tears had been mopped, and now it was the face that was reddening. 'I will not testify against my husband, so you can get that idea out of your head.'

My God! Here was a bolt from the blue. Otto affected not to be surprised, or delighted, by the implication.

'I know many think it was Joe what done it; probably even you, Detective. But I have four children here at home, and Joe is a good provider. He won't be if he's hanged.'

'Mrs Latham, you seem to be saying you believe your husband —?'

'I'm not sayin' nothin'. But if police and the judges can get one man wrong, they can get two, and I know there's many who think Joe killed Maggie. I'm not one of them.'

'I'd like to speak to Joe. When will he be home?'

Alice smiled. 'And I thought you was a good detective! Haven't you heard? Joe don't live here any more.'

'I see.'

'No you don't. He don't live here 'cause I told him to leave.'

'Where is he now?'

'Adelaide. Don't ask me for an address, 'cause I don't have one.'

'So, if he's not in Daylesford, why not answer my questions?'

Alice rolled her eyes. 'My, you're not so smart as you think. I'll explain it for you nice and slow. Joe Latham is the father of my children; he sends me money. If he goes to gaol, I get no money, 'cept what I earn doing laundry, which isn't near enough. Now, I've had enough of your questions, and I'm sorry to appear rude, but if you could be so considerate as to please finish your tea and be on your way.'

Otto nodded that, of course, he understood perfectly. He set down his cup, stood up, and collected his hat.

'Thank you, Mrs Latham. I do appreciate how difficult your circumstances are, and I apologise if I have intruded.' He stepped across to the back door and out into the yard. When he turned around, Mrs Latham was standing on the threshold.

'Before I go,' he said, 'we both know that George Stuart was very certain that your husband made violent threats against your daughter. And Joe did admit at the inquest to striking Maggie, and I have learned that neither were you spared his temper. So let us not fool ourselves, Mrs Latham — your husband is, by any reading of his behaviour, a very violent man. And violent men are dangerous. Good day to you.'

Of course, Otto knew she was lying; Joe Latham didn't sound the kind who would leave simply because his abused wife told him to. No, she had something over her husband that he didn't want revealed.

'WHAT ARE YOU FUCKING doing here, Berliner?'

Otto didn't need to look up from his coffee and sandwich to know that the man with the foul mouth was his former colleague Detective Thomas Walker. But he did look up anyway, after a suitable delay.

'Walker, charming as ever. I'm having lunch, if your detecting skills are still a little underdeveloped. Please, won't you join me, but if you could just keep your voice down …' Otto cast his eyes about the room, where half-a-dozen other diners were enjoying light refreshments and conversation. 'You see, a point of difference between the Argus Restaurant and the hotel counter lunch,' he said, 'is the quiet.'

Walker had a choice here, and both men knew it: walk out or sit down. Either was a capitulation. He chose the latter, and, by way of a smile, Otto allowed himself a modest gloat. But Walker had too much of a head of steam up to care.

'Look, Berliner, you left this town and now you're back, on some kind of private investigation, undermining the work and reputation of the local police. And as for putting the bereaved mother through her pain again, I thought that would be beneath even you. Just what are you trying to achieve?'

Otto listened with a deadpan face, but with a mind busy calculating how best to respond once Walker was done bleating. First, he would take a few moments before speaking; he always found it remarkable how a slight pause could give one the ascendancy, to have the other man waiting on one's words.

'Detective Walker, I know my presence causes you great discomfort —'

'Try, your very existence.'

'Very droll, but if you'll let me finish. Perhaps your discomfort is because you stand to be monumentally embarrassed should I prove everyone wrong about David Rose — which I admit, I may or may not do. Or it could be the reward you stand to lose that concerns you most? I should think that thirty or forty pounds of that two hundred might have your name on it, seeing as it was you, and only you, who discovered the pipe that condemned the man. But your discomfort, or the bereaved mother's, is not my concern; the truth is.'

Walker sat back in his chair and waved away Mrs Homberg, the proprietor's wife, who'd arrived to take an order. He looked at Berliner with a smirk.

'You're such a pompous prick. Is that a Bavarian trait?'

'It may well be, though my family's Prussian, so don't take my word for it.'

Walker leant forward, but Otto wasn't about to hand him the floor. He stood and took his hat and scarf from the stand. 'Naturally, I will be speaking to Superintendent Nicolson and Chief Commissioner Standish in due course.' He bent to Walker's ear. 'And, Thomas, you might even set aside your antipathy towards me and assist in my investigations. We are, after all, meant to be on the same side. Good day.'

Otto stepped out into a busy Vincent Street, the day cold but still bright. He turned and walked, and was in front of the Union Bank when a woman's voice spoke his name. He looked over his shoulder to see Mrs Homberg there. Beyond, Detective Walker was leaving the Argus.

'Detective Berliner,' she said, 'do you have a moment?'

'Of course, Mrs Homberg. By the way, I neglected to say that was a splendid sandwich.'

'Thank you. Do you mind if we … ?' She led Otto out of the pedestrian stream to a spot by the bank. After a glance back to the door of the Argus, she said 'I heard you were in town, and asking questions about Margaret Stuart's murder —'

'My, word does travel so fast!'

'Well, I do know Alice Latham; Maggie worked in the restaurant for a month or so. Did you know?'

'No. Maybe she served me.'

'You'd remember. She was a very pretty girl. Beautiful, I think. What happened to her was —'

'I expect many men paid her attention?'

'Of course, and often it was of the kind most unwelcome.'

'From anyone in particular?'

'None that made a habit of it.'

'I see. Is there something else you wish to tell me?'

She glanced behind again. 'I just don't want my husband to know I'm telling you this.'

'Mrs Homberg, what exactly is it you wish to tell me?'

'There was an incident, one night, not quite two years ago. Maggie's stepfather would come to escort her home on those days she worked late. This night, when she was leaving, a man called Serafino Bonetti was here. He works at a bakery, and he was delivering —'

'You do know Bonetti was arrested for a time on suspicion of Maggie's murder?'

'Yes I do, and Mr Homberg and I could not believe that he would ever hurt even a kitten. A fine young man he is, and Maggie did like his company. She'd have friendly words with him whenever he made a bread delivery.'

'And on this particular night?'

'Serafino was leaving and, like a gentleman, he opened the door for Maggie. I saw them, just out on the footpath, smiling and talking. And then I saw Joe Latham walk up. He would have been waiting for her, to take her home. He must have come from the Golden Age just there, because he seemed a little unsteady on his feet.'

'So, there was an altercation of some sort?'

'I couldn't hear much, but I was at the window, and with

the light turned down I saw Joe Latham pointing his finger at Serafino. He was threatening him. And then Maggie was arguing with her stepfather. Serafino left — I think because Maggie asked him to go. She could see that Latham was looking to start a fight.'

'Pardon my asking, Mrs Homberg, but why are you telling me this?'

'So you can know what a violent and jealous man Joe Latham is, and you can do something! You know he used to beat Alice, his own wife—?'

'Yes—'

'But I am not finished, Detective Berliner.'

'Do go on.'

'Two evenings later, when Maggie had to change her blouse — she'd had an accident with the sauce — I saw the most awful bruise on her neck. Like a hand had taken hold of it, like so, and squeezed.' Mrs Homberg demonstrated a claw-hold. 'She had a small neck. She knew I'd seen her, and she made me promise never to say anything to anyone.'

'And you don't you want your husband to know you've told me this because ...?'

'Only to avoid a row. He thinks a man was found guilty, and that is that. Joe Latham was a bad man, but he can't hurt Maggie any more.'

'I'm sure many people would agree with him.'

'But Detective Berliner, if David Rose had to answer questions, why didn't Joe Latham? I think there is something terribly wrong here.'

Otto nodded. 'And I'm most inclined to agree with you, Mrs Homberg.'

IF OTTO HAD ENTERTAINED the idea of being a father one day, he was feeling rather glad at the moment of the luxury that parenthood was still an option. It wasn't that young Henry

Chuck's company was intolerable; rather, it was just a little too much like hard work for Otto to prefer it over sitting alone. The pair of them — detective and child — were at the dining table, while in the kitchen Tom carved a chicken, and Adeline attended to the vegetables.

Otto persisted; something from the rules of social etiquette told him that as the guest it was his responsibility to entertain the lad while the parents were busy preparing the meal. He reminded himself that to his parents, having recently lost a baby, the young fellow was especially precious.

'How old are you, Henry?' Otto said.

'Ten next year.'

'Ten next year. Well, well. And do you want to be a photographic artist, just like your father?'

'No.'

Otto nodded, and wondered how far away dinner was.

'Where do you come from?' the boy asked abruptly.

'I came with my family to Sydney from Berlin when I was about your age—'

'I'd like to be a detective.'

The conversation had just turned mildly interesting.

'Oh? Tell me why,' Otto said.

The boy shrugged. 'I'm good at noticing things. I can tell you came here down Albert Street, from Camp Street.'

'Really? I am staying at the Albert Hotel, on the Camp Street corner. Did you see me walk down?'

The boy's parents had entered the room, each bringing two plates.

'Here we are at last, gentlemen,' Tom said. 'I know you both must be ravenous.'

'It looks most edible!' Otto said, not noticing that the boy was anxious to finish his account.

'No, I didn't see you walk down,' Henry said, a little piqued.

Otto turned to him. 'So, how —?'

'It's your trousers,' the boy said. 'There are spots of yellow clay on them from the where the footpath was dug up for the drains. That's how I know.'

Otto twisted in his seat to see the hem of his tweeds. 'So there are. That is very observant of you, Henry,' he said, genuinely impressed. 'I think you might make a fine detective. In fact, you're a detective already!'

AFTER DINNER, WHEN HENRY had been put to bed and Adeline had retired, Otto sat with Tom in the sitting room and, over a warming brandy, related the day's developments.

'Your inquiries have certainly attracted considerable attention, Otto. Does that concern you?'

'Not in the least,' Otto said, crossing one leg over the other and holding a palm to the gentle fire flickering in the grate.

'But should there be a murderer at large, might he not leave the district?'

'He might, or might not. But remember, David Rose has already been tried and condemned, so I don't know whether any killer at large would flatter me so much that he might think I could change that.'

'But it's what you intend to do, of course?'

'Of course. Criminals do tend to underestimate the police, which is why there are criminals.'

Tom chuckled.

'But then, in this colony, criminals have good grounds,' Otto added wryly. 'Anyway, who knows, my poking around may even flush a killer from cover.'

'Walker sounded most annoyed with you. Can the police order you to cease investigations?'

'Perhaps. But why would they? To pretend that it's to protect the likes of Alice Latham, maybe. No, they won't want to risk appearing to have something to hide. They'd be thinking that, in three days, Rose will be executed and it will all go away, me included.'

'A tipple more?' Tom said, reaching for the bottle after a minute's quiet reflection in the glow of the coals.

'Tempting, Tom, but I really ought to take myself off to bed.' Otto stood, and took his hat and coat from the hook.

'I feel I should be doing something,' Tom said. 'To help, I mean.'

'Feeding me a wonderful dinner is a good start!' Otto smiled, then grasped Tom's upper arm. 'Of course, I know what you mean, and just as soon as I have something for you …'

'But there is so little time, yet I wonder at times you seem to forget that — you seem so calm.'

Otto smiled. 'Would it reassure you if I turned a little frantic?'

They walked through to the front of the shop, and paused at the door to the street.

'So Joe Latham's your suspect?'

'Well, Tom, it is curious that a man who beat his stepdaughter, and threatened to cut her throat, should not have been investigated.'

'And he was charged with taking Maggie's belongings from the house three days after her death.'

'Yes, makes you wonder —'

'And she told the inquest Joe got up at ten-thirty or eleven to light his pipe, and she said he was only out of bed a few minutes. But then when the police came to her door at three in the morning, she said she and Joe had only just dozed off.'

'Maybe their marriage wasn't all violence!'

Tom frowned at the levity. Otto hastened to reassure his friend.

'It's all right, Tom. I'm just tired. But you're right, that is very curious. Maybe at 3.00 a.m. Joe had just come back from disposing of bloodied clothes? And a murder weapon, perhaps?'

27

FRIDAY 18th AUGUST
THREE DAYS BEFORE THE DAY OF EXECUTION

OTTO'S CHOICE OF ACCOMMODATION was made, he would say, because he knew the place to be comfortable and reasonable, with a good breakfast, and centrally located. That his former colleagues would see it as brazen and arrogant to take a room directly opposite their place of work had not been a consideration. But Walker's bearding him in the Argus had made him glad his visit had caused such irritation to the police; it was a measure of how much they respected him, however much they might deny it. And if the police could be agitated by his presence, a murderer at large might equally be anxious. And anxious criminals, Otto knew, make mistakes.

Yesterday morning, before his visit to Alice Latham, Otto had called in at the New Wombat Hill Company mine, just up behind the police camp, to leave a written message for George Stuart. This morning, at breakfast, he was handed a reply; George Stuart would be very pleased to speak to him, and was happy to meet at his former residence, the scene of his wife's murder, at ten that morning. Otto arrived at a quarter to; he preferred to be first at any rendezvous. If at a restaurant, for example, it allowed him to choose the table, and even the chair in which he would sit.

He might want to keep an eye on comings and goings of other patrons, or to gauge the state of mind of his interlocutor as he entered — whether confident, apprehensive, or otherwise. Otto was by a stump at the eastern side of the house when he saw George Stuart approaching along Albert Street. He'd never met the man, but he could tell by the determined, head-down step that the figure on the road was one keeping an appointment. As Stuart neared, Otto could see that he was thickset, round-shouldered, and not all that tall, as most miners seemed to be. He wondered idly whether the occupation selected the man or shaped him.

Stuart left the road and clambered up the embankment to the sloping ground that led to the windowless rear of the house. Otto was standing adjacent to the chimney, which he had decided would be the subject of his opening question.

'Hello, Mr Stuart,' he said. 'Thank you for coming. Detective Otto Berliner.' He extended his hand, and Stuart took it. He was a little out of breath; he may have been of robust musculature, but many a miner's barrel chest contained lungs scarred by the needles of quartz dust.

'Not often a man is thanked for coming to his own home,' he said, and Otto wasn't sure this was meant with wry humour.

'Chimney's repaired, I see,' Otto said.

'I fixed the barrel good this time. They're so sure the murderer knocked it over — the marks on the whitewash.'

'You don't agree?'

Stuart shrugged. 'I dunno. I don't care much now. I do know my wife used a brush to whitewash with; that could have made the marks, easy.'

'Do I assume, then, that you're back living here?'

'Not right at present, but will again soon enough. It's been near eight months.'

Here was a cue for Otto to express his condolences, but he let the moment pass; this wasn't a comfort visit.

'I suppose you're wondering why I'm here?'

'Because you know they've got the wrong man. And you know I agree with you. It's Joe Latham who killed my wife. That your reckoning?'

'He's a suspect.'

Stuart scoffed at Otto's equivocation.

'Did Latham know you were going on night shift?

'I didn't tell him; Maggie may have mentioned it to her mother.'

'Who did you tell?'

'I told Maggie. Joyce Pitman was there, too, and Louisa.'

'Your house doesn't have a cess pit, does it?'

'Not likely. There's a shaft back away over there.' He turned, and waggled a hand at the north. 'We used that, as did others.'

'The police search it?'

'I don't know how they could. There'd be forty foot down to twenty foot of shit.'

'Show me.'

Stuart grinned. 'You're the detective.'

They walked across Albert Street to a goat track along a ridge, Otto following. To the right was Wombat Hill and the young township at its skirts; to the left, the reason there was a township: goldmines, with their shedding and poppet heads, and the scalped slopes and mullock cones of their creation. Not quite fifty yards from the house, the track descended the mining side of the ridge, and in another fifty yards there it was, fenced by a desultory square of bush-cut saplings: the deep hole into which the human waste of a neighbourhood was tipped.

Stuart stopped back from the lip as Otto stepped forward to the peer into the blackness.

'It was sunk eight year ago; barely a colour come out of it,' Stuart said.

'How many houses does this serve?'

'Can't rightly be sure. There's mine, Rothery's, Clayfield's, and I'm sure Pitman drops a bucket from his brothel down there every once in a while.'

Otto walked to the other side of the opening and peered over the barrier.

'You're not going down there?' Stuart said. 'There's been eight months worth o' shit since, you know.'

Otto didn't know what he might do. He found a stone and dropped it. There was a delay of about a second, before an impact that was as much a smack as a splash. He craned for a better view, reluctant to trust the uppermost railing with all his weight. The shaft was narrow, barely a yard wide, and protruding rock precluded a view beyond a few metres. Stuart watched, bemused.

Otto stepped away, and with Stuart off-guard, said, 'Maggie told you that David Rose said he thought she was a pretty woman, that he'd like to marry her. Why didn't you speak with him about that?'

'Why would I? She was pretty, for sure, and there were many a man who'd have taken her for a wife. If I spoke to them all I'd be doing nothing else!'

While Stuart was amused by his observation, Otto kept his features straight.

'Unlike these other men, Mr Stuart, Rose made his intentions plain, to a point that caused her to speak to you about him, to say that he frightened her.'

'When she told him she was a married woman, he rightly made no more such remarks.'

'Yes, but she was still frightened of him. Didn't that concern you enough to seek him out and speak to him, if only to reassure Maggie?'

Stuart wasn't enjoying this interrogation. He shook his head and looked to the sky. Otto decided to prod a little more.

'Did you like other men coveting your wife, Mr Stuart?'

'What the fucking hell do you mean by that, Berliner?' Stuart was breathing heavily now, his nostrils flaring and his jaw jutting.

'It's a natural thing for a man to be proud to have won a woman other men could only dream of having. Maggie was a prize, and she was yours.'

Stuart advanced a few steps, to the opposite side of the barrier fence.

'You've a strange way of doing detective work, Mr Berliner, accusing me.'

'Of what am I accusing you?'

Stuart averted his eyes.

'Your wife was by nature a nervous, timid woman, wouldn't you say, Mr Stuart?'

Stuart nodded.

'I daresay that having Joe Latham for a stepfather would account for that, would you agree?'

'The man's an animal.'

'But I think you liked Maggie to be frightened. It's why you threw stones down the chimney that evening. You knew that would upset her, but you liked the feeling of power, of that beautiful young woman depending on you for protection.'

Stuart pushed off from the rail. He scratched his head, looked away and back to Otto, giving every impression that he was about to turn violent. Otto was undeterred. He pressed further.

'Only she couldn't depend on you, and now it is too late.' He saw Stuart begin to wilt. The widower dropped to his haunches and then to his knees, his face crumpling until it could not hold back the tears.

A SIGN IN THE window of the London Portrait Gallery proclaimed, 'All photographs produced in natural sunlight by the latest methods: no artificial light necessary.'

Otto hadn't taken any heed of it until now, on his return from his visit to the abandoned shaft with George Stuart. Tom Chuck asked what had raised his interest.

'I was hoping that you might have means by which to illuminate a very dark and very deep hole. It would seem from your sign that probably you don't.'

'On the contrary, my friend. But it's not a lamp — rather, a mirror.'

'A mirror. Of course. Tom, you're brilliant!'

'And you're very perceptive. But I confess it is no stroke of genius; I do use a mirror on occasion to reflect light into dark corners.'

'This is a special photographic mirror? I wouldn't want you to risk —'

'No, no, no. Nothing special — just an everyday household mirror.'

'All the same, I will tell you that should it be dropped, it will never be seen again.'

After a soup-and-bread lunch in Chuck's kitchen, and while the winter sun was out in a blue sky, the two men made a start for the shaft. Tom brought a ten-yard length of rope, which Otto considered sufficient for their first reconnoitre. As they walked the half-mile, Tom pressed Otto to share his thinking. Otto obliged, in his own circuitous way.

'Tell me again, Tom, the items produced to find David Rose guilty.'

'The pipe, the shirt —'

'Yes, the shirt. Did Pearson Thompson remind the jury that no soot was found on it, or on the victim?'

'Yes, he did.'

'The man's not a complete fool then. What else?'

'Hair samples, whiskers, spermato-whatever …'

Otto stopped and turned to his partner. 'What then, is missing from this list?'

Tom shrugged. 'Sorry, Otto, I'm no detective. I —'

'A clue, Tom. The victim's throat was cut.'

'Oh yes, of course. A knife. The murder weapon.'

'Very good, Tom! I can see where your boy gets his detecting ability,' Otto turned and resumed the mission. 'Not from you.'

They reached the shaft with the sun low in the north, an angle Otto reckoned most efficacious in collecting light for reflecting. With a heel, he removed two of the loosest of the sapling railings, laid them parallel across the mouth of the abyss, and secured them with the rope to posts of the barrier fence.

Tom was puzzled. 'Are you going down there —?'

'I just want to see what is to be seen.'

'A knife, you mean? Pardon my scepticism, Otto, but isn't that just a little optimistic?'

'Tom, I prefer "thorough" to "optimistic". My former colleagues are often optimistic, but seldom, if ever, thorough. I don't expect to see a knife, but think about this: if you were struggling to hold down your victim while you cut her throat, you would not end up with specks or spots of blood on you; you would be drenched in it. You would want to discard these clothes. And the knife, of course.'

'But here? Who would —? Oh, I see. Someone who knew of this shaft.'

'Precisely. And not many would know — certainly not well enough to find it in the dark.'

'Someone who lives nearby, you mean?'

'Or once did.'

'Joe Latham lived in George Stuart's house, didn't he?'

'He did. He built the place.'

'Don't you think that if clothes, or a knife, were thrown down there, they would have sunk out of sight?'

'Very likely, but how can we be sure? So much of solving crime is in the discovery of the unexpected. Now, enough talk. I'm going to sit astride these timbers and edge out over the shaft. When I am ready, you will hand me the mirror.' Otto climbed through the railings and mounted the boards, as if on a wooden horse.

‘That is a hellish smell coming from down there,’ Tom said. ‘You’re not afraid there might be toxic vapours?’

‘It could be worse; it might be summer. Can you imagine the flies?’ Immediately, he looked up at Tom. ‘Forgive me, Tom. I wasn’t thinking.’

With a shake of his head, Tom absolved him.

Otto crabbed forward. ‘Actually, I’m more concerned about these timbers. Can you hear the creaking?’

‘Please, Otto, let us not joke. If you fall, I’ll have to fetch you out.’

Otto was in position. ‘Now, the mirror.’

Tom reached across. His mirror was heavy; in its wood frame it had the dimensions of a washboard. Otto took it and steadied it on the timber between his thighs.

‘Now, I stand the mirror up, like so, towards the sun …’ Light flickered over lichen-covered rock that wouldn’t normally see sun till midsummer. ‘Now, I tilt it down …’ The beam slid down the uneven face of the shaft.

Tom watched, and decided that all this thoroughness of Otto’s came at the cost of rather a lot of effort, and very little promise of success —

‘Ah-ha!’

‘A knife?’

‘No. It could be clothing. It is impossible to tell from here.’

‘How far?’

‘Only twenty feet. It’s caught up on a rock or a timber, or something. It is fabric, I think. A bundle, covered in excrement, of course.’

‘So,’ Tom said, ‘I suppose you’re going down there.’

‘I see no alternative. Unless?’ He looked at Tom, who rolled his eyes and shook his head.

‘Then there is no alternative.’

‘When?’

‘Today, of course.’

OTTO AND TOM RETURNED to the shaft at five o'clock, with twenty yards of rope and a kerosene lamp. Otto had suggested that young Henry, being a lightweight, might be the best suited for the retrieval operation. It was a suggestion his father was never going to entertain.

'Yes, Otto, what could be more loving than lowering my only child into a cess pit to retrieve the blood-soaked clothes of a murderer?'

'He did say he wants to be a detective.'

Tom was appalled, and looked it.

'Maybe you could explain that to my wife.'

Otto slapped Tom's arm. 'As if I would send your boy on such an errand. Utter madness! Now, let us get to work.'

'You're very exuberant, I must say, for what you're about to do.'

'Yes, I am excited, Tom. I feel like a hound picking up the scent of a fox.'

With half an hour of sun remaining, and cloud increasing, light conditions at the shaft were gloomy. But as it was customary to empty the night soil in the morning, now was the time to mount this salvage operation. Otto removed his belt, hung the lamp from it, and rebuckled, forming a loop that would be his seat, with the lamp below illuminating the way. He tied one end of the rope to the loop, and wrapped the other once around the top rail and handed it to Tom.

'Take this back until it is taut,' Otto said.

When Tom was in position, Otto ventured out on the rails still positioned over the drop.

'You've done this before, I assume?' Tom said.

'Climb down into a cess pit?'

'You know what I mean.'

'It's time to concentrate, Tom. Brace yourself. Are you ready? Here I go.'

Otto stepped off into the void. But the only movement was a

gentle swing that took Otto's feet out and back to the rails they had just left.

'You'll have to let it out a little, Tom —'

Otto was suddenly six yards lower, and swinging hard into the walls of the shaft. His feet kicked soil and rocks free to drop into the stinking mire below.

'Otto! Are you all right?'

Tom was at the mouth.

'I'm sorry, Otto, it got away from me. I really don't think this was a good idea.'

With his stomach still in his throat and his pulse knocking in his ears, Otto wasn't disposed to speak. He felt the rope, under the strain as stiff as a steel rod, and creaking as it swung gently. The belt cut into his hips and buttocks.

'Otto?'

Otto hinged his head upwards. He could just see the top of Tom's head in silhouette. 'Still here!'

'Oh, thank God! I've tied the rope. I'm going for a horse, to get you out of there. I won't be long. Try to stay calm.'

And so Otto was left alone on his rope, hanging still but for a gentle twisting. His breathing had calmed, his heart no longer thumped, and he could believe that he was in no danger of falling. In fact, to look on the bright side, he was almost in the place he was intending to be, albeit coming to it rather sooner than he had expected. He stole a look below, to the burning lamp and the illuminated wall around it, and the bundle that had snagged there. If he reached out with his foot, he could just about touch the dirty fabric, and was almost close enough, if he dared, to reach out and hook his foot under it. He thought again. Ten or more feet below, the foul, black contents of the shaft lay glistening. If the bundle fell, this enterprise would come to naught. He would just have to bear the discomfort a little while longer, and on Tom's return he would simply be lowered a yard and a half, and the prize would be his —

A pulse passed through the rope to Otto's hands. And another. He looked up. A shadow crossed the opening.

'Tom?'

His own voice was the last sound Otto heard before he crashed into the muffled and unfathomed deep below.

Quickly he was at the surface, his lips pursed tightly against the filth, and his arms flailing for a rocky protrusion or an embedded iron spike to which he could cling. The rope, having been his lifeline, now threatened to drown him. It writhed around and over Otto, entangling his arms and pulling at his neck. Objects unknown brushed by his hands and cheeks — some solid, some disintegrating on contact. His kicking disturbed lower strata of the putrescence, and bubbles boiled to the surface, where they burst and released their acrid contents. Otto felt himself succumbing to the foetid air, and entertained the possibility that he might die there, like a fly in a pitcher plant, his tissues slowly liquefying and adding to the foul solution. God knows what it was doing to his delicate lungs. And then he saw his salvation — a cleft in the rock. He reached high, slid a hand in, and there he hung, like a gibbon on a vine, to rest a while and to wonder whether the rope had snapped or had been cut.

OTTO HAD SEEN THE first star before Tom returned. He first knew of his assistant's being there by the cry he made on seeing the rope gone. And then there he was, out on the railings, peering into the dark.

'Otto!'

'I'm here.'

'Thank God! I have a horse. And rope. I'll let it down.' Otto noted, with approval, Tom's good judgement in deferring any observations and questions.

The rope arrived, with a loop tied. Otto placed a foot therein and gave Tom the all-clear to pull, with the stipulation that the horse be paused after eight feet so Otto could collect the bundle still affixed to the wall of the shaft. The execution may have been unrefined, but this enterprise would be a success after all.

AT TOM'S INSISTENCE, OTTO was to make straight for the Victoria Swimming Baths.

'I'll take the evidence, and when you're good and cleaned up, we'll examine it, and decide what to do next, because ...' Tom held up the chopped end of the rope, 'someone tried to kill you tonight, Otto, my friend.'

Otto nodded his concurrence with the plan, and was privately grateful for Tom's taking matters in hand. For now.

'I shall bring you clothes from your hotel room,' Tom said. 'You take the horse. I'll return him tomorrow. And here's a shilling for the bath.'

All this attention was an unfamiliar experience for Otto, at least in his adult life. He expected it was akin to the kind a married man might have, and he fancied he might like more of it. Tom Chuck seemed born to deal with a crisis. A lesser man — Walker, for example — would be falling about in stitches at the sight and smell of him. Right now, though, his appearance was not his most pressing concern; the night was upon them, and with its chill air, Otto was already in a lively shiver. At least under the cover of darkness, he would go by the streets unnoticed. And not just because he was drenched in sewage; an attempt on his life had just been made, after all.

'Half a mile east along Raglan,' Tom said, and with a heave, helped Otto into the saddle and set him off at a brisk trot.

ARCHDEACON CRAWFORD WAS AT the cell door promptly after the evening meal. He'd learned that with their bellies full, the day done, and the promise of sleep, prisoners were generally rendered docile. He was hoping he might find David Rose in such a mood, or at least one of resignation.

While the clergyman had been deeply troubled by an obdurate resistance in Rose to the acceptance of his fate, he was even more deeply troubled by his own part in the publication of the letters to the paper, for these had only encouraged Rose in his delusion. Crawford had, naively he believed, thought that their writing may have been for Rose the catharsis necessary to clear the way to repentance. Alas, Crawford feared he had only exacerbated matters, for Rose was insisting that he write still more, as if innocence could be proved by repetition — and insisting even though the execution order had been issued. It was well past time, Crawford knew, to be indulging Rose's fantasy; the fact was that the court had found him guilty and that he would depart this earth in three days. It was time that his soul be readied for eternity. This, not the writing of impotent letters, or shielding the condemned man from the truth, was Crawford's sacred charge, and he was determined now, in the little time that remained, to carry it out. As the guard turned the key and slid the bolt, Archdeacon Crawford steeled himself to his mission.

OTTO WASN'T ENTIRELY HAPPY to have his clothes shoved into the fire. The cotton shirt was a gift from Helga, and the warm woollen trousers were of the most agreeable fit. Of course, he'd had no choice; no amount of scrubbing and soaking could ever remove the raw sewage now embedded in their warp and weft. And there were his leather boots, so very nicely worn-in, so very thoroughly ruined. Still, he could console himself that, at least in its demise, his erstwhile attire was serving him well by heating the sixty gallons of water in which he was now steeping.

Otto had paid for precisely twenty minutes' steeping, and he suspected that if he was ever to mix again in polite society, he would have to take every second of it. The bath was good and deep, and one of a dozen or more in individual cubicles that ringed a room-sized communal pool. Fortunately, this was unoccupied when proprietor Horatio Pensom had led Otto and his shit-plastered hair to his private compartment. Pensom handed him a quarter-brick of the yellowest soap, its smell as strong as its colour, and inspiring confidence in Otto that it would be equal to the task.

'I reckon you might need all o' that,' Pensom had quipped, with a once-over glance. Otto failed to find amusement in the remark, but smiled as if he had; the generosity was deserving of that much.

And so, at last, lying beneath the suds and scum, his most immediate concerns attended to, Otto could appreciate that his unforeseen plunge into the mire had in fact been a great leap forward — figuratively. The collection of a bundle of unknown content and provenance had been his objective, but the cutting of his rope had all but confirmed not only that the bundle was indeed connected to the case, but also that Maggie Stuart's real killer was still at large. And that he was right here in town! The adventure may have cost him his beloved clobber, but awaiting him in a bloody and shit-caked roll at Chuck's was an ensemble of inestimably greater importance.

BACK AT TOM'S, OTTO decided that Adeline's vegetable soup was indubitably the best soup he had ever sipped. Yet with urgent work to be done, he restricted himself to just the one bowl. Tom had placed the evening's pungent prize on the benchtop in his workroom, a space crowded with the paraphernalia, both arcane and familiar, of the photographic artist. Strong chemical aromas permeated the air, and for these Otto was appreciative, for they masked the odour he was sure still hung about his skin 'like a fog on the Spree', as his father might have said. With aprons on, and a lamp in position, the examination could begin. Otto played the surgeon; Tom, his assistant.

'Scissors?' Otto said. 'This is all tied tight in twine.'

Tom handed him a pair, borrowed from Adeline's sewing box. He looked behind to check she wasn't there.

'Otto?'

'Mmm?'

'Please don't think I'm making light of your misfortune today, but because someone cut the rope —'

'Hold these.'

Otto had cut the twine and handed the scissors back to Tom. He straightened.

'Yes, Tom, because someone cut the rope, we know there is someone who has a secret.' He turned to his work, slowly unrolling the sodden fabric. 'Whoever cut the rope didn't just turn up by chance; he must have known we were down there — and why. Which has me wondering, how did he know?'

'But who knew we were going to investigate that shaft? Otto, you can't possibly stay at the Albert tonight. Whoever tried to drown you will know soon enough that he failed.'

Otto smiled. 'Thank you, Tom, but I think I shall be safe; the Police Camp is right across the street.'

'You have some faith in them, then?'

Otto made no comment; his attention was to the job at hand. 'And what do we have here?'

The entire length of the bundle had been unrolled now, to reveal its composition: a cotton shirt lying face-up atop moleskin trousers, both garments heavily and darkly stained, and at the bottom end, at the hems, where the rolling would have begun, a knife.

'I am amazed,' Tom said, and put a hand on Otto's shoulder. 'You are a detective without peer!'

Otto leant over the filthy blade.

'See that, Tom? There's a hair stuck to it.' Otto reached for it, and drew it clear between thumb and forefinger.

'It's very long,' Tom said. 'Twelve inches or more.'

'What colour was Mrs Stuart's hair?'

'Red-brown, as that one appears to be.'

Otto laid the specimen on a sheet of paper. Tom thought to point out that it was paper — quite expensive paper — prepared for a portrait he'd be taking tomorrow, but thought better of it.

'This staining is blood,' Otto said, sweeping a hand over the shirt. 'I've never seen blood so long after it was spilled.'

'There's so much of it! And they found but a speck on David Rose's shirt. It really is astounding.'

Otto stood back from the bench. 'Astounding?'

'I mean, that the police didn't search the shaft. Don't you think that's astounding?'

Otto made a wry smile. 'If you knew the police as I do, Tom, unsurprising might be the word. Disappointing would be another.'

Otto lifted the knife and turned it in his hand. A sheath knife it was, the kind many a working man might use. And certainly one a murderer might employ. Its two-edged blade was six inches long, an inch wide at its broadest, and tapered to a sharp point. To it adhered a lacework patina of dried blood, which extended less obviously across the wooden hilt. It looked quite new, though the blade on one side had a chip in it, probably from inappropriate usage.

'We can be sure this is the murder weapon, can't we?' Tom said.

Otto returned the knife to the bench. 'Let's just say it's probably the murder weapon. That's sufficient to be going on with. The police were sure, and look where it led them. Now, where does Doctor Doolittle live?'

FRANK DOOLITTLE'S HOUSE WAS in Camp Street, midway between the Theatre Royal and the Court House, and a testing five-minute walk uphill from Chuck's London Portrait Gallery. At nine-thirty, it was well past time for social visits, but this was business and it couldn't wait. The evening was crisp and starlit, and the crunch of their footfall was sharp in the cold air. Daylesford was in quiet repose on this clear winter's night: yellow light spilled from windows; someone was practising violin. A dog barked; several replied. Otto and Tom reached the top of Albert Street, and turned left at the Albert Hotel into Camp Street. A new sound reached their ears. Otto stopped. He closed his eyes, and a peaceful calm settled across his features as the familiar strains of the *Hallelujah* chorus came to him across the stillness.

'Handel?' he said. 'In Daylesford?' He looked at Tom for an explanation of this unexpected treat.

Tom bridled at the implication of Otto's incredulous tone.

'Yes, the Daylesford Philharmonic Society are rehearsing. They're forty-strong — vocalists and players, and they've been performing for months now, at the Theatre Royal. I've heard they're very good, actually.'

Otto read Tom's irritation, and was quick to mollify him.

'I can hear that they're very good,' he said. They resumed their walking. 'You know, Tom, I've always thought that once a photographic artist sets up in a town, can a philharmonic society be far behind? Now, let's see what the good doctor makes of our bloody knife.'

28

SATURDAY AUGUST 19th
TWO DAYS BEFORE THE DAY OF EXECUTION

DAVID ROSE CURLED TIGHTLY on his canvas mattress and pressed his hands to his ears against the early-morning echoes of metal clanging and squealing, of the gritty footfall of the turnkey on the flagstones, of a mad inmate barking obscenities before being removed to the solitary cells, of another one whistling. He heard the metal flap in his door open, and saw the pannikin of porridge appear through it. He got up and hurried to it before the turnkey let it fall. He had yet to return with it to his mattress when the explosion went off outside and rumbled through the floor beneath his feet. In the silence of the aftermath, the turnkey chattered at him through the flap.

'Hear that, Rose? They've just blasted your grave.'

OTTO HAD AN EARLY breakfast at the Albert, and by seven he was on his way in the dawn gloom to the shaft. He didn't take up Tom's offer of accommodation — not in spite of the knowledge that his would-be killer was at large and likely to want to see his business through, but because of it. Time was short, and drawing the killer from cover was his objective now, but not to a household where a woman and child lived. Besides, he was hardly a tethered goat, unprepared and defenceless; he knew a move or two.

There'd been such heavy rain overnight he had grave doubts that any trace would be left of the rope-cutter's footprints. But if a knife discarded nearly eight months before could be found, it was a reasonable hope that after just fourteen hours, some clue might be lying there for the discovering.

The air was cold and still this morning, and the light thin with the hour and the season. Otto made his way west along Albert Street, past the West of England and Union Hotels, a bakery in full swing, a vegetable plot, several slab huts, and a vacant lot with a cow. He reached Pitman's at the West Street corner. Otto had no particular view of these so-called 'refreshment rooms', many of which were dispersed throughout the town. The standards varied, but the term was understood to be a euphemism for grog shanty, which itself was a euphemism for brothel. To Otto's mind, whatever particular nature of service was provided by any of these establishments, how grown adults amused themselves was their affair. A man was emerging from Pitman's now, tucking in his shirt and finger-raking his hair. He nodded a sheepish good morning to Otto, and shuffled off towards the town.

The road became steep here, rising in sixty yards to where George Stuart's cottage stood cold and empty. He crossed the street and joined the ridge track to the shaft. The going was heavy, and Otto's second pair of boots was barely up to the task of holding the shifting ground. He slipped and slid, but by and by made it to the scene of last evening's discovery and near-disaster. He approached the perimeter fence and stood by it while his eyes quartered the ground, rendered a coarse stucco by horse and human traffic.

A man appeared along the path. A short, thickset man he was, with sandy hair and a disposition to conflict, if Otto read his features right. A scowl looked to be his face's natural expression of repose, unless it was because he was lugging a night can. He reached the barrier fence without making any acknowledgement of Otto's presence. There he dropped the can to the muddy ground, flipped off the lid, and upended the pungent contents into the foul broth below. Some shit struck the railings that still lay across the mouth. The spatter prompted a 'Fuck!' and a little jump back.

Otto decided there was nothing to find here, and began heading back to Chuck's.

'You been speaking to my ol' lady,' the man said, in a tone that made any denial redundant.

'Well, seeing as I don't know who you are, I wouldn't know,' Otto lied, for this angry gnome surely could be none other than Joe Latham, though his wife had said he was in Adelaide.

'You know exactly who I mean, copper: Alice Latham.'

'Oh, yes. I did pay her a vis —'

Suddenly, the two yards between the two men had become half a yard, so quickly had Joe stepped across the mud. Otto felt himself flinch with the expectation of receiving a fist to the face. The man's diminutive stature made him all the more threatening, since it was clear he saw Otto's four inches' height advantage as no disadvantage to him.

'Who the hell are you, to be asking my missus questions? Have you no respect for a grieving mother?'

'First, I'm a detective, that's who I am, and secondly, of course I have respect.' Otto noticed that his cool defiance unsettled this angry little man. He pressed further. 'Why would you object to me asking your wife questions?'

'Because the murderer of my Maggie has been tried and convicted, but now you want to stir it all up and put her poor broken-hearted mother through all that pain again.'

'If the wrong man is hanged, that will be no comfort to your wife, or to anyone. Except the real killer.'

Otto was watching Joe's features very closely. Did they reveal a guilty conscience? It was impossible to tell, with the man's anger a mask.

'Do you always empty your nightsoil here, Joe? I'd have thought it a bit out of the way.'

'What's it to you?'

'Well, as this shaft would be the perfect place to dump evidence, maybe you've noticed some suspicious activity?'

Joe scoffed. 'Why don't you leave well alone? Didn't you coppers already get all the evidence you need?'

'That's what a lot of people think, Joe. But you know what, I think they've got the wrong man over there in Castlemaine. I think someone else killed your stepdaughter, and I'm going to prove it. You'd be happy to know the truth, wouldn't you, Joe? And your grieving wife?'

MUCH AS THEY LIKED, or wanted, to think of Otto Berliner as an irrelevance, some of Daylesford's police officers could not quite manage to ignore their former colleague when he made an appearance at the station at eight-thirty in the morning. His mere presence brought on a stiffening of faces, a muting of voices, and a quickening of steps. They'd resented his being called in by Nicolson to help with the hunt for David Rose, and they resented him now, coming to prove them all wrong about the very man he'd helped them to apprehend. It was unfortunate, then, for the locals that Superintendent Nicolson happened to be in town from Melbourne this day, for now Otto could ignore them right back. However, when Otto apprised him of his discovery in the shaft, Nicolson had promptly called Sergeant Telford and Detective Walker for a meeting.

'Gentlemen, Detective Berliner, as you are aware, has been in town these past few days — in his own time, mind — making enquiries.'

'Yes, we've heard, Sir. Into a case that's done and dusted,' Telford said, folding his arms and shifting in his seat as if preparing to fart. 'Crime must have taken a holiday in Melbourne.'

'Sir,' Walker said, 'while I think we should hear Berliner, it should be remembered that we are very busy, and manpower is limited enough without reopening cases that have been lawfully concluded.'

'And I agree with you, Walker. Though I think you'll find that what Berliner has to say at least warrants our attention. What happens thereafter is not under consideration. Berliner …'

'Thank you, Sir.'

Otto lifted his bag and placed it on the table. With the others standing at each of the other three sides, he took out the bundle and unrolled it, until the knife was revealed at the hems of the trousers, the position in which it had been originally put.

'These items, gentlemen, I recovered in the bundle I have just unrolled, from an old shaft up by the Stuarts. They used this shaft, as did others of the neighbourhood, as their cess pit. You'll note the staining on the clothing and the knife. While it might not appear to be blood, it is blood, as I would expect it to appear eight months after leaving the body. Doctor Doolittle has examined the knife, and confirmed that it could well be the murder weapon.'

'And these items were thrown down this shaft?' Nicolson said.

'Yes, Sir. The bundle snagged on the side of the shaft before it could reach the bottom.'

'Why the devil wasn't this discovered before?' Nicolson said. 'It would have brought Rose's trial forward by months, and silenced this clamour that the evidence was inadequate. Was the shaft even searched? Walker?'

Walker shrugged. 'Sir, I can only say that our investigations led to the pipe being the most promising evidence for a conviction. As for the delay in bringing Rose to trial, I think it was proved unnecessary anyway.'

Telford backed his colleague. 'He's right, Sir. It was the pipe that sealed it for Rose. The trial could have started weeks before. Months even.'

'Precisely,' Walker said, with a nod to the wisdom of the sergeant.

This, Otto thought, was the feeblest of arguments. But his concern was not with debating two petty men who would argue that black was white if it meant they wouldn't have to agree with him; it was with Nicolson's assessment of the evidence. He went to this now.

'Sir, we ought not assume that these items belong to David Rose. The possibility remains that they are not his, and while it does —'

'Detective Berliner, you seem to be implying that David Rose's guilt is brought into question by these items?'

'There have been questions about this, in the community. I think there may be more, if such evidence is not examined before sentence is carried out next Monday. And who knows what other evidence lies undiscovered?'

Walker scoffed elaborately.

'You're saying Rose has been wrongfully convicted!' He turned to Nicolson. 'I take offence at that, Sir.'

Otto paid no regard to this. He kept his remarks directed at the colony's most senior detective.

'Whether I think Rose was wrongfully convicted or not, Sir, is not important. I simply say that the ownership of the items, and how they came to be where they were found, ought to be investigated, and, while they are, there should be a stay of execution. After all this time, what is the hurry to despatch Rose?' To this question, Otto well knew that from Walker's point of view, the answer was a thirty or forty pounds reward.

Nicolson weighed Otto's words a moment, but Otto saw no sign that they were swaying him.

'Detective Berliner, you may not be aware that for three days the Executive Council — and that includes none other than Chief Secretary McCulloch and Attorney-General Higinbotham — have sat with Governor Darling, and Judge Barry, might I add, to ascertain whether there is any foundation for objecting to the verdict. They found none, which is why Governor Darling signed the death warrant on Tuesday last. Yet you expect all their deliberations, and those of the court, to be suspended because you found some articles down a shaft?'

'But these items were not —'

'Berliner! Enough! The whole of the evidence was meticulously reviewed: the clothes, the pipe, the movements of Rose, the words he spoke to the victim. Everything! Every pain was taken to arrive at a just decision.'

Otto could sense the movement of Walker's nodding head, and the glee within it at this dressing down.

Nicolson walked to the window. It seemed to Otto that the man was trying to convince himself as much as anyone. 'These items you've brought us don't alter anything. I daresay they probably only vindicate the verdict.' He crossed to the table and pointed to the trousers. 'Rose was seen wearing moleskins by several witnesses. And this shirt fits a description by several witnesses. And the size is right.'

'So is the state of 'em,' Walker said, with a smirk.

'Rose did have a habit of discarding shirts,' Telford added, lest he hadn't made it clear that his position was with the other two. 'The bastard has some standards then, eh Thomas?'

Nicolson ignored the levity; he was encouraged by the support, and seemed no longer agitated by Otto's challenge. He pointed to the knife. 'You say Doolittle confirmed this knife could have inflicted the wounds on the deceased?'

Otto nodded, but Nicolson pressed on.

'We know Rose had a knife. So this is probably it. Walker?'

'I'd say it was most likely, Sir, covered in blood like that, being found near the house —'

'And what if it isn't Rose's?' Otto knew, even before he'd said this, that no good would come of it.

'Then it's just a knife wrapped up in some clothes, and tossed down a shaft,' Walker said, prompting Otto to consider how curious it was that no one had asked how the items were retrieved.

There was a pause in the discussion. Nicolson began to gather his things. Walker and Telford stood. But Otto wasn't ready to end the discussion.

Hastily, he said, 'I thought you might have asked me how I managed to retrieve these items, but then I suppose you must have assumed that I lowered myself down into that hideous pit by means of a rope —'

'It's a pity it didn't break,' Telford said, eliciting a chuckle from Walker. 'I'm only jesting, Otto,' Telford added with mock contrition. 'That would have been no laughing matter.'

'Thank you, Lawrence. Your concern is comforting. But, you see, there is a saying, I think, about truth in jest —'

'Can we get to the point, please, Berliner,' Nicolson said, loading a satchel. 'I have ten minutes to be on the nine o'clock coach to Melbourne.'

'Very well then, Sir. I was suspended in that shaft when the rope was cut.'

Looks were exchanged, and when the thinking behind them — Walker's and Telford's — was revealed, Otto could hardly have been surprised.

'So you fell in?' Walker said. 'Into the shit?'

Telford was shaking his head, barely able to disguise his amusement. 'Jesus Christ!'

Otto looked to Nicolson. 'Well, Sir, of course you know what this means, surely?'

'Yes, Berliner, it would seem you're lucky to be alive.'

Otto's exasperation was leaking from every pore. 'Sir, someone doesn't want me investigating. Surely that much is obvious!'

Nicolson was having none of Otto's argument.

'Berliner, *I* don't want you investigating, but I won't stop you, or you'll be sure to be accusing me of a conspiracy. Though I must caution you, with these officers bearing witness, this investigation of yours has no official authority, and by its very nature only encourages speculation and disquiet in the community. The public must be confident in its police and judiciary. What you are doing casts doubt, and foments unease. The evidence presented established Rose's guilt *beyond all reasonable doubt*. This knife, these clothes — your falling into the mire — change nothing.'

'So why not prove ownership then, at least for our own consciences?'

'But my conscience is clear, Detective Berliner,' Nicolson said.

Walker was quick to fall in behind his boss. 'And mine.'

Telford stood and left the room, shaking his head.

OTTO HEADED TO THE London Portrait Gallery feeling disappointed, irritated, and outraged, though not surprised. This was the Daylesford police force, after all, fiercely incompetent and defiantly uncommitted. He knew there was no realistic prospect that police resources would be directed to follow up his investigation, much less that a stay of execution would be called. It was just that on finding Nicolson there — the Superintendent of Detectives, for heaven's sake — he had entertained a small hope of eliciting a favourable response, if only because the superintendent might convey concerns about the case more easily to those who had the ear of the governor. But then, in Otto's experience of the Victoria Police, rank was no indicator of ability or good judgement.

At least his conscience was clear; he'd simply had to inform the police of his discovery, and the circumstances of it. And now that he had, the burden of their inaction would be theirs. He was relieved that Nicolson hadn't barred him from continuing his inquiries; just why the superintendent hadn't was perhaps down to him being chary of provoking a man who might protest, take things to a higher authority, and embarrass him. It was a calculated risk, for Otto knew that if he were successful in saving

Rose, the superintendent, and many others, would be wearing embarrassment aplenty, and what a day of triumph that would be!

But could he save Rose, in just three days?

Tom Chuck was sweeping the veranda boards when Otto arrived at the gallery.

'Good news?' he said.

'In part. The police will not be interfering with my investigations; but, no, they will not be seeking a stay of execution.'

'So what can we do?'

'Find the owner of the knife.'

'By Monday morning?'

'If not sooner. How is the photograph?'

'Very good, I must say. The detail is excellent.'

'Of course! You are an artist. Show me.'

Tom led the way to his workroom. 'And may I say, what a masterstroke of yours it was to ask me to take it.'

'That is too generous; I knew the police would keep the evidence, so it was hardly —'

'You also knew Nicolson would be unlikely to stand in the way of your investigations if he knows you don't actually have the evidence.'

Otto hadn't thought of this. 'Quite right, Tom.'

They were at the table where the photograph lay. Otto bent forward to examine it closely.

'You know, I think the black-and-white image shows details not readily apparent in the real article. Can this be the case?'

'Indeed, Otto, it can. Colour can be a distraction, and the length of exposure can highlight certain features. Look at the grain in the hilt, and the chipped blade. I'd say it was dropped.'

Otto stood up. 'Most important, I think, is that the knife is not of a common look, so there are likely very few about. Also, it looks to be quite new, and thus, we can surmise, purchased recently — which increases the odds that it was sold here in Daylesford.'

A broad smile formed across Tom's face. 'Henry!' he called.

Footsteps rang on the floorboards, and presently the boy appeared in the doorway. On seeing Otto, he blushed.

'Let's show Detective Berliner what you found.'

Tom went to a drawer and took out a photograph. He brought it to the table.

'I took this photograph almost a year ago,' Tom explained. 'It's Kreckler's, the tobacconist. That's him there, with his assistant out the front of the shop. He wanted a portrait of his business.'

'So why —?'

'Isn't it hanging proudly in Mr Kreckler's shop? A good question. See that?' Tom pointed to a ripple in the paper. 'We had a little mishap, didn't we, Henry?'

The boy hung his head, but his old man was kind. He tousled his son's hair. 'It's all right now. We learned our lesson: no lemonade in the workroom! But now, my boy, show Detective Berliner your discovery.'

The boy set his embarrassment aside to explain, 'I saw Pa's photograph of the knife, and I remembered seeing this. Look there.' Tom pointed to the Kreckler image, near where the illicit lemonade had done its work. Otto took the magnifying glass offered by Tom and craned forward to examine the image. And there, among the smoking paraphernalia on display in the window, was a knife.

'My God!' Otto said. 'It's the same! Perhaps not the very same, but the same make. It's unmistakeable, no doubt about it: the hilt, the blade, the insignia ...' He stood back and put a hand on Henry's shoulder. 'You are indeed a detective, young man.' He turned to Tom. 'I shall go at once to Kreckler's, and see if he can recall selling such a knife.'

Otto noticed Tom's bewilderment. 'You have something on your mind?'

'Forgive my ignorance of police work, but we both agree that David Rose is not guilty?'

'Yes, of course.'

'But we haven't mentioned any other suspect. I was wondering whether we should have, by now? So that our investigation might be more focussed in a certain direction.'

On hearing this, Otto felt, of all things, a stab of irritation. Clearly, Tom saw himself as a partner, but in Otto's eyes he wasn't a partner; he was an assistant. There was a difference, and Otto knew he should have taken more care to delineate their respective roles. Now, he knew he had to be delicate lest he insult his friend or hurt his feelings, or, worse, lose his trust.

'Tom, if this case has proved anything, it is that in gathering evidence, one should not be biased in that endeavour by a premature settling on any particular suspect. David Rose was suspected, and evidence was then gathered and manipulated to vindicate that suspicion. Now, in our investigation we will not make the same mistake. We are gathering evidence and pursuing legitimate and logical lines of inquiry, uncompromised and unprejudiced by preconceptions.'

Tom nodded, though Otto saw that he wasn't entirely convinced by the verbosity.

'When the time is right, I promise, we will have our suspects. Then we shall discuss how we proceed from there.'

Tom didn't appear satisfied, and Otto was not a little peeved that he had the temerity to question him.

'But what about Joe Latham?'

'Latham does present as the most likely. But then, he always has, since even before Rose was arrested.'

'But if he's in Adelaide, he couldn't have cut the rope. I'm very confused, Otto. I just want to feel some progress is being made.'

'Actually, Tom, he's not in Adelaide. His wife misled me. He was at the shaft this morning.'

Tom made a look that could only mean that he felt snubbed. Otto hastened to reassure him.

'Tom, don't be impatient. Impatience is the enemy. We collect evidence, and we build a picture. It may seem blurred, a confusion of contradictions, and then suddenly it's all in focus, it all makes sense. I expect it's a little like taking a photograph.' He smiled. 'We'll talk tonight. Now, I should be on my way to Kreckler's. I'll have to take this.' He held up the photograph of the knife.

Tom nodded.

Otto slapped his friend on the upper arm. He waved the photograph. 'Never before did a detective have such an assistant!'

HAROLD KRECKLER'S TOBACCONIST STORE was near the top of Vincent Street. The front window, of which the owner was so proud, afforded passers-by a view into an Aladdin's cave of smoking accessories and apparatus. Dozens of pipes, from cheap clay varieties for the workingman to deluxe cherrywoods for the discerning gentleman, were displayed in rows on wooden shelves. There were also shaving accoutrements — from hand mirrors to strops, razors to shaving brushes — filling still more shelf space. And here and there, in the gaps, were tobacco pouches, combs, brushes ... and knives. Otto scanned the few on display, but there was none of the kind he'd found down the shaft. He stepped to the door and entered this crowded little world.

'Good afternoon, Sir.'

Otto peered through the dim interior to see that the wiry man with the round spectacles he'd spied in the damaged photograph had just greeted him from behind the counter. Otto approached, and a hand shot to the man's mouth.

'Are you Otto Berliner?' he said, with a remnant of a Westphalian accent. 'The detective?'

'I am.'

'I remember your face. But I'd heard you were back in Daylesford, asking questions about the Stuart murder. You know, I was on the jury at the inquest. A terrible business.'

Otto had only the faintest recollection of Kreckler from his time in Daylesford, which now surprised him, given the man's loquacity.

'Anyway, Detective, how can I help you?' Kreckler tilted his head, clasped his hands together, and stretched his mouth into a solicitous grin.

'First, by looking at this photograph. Have you sold such a knife?'

Kreckler took the image, and was immediately nodding in recognition.

'I did sell several of these. None left, I'm afraid.' Suddenly, a change in mood came over Kreckler like a cloud passing across the sun. His smile fell, and his eyes widened. 'Oh! Is this the knife that cut that poor woman's throat — Oh *mein Gott*! I sat through all that testimony, and all along it was the knife I sold —'

'Mr Kreckler, please. You are leaping to conclusions. Just calm yourself, and answer my questions.'

Kreckler nodded. 'Yes, of course. I apologise. Anyway, I can tell you now that David Rose was never in this shop. So if it was this knife, he didn't get it from here. And, you know, that pipe of his wasn't from here either.'

'Mr Kreckler, please, just answer my questions. Do you recall selling such a knife to anyone in particular sometime during last year, or even the year before?'

'I can tell you I didn't stock the knife before January or February last year. In any case, I had only four. I bought them from a trader up from Melbourne. They were excellent quality; you'll see there, it says *made in England* on the blade? Sheffield. This photograph is so detailed. Did Thomas Chuck —?'

'Can you remember who bought the knives?'

'Good heavens, no! Except for one. I remember because it was a woman. Not many women come into this shop, though Maggie Stuart did to buy her husband tobacco, just a day or two before — anyway, certainly very few women, none in fact, come in to buy a knife, at least not like this knife. Except there was this one woman

I remember, probably about a year ago now.'

'You know this woman?'

'I didn't, but I'm sure I'd seen her in town. She was the kind of woman a man'd notice — attractive in a certain way, if you know what I mean.'

'No, I don't know what you mean.'

'She was, you know ...' Kreckler made cups of his hands.

'Big-bosomed?'

'Yes. And very alluring. Is that the word I'm after?'

'Mr Kreckler, I haven't all day, so if you could —'

'Of course. I remember seeing her next when she was a witness at the inquest. That's when I found out who she was: Maria Molesworth. She works at Pitman's, a cheap little grog shanty in Albert Street.' He smiled, the remembering of the lady's name seemingly assuaging his horror that he might have sold her a murder weapon. And then he was aghast once again.

'You don't think she —?'

'Thank you, Mr Kreckler. You have been helpful. I would direct you to keep this meeting strictly confidential.'

Kreckler nodded. 'You have my word.'

Otto was certain that Kreckler's word counted for very little, but nodded his acceptance of it. He gathered the photograph and left. This talk had borne ripe fruit, but there was still so much to do, and only two days in which to do it. He'd been thinking about Tom and his eagerness to help. Well, Otto reckoned, now it was time to put their two heads together.

WITH HIS WOOD-CARRYING DONE and the turnkey's back turned, David Rose tore off the last rags of his calico shirt and trousers, and stuffed them into the firebox. He waited there, naked, before the boiling pots of the evening stew, enjoying the heat on his pallid skin, and a feeling akin to liberation.

'What the hell! Rose! What are you — Jesus Christ almighty!'

The turnkey stomped across the stone floor and tossed the prisoner a small tarpaulin. 'Cover yourself, you mad fuckin' piece of shit. There are women through there!' he bawled. 'Fuck you; you're going back to your cell. No stew!'

At the foot of the stone steps up to the ground floor, the condemned man was detoured with a push to the doorway of the two solitary cells.

'Looky here; both free. The governor might even give you a choice, a special treat, like.'

It was for answering back that Rose had done a 48-hour stretch in solitary — in Castlemaine, that is. At seventeen, in Tasmania, he did three days in one of these: not enough width to lie down, food served at odd times to disorientate the prisoner, and not the dimmest hint of light.

'Like your grave, Rose. All the darkness, and you'll even be standing up. But, eh, chin up, your corpse'll be facing out staring at them wide-open spaces. Forever.' The turnkey shook his head and chuckled. 'They think of everything.'

29

AT MID-AFTERNOON, AFTER A sandwich and coffee at the Argus, Otto was making his way back to Chuck's. He turned the corner from busy Vincent Street to quiet Albert Street, and was just outside the London Portrait Gallery when he felt a hand clutch at his elbow.

'Detective Berliner?'

Otto was looking at a woman in her mid-thirties, attractive in a regular way, with a kind, if troubled, look.

'Good afternoon, Sir. I'm Mrs Spinks, Sarah Spinks,' she said, a little tentative about making his acquaintance. Otto recalled the name.

'How do you do, Mrs Spinks,' he said, and doffed his hat.

She suddenly seemed more certain of herself after Otto's reception. 'You would know that I gave testimony at David Rose's trial?'

'I do know that. I also know that you were very concerned about how your testimony was presented by the prosecution.'

On hearing this, Sarah's whole being seemed to loosen, as if a great knot within her had been undone. Her eyes brightened with the confidence of one who knows she is being understood.

'It has troubled me so, Mr Berliner. See, it was I who first alerted the police to David Rose. Did you know that? It was my report that began the hunt for that man.' She shook her head, and Otto could see that she must have suffered great torment these past months.

'I do understand, Mrs Spinks. You see, it was I who led the search for Mr Rose. So, it seems, we share —'

'Guilt?'

Otto was hesitant, but nodded. 'Yes, I think you might call it guilt, if not responsibility.'

Sarah Spinks touched him on the arm. 'It's why you're here, to find the murderer?'

'I'm trying to, Mrs Spinks. But I have barely two days to do it in, and as my investigations are not officially sanctioned, I have quite a challenge. Now, you were at the Theatre Royal that night?'

'I was. On the way home, I saw a man not far from Margaret Stuart's cottage. I thought it may have been the man I saw with my children — David Rose, though I didn't know his name then — which is why I went to the police. But I wouldn't swear that it was him, and I said so at the inquest and at the trial. Now I wish I'd never said anything, because all that business about him walking in from Glenlyon would not be believed by the jury unless they took my words as proof that David Rose had walked all that way.'

Otto guided Sarah to the outer edge of the veranda; foot traffic had picked up, and this discussion was not for general airing.

'If you can recall anything else from that night —'

'Believe me, Detective, I have gone over and over that evening. I was with Angus Miller, and I have discussed it with him until I'm sure he is heartily sick to death of it.'

'What do you know of Maria Molesworth?'

The abruptness of the question threw Sarah, as Otto intended. Not that Otto had any suspicions about Sarah Spinks; he just found that much can be revealed by the unexpected question, simply in a look. For example, was Sarah surprised that Maria would be mentioned? Did she like Maria, dislike her, or feel indifferent about her? It seemed from his reading of Sarah's mild response that she and Maria were not acquainted; if there was any bewilderment on Sarah's face, it was because a woman might be of interest to Otto in his murder investigations.

'I don't know Maria,' Sarah said. 'Except that she works for the Pitmans. I saw Maria and Mrs Pitman were at Christy's Minstrels show together on the night of the murder.'

Otto nodded. Nothing new here. But then came a delayed revelation.

'I saw Maria talking to Maggie in the street.'

'When and where was this?'

'Late afternoon, the day Maggie was — they were just over there.' Sarah pointed down Albert Street. 'It was for less than a minute. I was in Gelliner's, across the street ... And now that I think of it, Maria Molesworth left the theatre early that night. Yes, near the end of the first part. But she may have just been going to the ladies'.

'Was she there after the performance?'

'I don't know. I wasn't looking for her. I didn't see Mrs Pitman after the show, either. Mr Berliner, your interest makes it impossible for me not to ask — does Maria Molesworth have something to do with the murder?'

'Mrs Spinks, I'm simply making investigations about the events of that night. And you've been much help. If you can think of anything else, I can be reached here, at the London Portrait Gallery any time. Leave a message if I'm not in.'

'I will. Thank you, Mr Berliner. I can't tell you how much better I feel for your being here.'

Otto tipped his hat, and with a smile bade Sarah Spinks a good day. He entered Chuck's premises to find the owner in the kitchen, sporting a blackened eye and a fat, bleeding lip. Adeline was attending to the wounds.

'My God! What on earth —?'

'Good afternoon, Otto,' Tom said, holding steady for his wife to dab at the blood.

'I told him not to go,' Adeline said.

'Go where, for heaven's sake? You look as though you've been in a drunken brawl.'

'Tell him, Tom.'

Tom sighed. 'I paid a visit to Mrs Latham,' he said, with a wince at the sting of carbolic.

'What! Why the devil would you do that?'

'I suspected you might not be happy about it. But only after the visit was a failure. Beforehand, I thought I was — ow! — I thought I was helping.'

'Nearly done, my poor darling,' Adeline said.

'What did I say about impatience, Tom?'

'Yes, Otto. You were right. I was stupid. Please accept my apology.'

Adeline finished her first-aid work, and Tom was free to sit up. Otto sat expectantly, prompting Tom to explain himself.

'Look, I wanted to encourage Alice Latham to speak up against her husband. He beats her, you know, and he beat his own stepdaughter. He threatened to cut her throat, for heaven's sake! George Stuart says Latham is the murderer; even Pearson Thompson thinks he is. But because his wife gave him an alibi, that's the end of the matter. Don't you see? She is the weak link, the one standing in the way of justice for her own daughter, for David Rose, for all of us.'

'Why would she lie? Why would she say Latham was home with her that night?'

Tom was on his feet. 'I don't know. She's afraid of him? She needs his support? You know, at the funeral, I heard she made such a show of praying that her daughter's killer was brought to justice, it had to be directed at her husband.'

This, to Otto, was an assumption too far. It was the kind of assumption that Tom had questioned at the trial.

'So what happened on your visit?' he said. 'I assume Joe came home and didn't approve of your being there?'

'Of course, and like the lunatic he is, he soon turned violent. And then he mentioned you, and then he good as admitted his guilt.'

'Oh?'

'He let slip something. He said he'd been looking forward to pouring — and dear, please pardon my language — a bucket of shit on your head.'

'Well, there's one mystery solved.'

'The one about who tried to kill you, you mean? Good God, Otto, why would he want to kill you, except because he was worried about you uncovering the truth? But he won't admit that, which is why I —'

'Paid his wife a visit? Yes, Tom, I see your thinking.'

'You know, Latham went back this morning to see if you were dead. He would have been surprised to see you there.'

'He was angry — which, I suppose, is one way of showing surprise.'

'Well, what do you think? He cut the rope, because he wanted to keep the evidence hidden, surely?'

Otto shook his head. 'We've made no link between Latham and the knife and clothes, yet here you are, jumping to conclusions that there is a link. Just like David Rose and the pipe!'

'I'm sorry.'

'I just wish you hadn't gone to Latham's. I'd already spoken to Mrs Latham; your visiting her only provoked the man.'

'I said I'm sorry. I just had to do something, seeing as you don't seem to want me to do anything.'

'What are you talking about! I'm the detective. What do you know about police work?'

'More than the average Daylesford trap.'

Otto thought this wouldn't be so hard. He smiled at Tom's quick wit, but Tom had up a small head of steam, and the moment of relief was short-lived.

'Otto, have you forgotten so soon? I was at the trial. If I hadn't been there, you wouldn't be here now. And on Tuesday you'd be reading about how David Rose was hanged.'

'I just wish you'd not acted without consultation.'

'Like you?'

'I'm in charge of this investigation! I don't have to consult!'

Tom hung his head, and Otto wondered whether he'd been a little strident. In the silence, he had room to think, and it occurred to him that maybe Tom's little expedition wasn't so ill-advised after all.

'You know, I don't think Latham wanted to kill me. He's an angry man, a bully. I trespassed in visiting his wife, just as you did. He didn't cut the rope to silence me. He cut it for the same reason he hit you — he hurts anyone who crosses him. He must have followed us to the shaft, so he would have known you'd be back to pull me out.'

'Then wouldn't he want to tell you it was he who'd dropped you in the muck, just to let you know he wasn't to be trifled with?'

'I'm sure he would. But I think he's smarter than to give me a reason to arrest him for attempted murder. He must have thought about that.'

'If he didn't want to kill you, then can he still be a suspect? I'm really quite confused, because who else could there be?'

'Well, Tom, after my visit to Kreckler's, I can tell you.'

ON REACHING PITMAN'S, IT occurred to Otto that he should have dressed down; the Saturday-night clientele sported a standard of attire well below his, more in keeping with the décor of bush poles, bark sheets, and rustic furniture. Not that he was there *incognito*; it was just that, with the police hostile to his presence, Otto thought there was a good case for subtlety. But owing to his recent plunge into ordure, all he had left were his tailored jacket and trousers, making him look a city gentleman who'd lost his way. But then came an unexpected benefit from standing out from the crowd: Maria Molesworth appeared from the throng and introduced herself. Otto had guessed her name before she'd said it, thanks to Kreckler's summary word-sketch.

'Would you care for a drink, Sir? Some company?'

'Thank you, no. You're Maria Molesworth, I presume? I wonder whether I might ask you a few questions?'

The smile fell from Maria's made-up face. 'What are you, police?'

'I can't deny it. Detective Otto Berliner. Is there somewhere private?'

A woman of dowdy appearance and frayed demeanour intruded. 'She's working, so her time's not hers to give. Meaning, Detective, mind you pay.'

'And you are?'

'I'm the proprietor, and as my husband is not here at present, and it's Saturday night, we've no time for questions from the police. Except paying ones, o'course. I'm sure you'd understand.'

Otto made a slight bow, and Mrs Pitman shifted herself away to serve at the bar. Maria looked ready to move.

'I won't keep you long, Maria.'

Otto reached into his jacket pocket to retrieve the photograph of the knife. He showed it to Maria.

'This knife, which I know you bought from Kreckler's, was the knife that killed Maggie Stuart, who you were seen talking —'

Maria silenced Otto with a hand on his forearm. 'Please, not here.' She turned and wove a route between and around the half-dozen or so patrons variously sitting, standing, or leaning as they chatted and laughed, and drank their way through their pay.

'Don't be long, Maria,' one called, 'I can feel something coming on!' Similar remarks were made, each drawing more snaggle-tooth chuckles and back-slaps.

Maria pushed open the door at the back of the room and led them into the small yard between the Pitmans' cottage and their business. Therein stood a room, with a lamp burning weakly in the window. Maria pushed the door open and led Otto inside. It was small and cosily furnished.

'Your boudoir? Very nice.'

The compliment did nothing to quell Maria's manifest discomfort. Her breathing was shallow, her chest heaving, and eyes wide.

'Listen to me, Detective. I bought that knife because Mrs Pitman sent me for it. She told me it was a present for her husband on his birthday last year. I haven't seen it since I gave it to her. And as for speaking to Margaret Stuart, I won't deny it.'

'What were you speaking about?'

'I can't rightly remember, but I do remember I was not very pleasant to her. I regret that now. Naturally.'

'You didn't like her?'

'I didn't know her well enough to like her or not. I get down at times, see. I was jealous of her, being pretty and married and everybody's darling.' She looked away, into the lamplight. 'And now she's dead. I must sound like a bitter old woman —'

She turned quickly to Otto.

'You think John Pitman killed her?'

Otto disregarded the enquiry. 'On the night of the murder, you were seen leaving the Christy's Minstrels show early. Where did you go?'

'What! So now you think *I* did it! This is absurd. There's a man already in gaol for Maggie's murder, and he's going to hang for it.'

'Yes, he will, at ten o'clock Monday morning. But I, and others besides, believe him to be not guilty. This knife is not his, and unless it can be shown that he ever had it in his possession, he will be executed as an innocent man. Would you want that on your conscience, Maria? Because it will be if you don't tell me all that you know, beginning with where you went when you left the theatre early that night.'

Maria was on edge, but with a nod she seemed at last to

understand that her best hope was in cooperating.

'I came home, here. I had an awful headache. I get them on occasion.'

'Can anyone verify that you were home?'

Maria hesitated.

'Maria?'

'John Pitman.'

'John Pitman saw you arrive?'

Maria nodded.

'Time?'

'Time. I don't know. It must have been soon after nine o'clock.'

'And you went to bed?'

'Yes.'

Otto scribbled in his notebook.

'Then why did Mr Pitman tell the court that you and Mrs Pitman arrived home just after eleven?'

Maria's face was blank. She shrugged.

'Where's Mr Pitman this evening, Maria?'

'In Melbourne. He told me he'd be coming back tomorrow.'

A knocking set the door wobbling in its flimsy frame, and a woman's voice barked. 'Maria!'

'I'll be there in a moment, Mrs Pitman.'

'It's all right, Maria. I'll be going now,' Otto said. He handed Maria three shillings. 'This ought to cover your time. Thank you, I'll see myself out.'

30

SUNDAY AUGUST 20th
THE EVE OF THE DAY OF EXECUTION

'YOU SHOULD NOT HAVE to be in this condition, David.' Archdeacon Crawford gestured at the irons clamped to Rose's ankles, and at the chains that linked them and clinked with his every movement. 'But you do know you gave the governor no choice; all that screaming and cursing, burning your clothes and such.'

Rose looked up. He was sitting on his thin mattress, in convict garb, his back to the wall. 'What do I care for a murderer and his rules?'

Crawford lowered himself and sat on the floorboards, his back against the wall, his legs drawn up —

The flap fell open, and a face appeared. The bolt squealed, and the door was swung in. Crawford was quickly to his feet.

Into the cell, stooping to avoid the lintel, stepped Governor McEwen and Sheriff Colles.

Rose drew his knees up to his chest, his chains rattling like coins in a sack.

'Excuse us, Mr Crawford,' McEwen said. He addressed Rose.

'Prisoner Rose, I'm here to warn you that should there be a continuation of your violent conduct this evening — stamping about, cursing and the like — I will have to put you in handcuffs.

Do you understand?'

Rose eyed his gaolers with a fierce look, and then in a transformation of his features, burst into convulsive laughter. The visitors watched, bemused, and waited for it to abate. Rose stood, and his ferocity was back. He stepped forward.

'I understand all right,' he spat, glaring at McEwen and Colles in turn, 'that you are my murderers. Do you understand that?' He looked at McEwen, and held out his wrists to him. 'Cuff me. I don't give a fuck!'

OTTO HAD SLEPT SATURDAY night on the floor at the London Portrait Gallery. He'd wanted to apprise Tom of all that had transpired that evening, of the inferences and deductions he'd made, of the uncertainties that remained. He'd wanted to discuss what was yet to be done on this last day, the day before David Rose's scheduled execution. He awoke early, after a fitful night; for the first time in the three-and-a-half days since he'd arrived in Daylesford, he was feeling a sense of urgency, of dread that all his efforts would come to naught. Before today, there'd always been tomorrow; now, tomorrow would be too late.

'Maria Molesworth and John Pitman have something more than an employer-employee association, I'm sure of it,' Otto said over boiled eggs and black coffee. He consulted his notebook: '"He told me he'd be back tomorrow,"' she said. That sounds intimate to me, something a wife or a lover might say.' He knew he might be reading too much into Maria's words, but the exigency of the situation called for him to trust his instincts, because never in his detective career had time mattered so much, and never had the consequences of failure been so grave. Besides, self-doubt was territory generally unfamiliar to Otto.

Tom was silent; he'd learned that when Otto was on a train of thought, he should be allowed to ride it uninterrupted to its destination.

'Maria went home early from the theatre, and said John Pitman would attest to that. So why did he tell the court that the women returned at eleven?'

'Because he had something to hide?'

'Precisely — an affair. Which would seem to have nothing to do with Maggie Stuart's murder, except that it was committed within an hour and a half of Maria leaving the theatre.' Otto stood. 'We know the knife was Pitman's, but what possible motivation would either of those two have to use it on that poor young woman?'

Tom was to his feet. 'Surely John Pitman is the killer? Surely now, we know this?'

Otto thought to observe that only yesterday Tom had been just as certain of Latham's guilt.

'If a pipe can hang an innocent man, Tom, a knife could do the same. Just because the knife is Pitman's —' Tom was nodding that he understood, and grimacing to show his frustration.

'Nothing is sure, Tom, not yet. But we do know at least that the murder weapon was John Pitman's, and we can assume that Maria Molesworth would not have been strong enough to hold down Maggie Stuart with one hand and cut her throat with the other.'

'Not on her own.'

Otto nodded. 'There is that possibility, yes. Let's just see how this string unravels. But Tom, we'll have our killer, I'm sure of it!'

He pulled the photo of the knife from the inside pocket of his jacket. 'You know, I should have asked you to make a photograph of the clothes. *Scheisser*!'

Otto was so caught up in this annoyance at himself that he didn't wonder why Tom now dashed from the room. He was back suddenly, and beaming like a naughty child who has been very, very good.

'There,' he said, placing on the table a photograph of the bloody garments. 'Will this help?'

Otto's mouth fell open, and his eyes sparkled. 'Tom, you are — well, words fail me!'

'I did wonder why you didn't ask me.'

Otto took the paper in his hands. 'I wonder myself, now that I have it. I thought the knife would be enough. They are unremarkable clothes, after all; anyone could be wearing these.' He gazed at the image and shook his head. 'Tom, you remind me that a good detective must always keep up with new methods!'

Tom smiled. A compliment from Otto was a rare delight, and what was more, he had never before felt so confident that Margaret Stuart's killer would be found and that David Rose would have justice.

VINCENT STREET EARLY ON Sunday morning was the scavenging ground of crows and stray dogs. That humans frequented the streets was evident only in the footprints and wheel ruts pressed into the winter mud. Soon, as beaks and maws cleared away Saturday's scraps, even the animals would abandon the town centre. But people would reappear at ten o'clock, when tolling church bells summoned them to services. As the Pitmans were sure to be among one congregation or another, Otto would delay his visit to their premises until midday. He understood that with time so tight, such forbearance would seem to some an unaffordable luxury; but Otto knew that where time was concerned, tight and ample were not mutually exclusive. It seemed that the unexpected photograph, the nourishing breakfast, and the sharp morning air had cohered to bring about this optimistic perspective. He could even see how the day would unfold to its satisfactory conclusion; it would begin now with a visit to the police station.

Otto found Sergeant Telford in the mounting yard, polishing a saddle slung over a railing. The big man looked up as Otto arrived, applied more oil to his rag, and continued. Otto stood by silently; he knew better than to submit to a petty power play. He also knew Telford couldn't hold out, and in less than half a minute the sergeant stood and spoke.

'This about the Stuart murder?'

'It is.'

'I've something to show you. Follow me.'

Telford seemed tense, which Otto found hard to fathom. He would have thought that news unpalatable to Telford had to be welcome news for David Rose.

Inside the station house, Telford handed Otto a sheet of paper on which was written, 'Schedule of Reward Payments'.

Otto looked down a list of names, alongside each of which was an amount presumably adjudged to be commensurate with each recipient's contribution to the apprehension of David Rose. He saw his own name, with '£5' written alongside it, and felt revulsion, which Telford misread.

'Not enough, Berliner, eh? I never thought I'd say it, but I'm on your side. I mean, you were the one who pointed the search in the right direction, after all. And look at the thanks I get: three lousy quid! Jesus Christ! It's bloody criminal, that's what it is. Brady gets thirty-five, Walker thirty. Fuck! Even those scoundrels Hathaway and Wolf get ten apiece.'

Otto handed back the sheet without comment. In this mood, Telford had to be handled carefully. He waited for the jealous pique to abate, and then spoke.

'I'm not here about the reward money, Sergeant. I don't want any part of it; I'm sickened that police should profit from the execution of an innocent man.'

This brought a smirk to Telford's face.

'Jesus, Berliner. You're a mad fucking detective, you are.'

Otto smiled limply, a response too subtle for the sergeant, and proceeded with the business he had come to transact. But then he saw a constable by the door.

'Your name?'

'Constable Dawson.'

'Stay there, Constable Dawson. I want you to witness what I am about to tell the sergeant here. Understood?'

'Sir.'

Otto turned to Telford.

'Later today, I will be arresting the murderer of Margaret Stuart, and the prisoner will be detained here until the arraignment.'

Telford was a picture of open-mouthed incredulity.

Otto pressed on.

'What you are to do today, Sergeant Telford, is to alert Superintendent Nicolson or Commissioner Standish, and, I suggest, the governor at Castlemaine Gaol. There is to be a stay of execution.'

Inadequate rewards had suddenly fallen by the wayside in Telford's head, which was now shaking in disbelief and, Otto suspected, contempt.

'Are you serious, Berliner, or really just fucking mad?'

'My advice to you, Sergeant, is to do as I say.'

'But it's too late, Otto! The trial, the guilty verdict, the death warrant from the bloody governor, the reward allocation ... all there is left is the noose, and that's tomorrow!'

'Which is why you will act today, or have the death of an innocent man on your head.'

Otto sensed in Telford the slightest wavering. It was a good time to leave.

'Just do your duty, Sergeant.'

OTTO'S STOMACH WAS SUDDENLY in his gullet. Joyce Pitman had just told him and Tom that her husband was in Melbourne, and that he wouldn't be returning until the one o'clock coach, Monday morning.

'There are no coaches on Sunday, Mr Berliner,' Mrs Pitman said, wiping a bench top with a rag. 'I thought you would have known that, being a detective.'

Otto knew he should have known that; it was careless of

him. Coming back on Sunday was not the same as *being* back on Sunday. He gave Maria a reproving glance, at which she flinched. She knew the urgency, all right.

Mrs Pitman straightened, her face flushed from the effort. 'But perhaps I can help you,' she said. 'This establishment is as much mine as my husband's, though he might not tell you that!' She laughed in a kind of squawk that had Otto thinking that the fewer times she was amused, the better.

'Very well, Mrs Pitman. It is a grave matter, the murder of Maggie Stuart —'

Mrs Pitman's hand was suddenly up, her face souring. 'Look, Mr Berliner, I'll not pretend any longer. I do know what you're here for. Do you think working in a place like this, I don't get to hear things? All your asking questions around town? I'll tell you one thing, and you won't like me sayin', but you deserved to be dumped in that hole, stirring up things for poor Mrs Latham. I never had no time for Joe, but after what he did to you, I could kiss the man. And Maria here told me all about the knife, so I know why you want to speak with my husband.' She moved to another bench and began to wipe.

Otto pulled out a chair and settled into it. Calmly, he said, 'Mrs Pitman, I've made no allegations against your husband. I just want to ask him, and you and Maria, some questions. You have nothing to fear if you have nothing to hide, I assure you.' He motioned to Tom for the photographs. He placed the first face up on the table for Mrs Pitman, if she would take the trouble.

'This knife, I found in the shaft, wrapped up in these clothes.' He placed the second photograph on the table. 'The knife and the clothes were bloodstained. Maria tells me you bought the knife for your husband.'

Mrs Pitman had finished wiping. She made a desultory study of the pictures.

'There must be hundreds of such knives, but yes, I did buy one like that as a birthday gift. But, you see, my husband was at home the night poor Maggie …' she pulled out a chair and slumped into it, her face in her hands.

'I can verify that,' Maria said. 'I already have. I told you, I had a terrible headache —'

'Yes, I know,' Otto said, 'both you and Mr Pitman were here while Mrs Pitman was out. What I don't understand is why Mr Pitman lied in court — why he said you, Maria, returned home at eleven.'

Otto noticed Mrs Pitman's silence, and the furrowed look that revealed a mind busy either with confusion or calculation. It was Maria who took up the challenge.

'I think, Mr Berliner, that is a question for Mr Pitman. So perhaps you can come back tomorrow?'

'By which time it will all be too late anyway, because the murderer will be dead,' Mrs Pitman said. 'And I've never seen my husband in these clothes,' she added, stabbing the image with a blackened and chipped fingernail. 'So, you two can piss off, or I'm going to call the police down here and make a complaint.'

Otto exchanged a look with Tom. They were agreed; they were washed-up here, and their investigation seemed to be lying in tatters.

SERGEANT TELFORD, DETECTIVE WALKER, and Constable Brady invited themselves into Otto's room at the Albert Hotel. There was threat in their number and swagger, and, at eight o'clock on a Sunday evening, in their timing. Otto had just returned from Chuck's, where the disappointment of the day had been put behind them with a discussion of strategy for the morrow. They would be at Pitman's early in the morning, and an arrest would be made — of that, Otto was convinced. But for now, he had this tableau of folded-arm menace before him, and if he didn't take care, there would be no tomorrow for his investigation.

'We've had a complaint,' Walker said.

'Just the one?'

'Don't be clever, Berliner. Pitman's ol' lady says you've been making accusations about her husband.'

'I've made no accusations. I simply asked her some questions about the knife and the clothes — which you have — and importantly, why her husband lied in court. Did you know he lied in court?'

'Only yesterday, you were cautioned by Superintendent Nicolson not to go upsetting the public, undermining the court —'

'I think Berliner's in contempt of court, actually, Detective Walker.'

'I think you might be right, Sergeant Telford.'

'So, are you going to arrest me?' Otto said. 'Is that why you're here?'

Walker and Telford exchanged a smirk. Brady stood by, wanting to join in, but too uncertain of his place. Otto fancied the young man was intimidated.

'No, Otto, the sooner you're out of town the better,' Walker said. 'Can you imagine, Lawrence, having Otto Berliner in the lock-up? Having to listen to his shit ...'

'Having to empty his shit,' Brady ventured, and was rewarded by his colleagues with a snigger.

Walker let the smile slide from his face. He stepped forward so that he was toe to toe with his rival.

'Tomorrow morning at ten o'clock, David fucking Rose will be dead, and you, Detective Berliner, will be where you can do no harm, on the Melbourne coach halfway to Malmsbury. Brady here will be with you, to make sure you get away all right.' He donned his hat, and turned to Telford. 'We done?'

Telford nodded and led Brady out.

'Only three pounds reward for you, Lawrence, don't forget.' Otto called, to no response.

Walker was at the door.

'So, the coach leaves at nine tomorrow morning, Otto. You be sure to be on it.'

31

MONDAY AUGUST 21st
THE DAY OF EXECUTION

DAVID ROSE AWOKE AT seven to a breakfast of sausages, fried eggs, and bread, and a mug of tea, brought by the turnkey who had kept watch over him overnight.

He also brought a bible, from which he began to read. With a grimace and a flourish of his fork, Rose bade him stop.

'Not now.'

The turnkey closed the book.

'So,' Rose said, 'this be the last morning I got to see.' He chewed as he stared thoughtfully into the candle flame. Suddenly, he turned to the gaoler. 'Mind now, you keep well away from women. It's what's brought me here.'

AT 7.00 A.M., WITH the dim glow of the rising sun at the back of Wombat Hill, Otto Berliner was striding down the hill through cold and thickening mist to the London Portrait Gallery. Despite the damp atmosphere and the urgency of his mission, there was a bounce in his step, for he had a plan that would catch a killer. It satisfied Otto that, for all their menaces, the three policemen had not caused the minutest waver in his resolve, and he would certainly not be departing on the nine o'clock coach. At the gallery, Tom was waiting outside, as had been arranged the day before.

'What if Pitman wasn't on the coach from Melbourne last night?' Tom said.

'But he was on the coach, Tom. I even know it arrived five minutes late.' He brandished a scrap of paper. 'A little note from the driver was awaiting me at breakfast.'

Tom slapped Otto's back, and the two men allowed themselves a small celebration that the day had begun as well as could be expected.

Pitman's was a bare three hundred yards from Vincent Street, and Otto and Tom stepped beneath its flimsy veranda as a curtain of rain from the west swept into town. Otto knocked hard, and, a half-minute later, Maria Molesworth unbolted the ill-fitting front door and let them in. In her face, Otto sensed there might even be some relief that he had come. In the early morning, without the yellow candle glow, the room was a cold and austere place. Rain pattered on the bark roof and smacked the ground as it cascaded from the overhang.

Otto removed his hat. 'Morning, Maria. Would you mind fetching Mr and Mrs Pitman? I must speak with them.'

She nodded and left.

'Thank you,' he called after her.

'I think we should brace ourselves for a storm,' Tom said. Whether he meant one of a meteorological kind, Otto didn't wonder; he was steeling himself for what he had to do.

Husband and wife appeared as two halves of a wild-haired beast roused from its den. John Pitman's socks were holed, his trouser braces dangling; Joyce was in her petticoats, with a little modesty lent by a shawl. She led the objection to this early-morning intrusion.

'I'm not having this harassment, I tell you, Berliner. Maria, you go fetch Sergeant Telford —'

'That won't be necessary, Mrs Pitman,' Otto said, 'because I'm here to arrest your husband for the murder of Margaret Stuart.'

All eyes, Tom's included, were on Otto, who wondered whether it would have been possible to throw a bigger cat among the pigeons.

Joyce Pitman slumped into a chair and turned a stricken look on her husband, who looked unconvincing in his expressions of outrage.

Maria was the first to speak in protest. 'No, it's not true!'

'Convince me then,' Otto said.

John Pitman spoke. 'Well, I can tell you, Detective, as God is my witness, I never killed that poor woman. I'd never so much as harm a hair of her pretty head.'

Otto showed Pitman a photograph of the knife.

'Is this yours?'

'I told you it is already!' Mrs Pitman said, heaving herself to her husband's side.

'Yes,' he said, 'like my wife says. It's my knife. It looks like my knife.'

'And these clothes?' Otto handed him the photograph.

'I've already told him they're not your clothes, John,' Mrs Pitman said, with great exhalation.

Pitman was studying the image, while Mrs Pitman remained in a state of irritation alongside.

'Yes, Detective, these are my clothes.' He turned to his wife. 'Look, on the shirt, that's that odd button you put on. And that little tear on the leg. Don't you remember, you stitched that? How you could get that wrong?'

Mrs Pitman craned for a closer look. 'Oh, yes! You're right, love.' She straightened. 'I've made so many repairs to your clothes, I forget! Goodness me. But these are so dirty —'

'When I tell you that your knife, Mr Pitman, was found by me and Mr Chuck here, wrapped within these garments, in a mine shaft within a hundred yards of Stuart's cottage, you'll understand why we're asking you these questions. You see, the knife has been identified by the eminent Doctor Doolittle as one that could well have inflicted the fatal wounds on Mrs Stuart. And you see those stains? They're not dirt, Mrs Pitman. Some are excrement, but most are blood — Maggie Stuart's blood, we can be certain.'

Pitman began to pace. He ran a hand through his greasy hair and across his thick stubble.

'This is madness. A man has already been convicted, for Christ's sake!'

'That's right, love,' Mrs Pitman said. 'Say nothing. David Rose will be dead by ten.'

It was good advice, Otto had to concede. He would just have to provoke them all the more. And bluff.

'I'm sorry, Mr Pitman, but if no one can corroborate your whereabouts between ten and eleven on the night of December 28th, I shall order a stay of execution while your involvement is investigated —'

'You can't do that,' Mrs Pitman scoffed. 'He's bluffing, love —'

'For Christ's sake, be quiet, Joyce! Look, Berliner, they are my clothes, all right? But I never killed Maggie! I was here, the whole evening.'

Mrs Pitman was on her feet, moving to her husband. 'Of course you didn't! Tell him nothing, love,' she said. 'Detective Walker told me Berliner's got no authority.'

Pitman pushed his wife's reaching hand away and turned on her.

'Why do you care so much what I say? I have nothing to hide.'

She reached for him again, and again he swept her away.

'Mr Pitman, if you can prove that you were here between ten and eleven that night, you will have no case to answer, and I promise you Mr Chuck and I will leave you in peace.'

Otto looked to Maria, and saw in her quivering lips and ashen face a woman in conflict. He was certain now of his hunch; she had come home early, and had spent those hours with her employer, her lover. *My God*, Otto thought, was she really weighing her secret affair against a man's life?

'I was with him,' she said.

The room was silent. Outside, water dripped and the wind whistled.

Mrs Pitman stood heaving, as a volcano blows ash before erupting. But Maria wasn't waiting.

'Don't worry yourself, Mrs Pitman, I'm not proud of myself. There was no love in it; it was a one-time business arrangement.'

'I know you're lying,' Mrs Pitman said.

'What the hell, Joyce? Don't you see, she's just given me an alibi!'

'I might have known she'd be turning tricks behind my back.' Mrs Pitman was glowering — a fearsome sight with her hair all awry.

'So what, Joyce, we had a fuck! We run a brothel, remember!' Pitman couldn't suppress the merest chuckle, though he was red-faced in disbelief and fury at the woman he suddenly seemed to find so repulsive. Tom readied to intervene lest he assault her. Otto signalled to stand to and let them have it out. Far from being intimidated by her spouse, Mrs Pitman met the challenge full-on.

'I don't care now if they hang you, John. Now I think about it, you probably did kill Maggie Stuart, 'cause she would've turned you down. She had too much class for the likes of you —'

Pitman had been thinking. He looked at his wife, his eyes a window to a brain recalling events and making calculations.

'How did you know, eh?' he said, waggling his index finger at her. 'How did you know?' He walked away, agitated, muttering. Something occurred to him. He spun to face her. 'The day after the murder, in this room, I remember, you said Maggie was drenched in her own blood, and "lying up there like that", exposed, violated. How would you know how she was lying? How would you know her nightdress was up, that she was violated? How would you know that?'

Mrs Pitman affected puzzlement. 'Everyone knew. Word gets around.'

'Not that fast! You knew hours after she was found, how she was lying — across the bed, legs apart, dress up, like someone had raped her. You knew all that! So who told you? Because I didn't!'

Mrs Pitman approached her husband. 'John, you've explained where you were that night, so the police can leave now.' She faced Otto. 'Like you promised.'

Otto tore a page from his notebook and dashed off three lines. He gestured for Tom to come.

'My colleague will take this note to the Telegraph Office. The message will be transmitted to Castlemaine, ordering that the execution of David Rose must not go ahead. He will then summon the police here to make the arrest.' He glanced at the clock above the door. It was a minute to nine. He knew the police would see he wasn't on the coach, and would be here within ten minutes anyway.

Tom took the note and departed.

DAVID ROSE WAS LED from the condemned cell directly onto the first-floor gallery of the gaol's central wing. Before him lay the drop; it formed a metal bridge across the corridor to the gallery on the other side. Above it was the beam with the fateful rope dangling from it.

He stood calm and composed outside the cell door, dressed in prison garb, with only socks on his feet.

'I'll not be hanged in my shoes,' he'd declared, and no one had denied him.

Alongside him was Archdeacon Crawford, given the signal now by the sheriff to guide the prisoner forward. Rose moved unassisted, though he'd been pinioned, his ankles strapped and arms pulled in a hug across the front, with his wrists tied at the back. He shuffled onto the bridge, keeping to the iron railing, and at the centre he stopped. He looked down at the sixty witnesses looking back at him from the ground floor. He did not flinch, nor sway, nor pant.

Crawford read a prayer, then gathered himself to address the prisoner in an unsteady voice.

'David Rose, in the name of God, just and merciful, who knows all things, and into whose awful presence your soul is now about to be sent, and before whom I warn you not to appear with guilt unconfessed, and with a lie. In his name, as his minister, I call upon you to answer in truth this question, ere it be too late. Did you murder Margaret Stuart?'

Into the cold silence, Rose replied, distinctly and deliberately, 'I did not.'

MRS PITMAN WAS AT Otto's ear. 'Arrest? What are you talking about, Berliner? My husband was home all that night, even if it was with this cow.' She rounded on Maria. 'There's nothing lower in this world than a cheating whore.'

'Mrs Pitman,' Otto said, blocking her line of sight to Maria, 'George Stuart told me that the only people he told about his night shift were his wife, the girl Louisa Goulding, and you. No one else.'

'I don't remember it.'

Otto saw her glance at the clock. Ten past. He could sense that the moment of resolution was very near.

'Mrs Pitman, you're a jealous woman, aren't you? Jealous of Margaret Stuart, in particular, the beautiful young neighbour who walked by this house every day. You couldn't compete with that; you knew your husband had designs on her, and, like many men, would have been intimate with her if she allowed it.' Otto turned to Pitman. 'To be fair to you, Mrs Pitman, I think such a conviction would be well founded. Your husband is most probably a man of considerable moral elasticity.'

Pitman shook his head, in a concession that any words of protest he might utter would ring hollow.

Otto turned back to Mrs Pitman. 'But surely not so morally

elastic that he would countenance murder of the woman he desired?'

Here Pitman found his voice. 'I told you I would never harm that girl.'

Mrs Pitman had been silent and still, offering no protest, and Otto knew it was time to increase the pressure. 'Mrs Pitman, I believe you left Christy's Minstrels early that night, changed into your husband's clothes — you had them secreted somewhere, in your woodshed maybe — and, so attired, you paid a visit to the Stuart cottage.'

'Dressed as my husband? That is ridiculous.'

'No, Mrs Pitman, not dressed as your husband, but as a man. These were ordinary clothes that any man could have worn. Even you didn't recognise them,' he added, allowing himself a smirk.

Mrs Pitman jabbed a finger at the photograph. 'There's no soot on them clothes. How can that be when the killer came down the chimney?'

Otto shook his head. 'You came through the front door, Mrs Pitman. I know this, because while there was blood on the doorknob, there was none on the key, which meant that Maggie must have unlocked the door to let her killer in. This means she knew who it was who'd come knocking at that late hour. Further, George Stuart said the marks on the chimney were not made by clothing, but by the brush his wife used to whitewash with; I've read the trial reports, the inquest transcript, and, most importantly, heard Mr Chuck's meticulously detailed first-hand account, so be assured that I am fully informed.'

Pitman was staring at his wife. '*You* killed Maggie?' He spun away from her, turning his head this way and that, as if searching for explanation amid the furniture. Maria Molesworth sat in a corner, stricken and motionless.

Mrs Pitman was on her feet, glancing at the clock. Otto finished what he'd started.

'You took that knife, and you went in disguise because your

intention was to kill Maggie Stuart. You could have changed your mind, but there you were, in her house, this beautiful young woman in her nightdress. And there's you. What else could you do, but kill her? You're a large and powerful woman, Mrs Pitman, and you used your advantage to hold Maggie down, while you stabbed this knife again and again at her throat. And when you were done, you arranged the body of this virtuous young woman in the most egregious manner. What a cold, calculating woman you are, Mrs Pitman.'

Joyce Pitman stood very still, her face unreadable. Was she simply dumbfounded by outrageous allegations, or pondering what she should do, now that the truth was out? And then she removed all doubt with a glance at the clock. She smirked. 'Twenty-five past nine, Detective. Looks like your assistant has failed —'

John Pitman's hands were at his wife's shoulders, swivelling her so close that she could breathe his rage and incomprehension.

'Please, Joyce, for pity's sake, tell me you didn't do it,' he said in breaking voice.

For a moment, it seemed that Mrs Pitman was considering a denial, but even she could see it was too late for that, and now the whole horror of her jealousy spilled from her mouth.

'How could I go on living in this place, while ever she was next door! I saw you, looking at her, and don't you deny it—'

'You murdered her for that! You stupid, mad woman! Of course I looked at her. And I'll tell you this, Joyce, I imagined her in my bed. What man wouldn't? She was beautiful—'

Here was a word above all words to stab into Mrs Pitman's very heart. She broke away, angry and fierce, as if her husband's admission had vindicated her crime.

Horses came to a stop outside. Loud knocks set the front door shaking.

Mrs Pitman hurried to open it, to Telford, Walker, and Brady. Otto saw what she was up to. If she got away long enough for

Rose to hang, she'd be untouchable.

'Sergeant Telford, thank God.' She pointed at Otto. 'That man is harassing me and my husband.'

She bustled by the policemen and into the street.

'Stop her, Telford, for heaven's sake!'

But Telford was having none of it.

'Give up, Berliner.' He grinned as he advanced on Otto, while Walker and Brady stood guard at the door. 'We gave you fair warning, Otto, but you're just too bloody pompous for your own good.'

Telford was close now. Mr Pitman was making for the door, to set out after his wife. Walker and Brady stood aside to let him through. Otto saw a chance, and took it. In a moment, he was at Pitman's side and slipping out with him.

On Albert Street, the rain had eased and traffic had built up. Mrs Pitman was thirty yards towards town, glancing behind as she bustled on. Her freedom was a matter of the smallest delay. Had the telegram got through to Castlemaine, Otto wondered. Had Tom even sent it? He should have been back by now. Otto felt Telford's meaty hand on his shoulder. He broke away in pursuit of the killer.

'Berliner!' Telford barked, as Otto closed in on his suspect. Mrs Pitman saw him, and struck out across the boggy street. An outbound coach was approaching. Mrs Pitman made her dash, but hadn't reckoned on the thick mud; her dress and feet anchored her, and she fell flat to the road before the pounding hooves. The driver shouted, but he was too late; his wheels had already ridden over her limp body.

'PRAY FOR ME.' THE words were softly spoken, for Crawford's ears only. The archdeacon squeezed Rose's forearm, and saw that the condemned man's hands were twitching. Crawford stepped away to the wall. The hangman stepped forward, pulled down the cap, and deftly fitted the noose over the head. He drew it tight, and there were gasps from below when the semblance of a human face appeared against the shroud. Breathing drew in the linen and blew it back out. The hangman stepped to the side, withdrew the bolt, and David Rose was suddenly a dead weight gently swinging.

Epilogue

WEDNESDAY 23rd AUGUST 1865
LINDEN'S GENTLEMEN'S SALON, COLLINS STREET MELBOURNE

> The murderer had a very bad head. The forehead was low and retreating, there was very little crown, while the animal bumps at the back of the skull were largely developed.

Otto put down his newspaper, closed his eyes, and expected to yield to the rake of the comb across his scalp, the soft, padded leather beneath him, and the muffled rhythm of the street outside. Yet his troubled mind would not cease its wandering over the deflating disappointment of the week just past.

What profit, he wondered, was there to be salvaged from this failed mission to save a man? The knowledge that he had been right, his detractors wrong, and that he had stood by his conviction in the face of menace and ridicule? Yes, for this he could rightly be proud. He'd tried, but they wouldn't listen. The telegram had been sent, but no one had read it. Otto sighed. *So much incompetence!* And so, there would be no accolade for exemplary detective work, no reflected commendation for his Private Inquiry Office. And no public condemnation of Joyce Pitman, nor justice for David Rose. No, all Otto's good work of the past few days would remain forever unsung ...

A thought struck him: this would be his penance, not just for bringing in an innocent man, but for the hubris that had been his motivation for doing so. Yes, from this he would profit, being reminded of the simple lesson never to mind what lesser men might think of him.

It was small consolation, but that's all there was, so now he did surrender to the chair and thought of brighter things: of the friend he had made in Tom Chuck, and of his future. He would remain a detective, but one unencumbered, unhindered, unfettered by police department inefficiencies, pettiness, and ineptitude. He'd already decided long ago that while ever he remained a salaried employee, he would never be free of the likes of Telford and Walker. So why was he waiting?

Today he would write and tender his resignation, and tomorrow his very own Private Inquiry Office would officially open for business. There was nothing in the way of it; he already had his first commission to be getting on with. The minute he was back in his office, he would open the folder on his desk. A case of fraud; it would make a welcome change from bloody murder.

So yes, the future was bright, but Otto suspected that much time yet would have to pass before he could embrace it to the full.

Acknowledgements

I AM INDEBTED TO Les Pitt (Daylesford and District Historical Society) for the many details — from the mundane to the extraordinary — of Daylesford life in the 1860s.

I thank the State Library of Victoria for ready access to its collection of newspaper records and historical publications.

To Bob Gott, my gratitude for the many weighty discussions of plot.

And to Henry Rosenbloom and the staff at Scribe — including Anna Thwaites, for her keen-eyed editing — thank you for a delightful collaboration.